V

D1595993

2001/02

16.95

F Man c.2

Jacob's Blood

Jacob's Blood

by

Brad Mangum

ISBN: 1-55517- 478-7
v.2

Published by Bonneville Books

Distributed by:
925 North Main, Springville, UT 84663 • 801/489-4084

CFI Publishing and Distribution Since 1986
Cedar Fort, Incorporated
CFI Distribution • CFI Books • Council Press • Bonneville Books

Typeset by Virginia Reeder
Cover design by Adam Ford
Cover design © 2000 by Lyle Mortimer

Printed in the United States of America

Dedication

To Papa, who taught me the value of laughter in
the face of adversity.

"I found *Jacob's Blood* to be a real treat. The momentum just kept building from chapter to chapter. I recommend this book to anyone. It teaches great principles in the thrilling setting of the post Civil War era. Though written about that particular period in American History, this book is truly timeless. It has application for us today as well. The only time I was disappointed was when I read the last two words, 'The End'. It's one you don't want to end. I'm ready for the sequel."

Oklahoma State Senator
Ben Robinson

For further information regarding *Jacob's Blood* go to www.bradmangum.homestead.com on the internet.

For other CFI, Council Press or Bonneville Books see www.cedarfort.com.

Foreword
by

Lee Nelson

Brad Mangum is one of those rare people who rolls up his sleeves and does the things others only talk about doing.

The only time Brad ever surprised me was the day we met. He showed up on my doorstep, jeans tucked in the tops of his cowboy boots, a red bandana around his neck, looking like a buckaroo on the high plains of New Mexico where he grew up. He announced he had come to team rope.

It didn't surprise me a year later when Brad drug Heisman Trophy winner (college football's highest award) Ty Detmer into the arena, announcing Ty was going to rope with us. Nor was I surprised a few years later, while driving across the Navajo Indian reservation in the middle of the night, when the local radio station began playing one of Brad's newly-released recordings, sung by his wife, Lisa.

Nor was I surprised on the eve of the new millennium when Brad called from Oklahoma to tell me he was writing a historical novel dealing with social turmoil in Georgia following the Civil War. As I said, Brad Mangum does the things others only dream about.

Brad sent me the first draft. I was pleased, but not surprised, at his fresh and original approach to Civil War history. His main character, Jake Brady, grew up in the south, but sided with Abraham Lincoln instead of Robert E. Lee, and became a decorated officer in the Union Army. Brady only thought the war was over until he tried to return to a southern community that had been devastated by the Union Army, finding himself fighting a different kind of war while battling to win back the love of his wife, and the trust of his own son.

Civil war buffs will find *Jacob's Blood,* a fresh and highly entertaining look at a frequently overlooked side of Civil War history. Others will simply enjoy a good story by an author with a do-anything mentality, a good sense of humor, and who loves history.

CHAPTER 1

After I opened the gate to our corral, I took a seat on the fence. My mind wandered; from things Ma had said about him, that were contrary to the things Jay had told me, to picturing how nice it would be to have a father. Why couldn't my Pa have been just like all the other kids' fathers? If he'd been born in the North, then he should have fought for the North. But he was born in the South, so he should have fought for the South, I told myself. I'd have been a whole lot better off if he'd have fought for the South and gotten killed, at least then I'd be like all the other boys who'd lost their fathers in the war. People look at them with a sympathetic eye and say things like, "Your Pa was a brave man, son", and, "Your dad was one of the finest men I've ever known". But there were no such comments for Ben Brady. Instead, the looks I got were those that would be aimed at a half-breed. Some of the other kids' folks had told their boys to not get too chummy with Ben, "He's got bad blood". Well at least I know Kenneth's folks won't ever say that.

I was so confused! Most people around here hated Jacob Brady, including Ma. But when Jay talked to me about him, he talked as though he were some kind of hero. He'd told me time and time again, "Ben, don't you let nobody make ya ashamed of him. I know him as good as anyone, or I knew him, I should say, and right or wrong he did what he had ta do." When Jay would say this, it would make me feel good about Jake, almost proud. Many times these words were the only consolation I had.

Grandpa Beck, on the other hand, couldn't say enough bad things about him, but I couldn't put much stock in that. Grandpa didn't have much good to say about anybody. Just the same, it sure got old hearin' the same stuff that I heard at school from people that claimed to love me. I knew he didn't mean to hurt me, but when he said things like, "Don't worry about that snake, Ben. Shoot! You're half Beck, that gives ya a fightin' chance." All that kind of talk did, was make me feel like a newly-freed slave.

Ma never said much about him, but when she did, it wasn't good. She'd never once disagreed with Grandpa, who was always much more vocal on the subject. I'd quit even askin' Ma about him anymore because she just said, "You've been talkin' ta Jay again, ain't' ya?" or, "He's dead and gone, live your own life and don't worry about him. He didn't worry about you much when he left here."

Oh, how I wished sometimes he was home. I'd either get the gun, and have the pleasure of shootin' him myself for all the sufferin' he'd caused me, or give him a hug and tell him how much I'd missed havin' him around. I felt so...

"Oh, Ma, ya scared me."

"I just came ta tell ya that supper was ready. Are ya feelin' poorly?"

"No, Ma, just thinkin'."

"What are ya thinkin' about?"

"Nothin'. Just stuff."

"Someone been botherin' ya at school again?"

"No, it's not that. It's just that, well, I'm just feelin' sorry for myself, I guess."

"Why, what in the world for? We've got a whole lot more than a lot'a folks around here. We've got a roof over our heads, three fat steers and a milk cow in the pasture. Yonder's a barn, with a fat hog and a host of chickens and you've got a horse; which few boys have ta ride ta' school on. Now what more could a growin' boy want?"

"A father, and a name that was respected."

"Now, you wait just a minute there, Ben! We've talked about this before and ya know full well that you're just gonna have ta be yourself and quit worryin' about things that ain't a gonna change. Try ta start countin' your blessings just a little. The war took a lot from folks in these parts, and I'd think you'd try ta' think about that instead of...wait, have you been talkin' to Jay again?"

"No, ma'am."

"Well I suggest that you finish up your chores and get on in the house!"

Ma turned and headed for the house. I turned my head away from her. I didn't want her to see the tears in my eyes. I guess she just didn't understand what it felt like to be the black sheep of the whole county.

"Hurry up, Ben, your supper is already gettin' cold."

I heard the front door to the house close. Maybe I should just leave and go away somewhere. Some place where nobody had ever heard the name "Brady." Maybe I should go north, like he did. It was plain to see that I would never be accepted here.

I was finally beginnin' to realize why Ma had been able to stay here, and why she couldn't understand the way I felt. It seemed like people weren't mean to her. They just acted as though they felt sorry for her. But with me it was different. I must remind people of him or somethin'. She could never understand. She had never been treated the way that I had.

If I didn't go now, then someday I would have to. Yep, I was gonna go. I'd go up north and find where he had spent some time and see what they thought of him up there. Besides, what difference would it make? I was sure they couldn't hate him there any worse than they did here. And who knew, they might even like him up there somewhere. They ought to; he fought and died for them.

I drew some water from the well out back of the house and went in for my last meal at home.

Ma and I ate our supper without saying much.

"Do ya want some more beans, Son?"

"No, ma'am, I'm full. I think I'll go check and make sure I shut the door to the saddle shed."

"Okay. Don't be long, it's gettin' dark."

I hurried outside. I wanted to get my things together. I walked down the path to the barn. All I could hear were the sounds of crickets and the croakin' of an old bullfrog in the pond. The grass was already growing fast, even though it was still early spring. It was a good three hundred feet from the house to the barn, so I was sure Ma couldn't see what I was doing. I took out my saddle and gave it a quick oilin'. The long trip north was bound to be wet this time of year. I took a couple of gunnysacks and tied them together with twine to make me some saddlebags. We generally just fed oats in the winter, but I put some oats in one side for Dungeon, cause I knew it would be a long trip and he would need the extra boost. I'd fill the other side with food and clothes that I'd have to get from the house late tonight, after Ma was asleep.

It was dark, so I put the saddle, gunnysacks, blanket and bridle all in a neat pile just inside the saddle shed. I ran around and shut the gate to the pen where Dungeon was still eatin' his hay. I was all set. All I had to do was wait until Ma was asleep, then get my stuff from the house and head north. I ran around the barn and headed up the path to the house with great expectations of where I would be tomorrow night at this time.

I was half-excited and half-scared. I really didn't know where I was even goin'; just north. But I had made up my mind and I was goin' to go. I figured I would tell Ma that I was goin' over ta Kenneth's house so she wouldn't know I was gone until it was too late. I went in the house.

As I shut the door, Ma asked, "What took ya so long? I was just fixin' to come lookin' for ya."

"I was just cleanin' and oilin' my saddle. I figured it needed it, bein's the rainy season's here."

"Yeah, it is. And it probably needed it purdy bad."

"Yeah, it did."

"Well, it's good you're takin' care of it cause we sure can't afford a new one. You know, that's the one thing I can say for your father. He always had things neat and orderly."

I was surprised! I think that was the first time I had ever heard her say anything good at all about him.

"It looks as though you may have inherited that one quality. Would ya clean the cinder out of the stove so it'll be clean for mornin'?"

"Yes, ma'am. Ma, I was goin' to go over to Kenneth's house tomorrow and go squirrel huntin'."

"What time?"

"I told him that I'd try to be over there at first light."

"Why can't Kenneth ever come over here, instead of you always goin' over there?"

"Cause he don't have a horse."

"Surely Jay could let him have one now and then. He's got a couple."

"His Pa says that they're too good a horses for a kid to take out and lame."

She paused for a moment. "Well, okay, but I want ya home before dark, ya hear?"

I sat in silence. So far I had gotten by without openly lying and I hated to start now. Truth was, I wasn't goin' to be home at all.

To my relief, she broke the silence, "It'll probably do ya good

6

to get out."

"Yes, ma'am, it probably will."

It was all set now. All I had to do was get up extra early and get gone before I had to answer any questions.

Early the next mornin' I slipped out of bed quietly, so I wouldn't wake Ma. I opened the trunk at the foot of my bed and got out two shirts, a couple of pairs of pants and socks and walked slowly toward the door. As I passed our kitchen table, I noticed a piece of paper lying next to a cloth, bundled up with somethin' in it. I stopped and looked at it.

Dear Ben,

I thought you and Kenneth might could use a lunch. Son, I'm sorry for bein' so harsh yesterday evenin' out at the corral. I know it's been hard on ya livin' here, but it's the only home we've got and I'm just grateful to have it. And I want you to know, Ben, that I'm grateful to have you, too. You've been a real strength to me. I know at times it feels like you're overworked, and you must think that I'm terrible to ya. Please try to remember, Son, that I love you very much. You're the only child that I have, and my world is centered around you. I want nothin' more than for you to be happy. You must realize though, Ben, that there are things that can never be.

I know I'm always throwin' other folks' problems in your face, but we live in hard times and I'm just so thankful for the things we've got. Sometimes when I look outside and see ya out there doin' chores, I thank God above that you weren't old enough to fight in that damnable war that ruined so many peoples' lives. I can't help but think of people like Edward Johnson and his poor wife, Edith, who lost their only two boys. It's practically ruined Edward. He never smiles anymore. And when I think of our old house and barn, though they ain't much, I'm grateful for 'em and grateful that they weren't destroyed. And I'm proud that our barn ain't stalled no Yankee horses and our house ain't sheltered no Yankee soldiers!

You have a good day and I'll see ya this evenin'. And remember, Ben, that I love ya and want only what's best for ya. I know sometimes ya get angry with me, but try to remember that I'm the only mother you've got and I'm doin the best I can.

Love,

Ma

I laid the letter back on the table, turned and walked over to the foot of my bed and sat down on my trunk. Tears welled up in my eyes and I had a lump in my throat. I didn't want Ma to be like Mr. Johnson and go through life miserable because I had left. I was goin' to come back, someday. After all, it's not like I'd be dead. I just wouldn't be here. I knew she'd understand, someday. Why'd she even have to write that letter? One thing was for sure; I couldn't stay at home after telling Ma I was goin' squirrel huntin'. Maybe I'd ride over to Kenneth's and talk to Jay and tell him what I was doin'. He was the only one that really understood how I felt. Maybe he could explain to Ma why I had to leave. My mind seemed to ease. That's what I needed to do, go talk to Jay.

I got up and picked up the lunch Ma had made for me, grabbed my squirrel gun leanin' against the door, and with my clothes under my arm, I headed out.

It was just before dawn when I left. There was still a full moon and it was a perfect mornin' to be out ridin'. Just before the sun came up I rode up the lane to Kenneth's house. They had a real nice place. Jay had done real well with his livery stable and blacksmith shop in town. As I rode through their gate I saw someone come out of the house. It was Jay's unmistakable walk. He always rolled his right hip and walked with what appeared to be a limp.

I had asked him before, if he was hurt, and he'd said, "No, boy, it's just the way I travel."

Jay headed toward the barn. I was glad when I saw he was alone. This would give me a chance to talk to him. I rode up to the barn and tied my horse on the corral fence just outside the barn door. I paused for a moment to consider whether I was doin' the right thing by talkin' to him. I came to the same conclusion I had come to a hundred times while ridin' over here. I needed to talk to Jay! So I went on in through the barn door.

I could hear the sound of milk splashin' on the side of a bucket comin' from behind a stack of hay. I walked on around the end of the stack.

"Well, good mornin', Ben. What brings ya over here so early? Is everything alright at home?"

"Yes, sir. Everything's fine. I just thought I'd better stop by and talk to ya."

He stopped milkin' and turned on his little stool toward me, "What about, Ben? What do ya mean, stop by? Are ya goin' somewhere?"

"Yes, sir, I'm plannin' on goin' up north."

"Up north? What in the sam hill do ya want to go up north for? Does your Ma know where you're at?"

"No sir. That's why I'm here. I thought I'd best talk with ya and maybe you'd be able ta tell her easier than me."

"Well, it's a dang good thing ya did! Sounds like you and I need ta have a talk."

"Yes, sir."

"Did ya loosen the cinch on your horse?"

"No, sir."

"Well, go do it, and then come back in. You and I need ta talk awhile. I'll finish up here and be right with ya."

I knew what Jay was thinkin', but nothin' he could say would make me change my mind. I knew when I explained my feelings to him, he'd understand. I'd had the whole ride over to think about it and my thoughts were all in order.

"Tell me what happened ta bring on this earth-shatterin' decision."

"Nothin' certain, just a whole bunch of stuff together."

"Well, start from the top and work your way down, then."

"It's just that I've finally realized that I can never be happy around these parts. People here will always look at me as the son of Jacob Allen Brady. The only way that I'm ever gonna get anywhere is if I leave. Go somewhere that people don't know the name Brady or maybe even find a place where somebody likes the name."

"Have ya thought about your Ma and how she's gonna take care of that place by herself?"

"Yes, sir, I figured with me out of her hair, she wouldn't have near as much work ta do, and any big stuff could wait until she could get you or maybe Grandpa to help her with it."

"Your grandpa's gettin' on up in years and can't do a whole lot, and I'm awfully busy. It might be a month-a-Sundays before I could get over there."

"I figure if it's a real emergency that you won't be too

busy, least wise ya never have been before."

"Yeah, I suppose you're probably right there. Well, if you're not really worried a whole lot about your Ma gettin' by, are ya worried about yourself? You've never been away from home before and it sounds like ya really ain't sure where you're goin'."

"I've got my gun, and I'm a fair shot. I can live off the land a little bit and when I need ta buy somethin' I can get a job doin' chores or runnin' errands for somebody."

"You've got it all figured out right well, don't ya? Let me ask ya somethin', Ben. Do ya feel like you're a man or at least man enough for you and I to talk man to man?"

"Yes, sir."

"Okay then, I'm gonna tell ya how I feel and I want ya ta know that no matter what you're gonna think of me after I say this, I'm still gonna like the heck out'a ya, no matter what ya do. Ben, I think you're bein' dang selfish. Your Ma has worked hard to make things comfortable for ya. She deserves more than to have the only thing that she really loves in this world take off and leave her. You're probably right. Without you around, she probably wouldn't have as much work ta do, but her burden would be three times what it is now just worryin' about ya, and wonderin' if you're warm and safe at night. I think you're turnin' your back on a God-given responsibility of takin' care of her needs. You know, Ben, you'll never be happy in life anywhere you go if you're the only person you think about. Real happiness comes from holdin' up your end of the responsibilities and helpin' other people down the road of life."

"Why didn't your friend, my Pa, hold up his end, then?"

"I've never met a man yet that could hold up his end of the work and responsibilities and still find plenty of time to help other folks, better than Jake Brady."

"Then, why did he leave me and Ma alone to take care of ourselves?"

"All I can say is, he did what he had ta do. And it was really the only thing he could do."

"Why? Surely he could have done somethin' else. He didn't have to go, did he?"

"Yeah, I think he did the right thing at the time. Ben, I know it must be hard, but I've never lied to ya before and I'm not lyin' to ya now. Your Pa was respected around here by everyone and had a good name. He's as good as any man that ever set foot in Georgia.

Now don't worry about him anymore. I know if he were here, he'd tell ya the same thing as I've told ya. Go back home and take care of your mother. Things will work themselves out, I'm sure of it."

"I think you're probably right. I don't know if everything will work out or not, but I guess I knew before I talked to ya that I hadn't oughta leave Ma by herself."

"Well, good, you are a man, ALMOST! Then you're gonna go back home?"

"Yes, sir, I reckon so. I probably ought to stay and do some huntin' since that's where I told Ma I was goin'."

"Good, good, and you don't feel hard towards me?"

"No, sir, I'm not sore."

"Yep, almost a man. Kenneth should be up and around, by now. Why don't ya go on in the house and get some breakfast. We'll just keep this to ourselves, if that's alright with you."

"Yes, sir, that's the way I'd like ta have it."

I turned and started toward the barn door.

"Ben! If you're ever lookin' for a place where somebody likes the name Brady, just ride on over here to my place. We like it right fine around here."

I smiled and walked on out the door.

CHAPTER 2

He rode in one evenin' about sundown. He was a tall, slender sort of fellow, with a salt-and-pepper beard. He was a Yankee soldier, at least he had the Yankee pants on. As he tied his horse and turned to walk toward Ma and me, we couldn't help but notice the blood. He was wounded. It was obvious he'd taken one in the belly.

I turned to look at Ma, tears streamin' down her face, but she was motionless. I was lost. Why wouldn't my mother help him? I had seen her help strangers before. Could it be that this was no stranger? Ma stared at him as though she had seen a ghost. Surely it wasn't him! I was told he was dead, but somehow I never believed it.

He stumbled and almost fell. Ma started forward, but restrained herself. Then he fell to the ground. He tried to get up but couldn't. She rushed to his side then yelled back at me to come and help her. I got on one side and Ma on the other. We struggled under his weight, even though he helped all he could. We got him inside and laid him on the bed in the front room. Was it him? Deep down I knew it was.

We took care of him as best we could, and tried to make him comfortable. I couldn't get the nerve to ask her, and it was plain she wasn't volunteerin' any information about this wounded man. I helped her get a few blankets out and some water in the tub and then she sent me to bed.

I was up most of the night. I couldn't keep my racin' mind from stealin' sleep from me. Ma made me sleep in the upstairs loft where she usually slept. She was going to sit up with our new guest. The next mornin' I had to ask her. As I climbed down from the loft, Ma looked up at me and smiled.

"Good morning, Ben."

"Good morning, Ma. How is he?"

"Not good."

"Is he my father?" I asked, timidly.

A cold silence came over her that seemed to last forever. Then she turned toward me and reluctantly said, "Yes."

"Why did you tell me he was dead?"

"Don't you understand? He is dead to us!" She turned and stared out the window with tears in her eyes.

I looked at this man lying on my bed. He was a rough looking man with wrinkles on his forehead and hands. His cheekbones were prominent and his hair was brown with a grayish tint. One thing was for certain, his six-foot-two-inch body had not seen water in a good long while. He was filthy from head to toe. Then my eyes focused on the blood-soaked bandage on his wound.

"Will he live Ma? Do ya think he'll live?"

I wanted so much for him to live. There was so much I wanted him to tell me. I'd heard good and bad about him all my life, mostly bad. But he was a mystery to me. To listen to stories of his life would be an adventure that I certainly wouldn't want to miss.

"I doubt it," Ma replied. " Not many men live when they're gut-shot. But I guess we should try to do all we can for him. Get your boots on and go out and saddle up old Dungeon, and ride to town and find Jay. Tell him that Jake is here and needs a doctor. He's one guy in town that still loves your father. Tell him that Doc Adair is in Blue Ridge on Wednesdays. If he hurries, he can probably catch him there."

The door didn't touch my tail end; I was out of there in a flash. I could hear Ma yellin' for me ta hurry back and help with the chores. Chores, I thought; that was the last thing on my mind! I saddled up in a hurry and covered the three-mile trip ta town in record time. I found Jay in his blacksmith shop, as usual, with beads of sweat as big as my fist, rollin' off of his chubby, red face. He looked up and noticed me comin' towards him.

"What do ya know, Ben?" he asked.

"My Pa's at the house! You need to get Doc Adair. Ma sent me to fetch ya!"

"Whoa, just a minute there, young'un. Start over, and try about half speed this time."

I tried to calm myself, somewhat, and started again. I looked around to make sure we were alone. "Pa is at the house. He showed up last night gut-shot, and Ma sent me to fetch you so as you could fetch a doctor. She said, Doc Adair was at Blue Ridge on Wednesdays, and if ya hurried, you could catch him there."

I could see the panic in Jay's eyes. He looked at the horse standin' next to him and then back at me. "Dang! I'd better get out of here. Would you go over to Mr. Fletcher's barbershop and tell Olie.... You know Olie Jacobson?

"Yes sir, I know Olie."

"Tell him that I'll shoe his horse, first crack a dawn tomorrow, okay?"

"Yes, sir."

As I headed for the door, he said, "Oh, Ben? Don't say anything about this to anybody; might cause problems!"

"Yes, sir...I know."

I then left promptly for the barbershop, delivered my message to Olie, and started my three-mile journey back home. This time I took it a little slower.

As I turned Dungeon to the north and started for home, it was a typical spring day in Georgia. A light mist was fallin', but my mind was far away from the weather and deep in thought. Who was Jacob Brady? Was he a coward and a traitor? Was he a worthless bum that had left his family to fend for themselves, while he went his own way, seekin' for self-satisfaction? I'd heard this from both my mother and Grandpa, and insinuations of much the same from some of the townsfolk of Clayton. But I must determine the truth for myself, I decided, as I could never be satisfied with the opinion of others. I chose, for now, to believe more on the things that Jay had, intermittently, told me at my request, over the past few years.

Jay and my Pa had grown up together and were as close as brothers. Jay had told me of the many experiences they'd had growin' up and, most times, would throw in a little fatherly advice, such as, "It wouldn't pay to try that these days." I didn't mind that, though, because many times he did seem like a father to me. This, however, didn't please Ma much, because of his love and respect for Pa. Ma would rather that I look to Grandpa Beck for my leadership and guidance. But Grandpa Beck was such a negative sort of fella that always seemed to find somethin' depressing to talk about, or somebody that wasn't doin' things the way he would do them. Jay, on the other hand, seemed always in a good mood and willing to help whoever he could. Most everybody in town liked Jay. You would hear him laughin' and jokin' with people, and talkin' about things that had happened in the past. Pa (although I knew he had probably been there) was seldom mentioned, and on those rare occasions that Jay might mention him, there came a slow coolness over the laughter, and the subject was changed or the crowd would disperse. Jay often said he would never understand how people who once loved Pa, and some who even watched him grow up, could so rapidly turn on him without a forgiving bone in their bodies; although he wasn't even sure that Pa had done anything that he needed their forgiveness for. Should a man ask forgiveness when he has the courage to stand up for what he believes to be right, and to boot, he's got a half a million people that are God-fearin' Christians that think just like him? Only God could judge that. Jay never talked to me about Pa when other people were around and he had told me that Ma had asked him not to talk to me at all about Pa. But I was much too inquisitive, and Jay liked tellin' his stories too much for that to have happened. So I learned a great deal more about Pa over the past few years than Ma knew about.

I rode into the barnyard with many questions on my mind. I knew that the only way those questions would ever be answered, was if Pa lived. I prayed to God above that he would let him live.

I unsaddled and fed my horse and headed over to check the stock tank. I was gettin' ready to tend to the rest of my chores when I heard Ma yell from the porch.

"Ben, I've done your chores, already. Just feed and water Dungeon and come on in."

I ran up and kicked my boots off by the door.

"Is he any better?"

I walked in and immediately looked over at Pa. Ma had taken his blood-soaked coat off and layed it at the foot of the bed.

"He's tried to stir a couple times, but that's all."

"Has he said anything?"

"No, just a bunch of mumbling, but nothin' you could understand. Did ya find Jay?"

"Yeah. He left right away to Blue Ridge."

"That should put 'em in here late tonight sometime, if Doc Adair can leave right away. Ben-- Well, never mind. I'll talk to ya later. Are ya hungry?"

Ma looked tired. She walked over to the table and uncovered some freshly-cooked sourdough biscuits in a tin.

"Yeah. I'm starvin'!"

"It's no wonder, ya left without eatin' a thing."

I sat down at the table and stared at Pa. I noticed Ma lookin' at me with that disapproving look, as though I was doin' something wrong. But she said nothin' as she busily worked by the stove. I could tell she wanted me to have nothin' to do with Pa and thought it unfortunate that I had even seen him.

She handed me some eggs, sausage, and gravy for the sourdough biscuits. "Here. As soon as you're done, I'd like ya to come outside and talk with me."

"Yes, ma'am."

Mom walked out the front door. I occasionally caught a glimpse of her, pacing back and forth in front of the window with her arms folded. While I ate, my mind raced through the many things I thought she might say to me. At the same time, I rehearsed my speech as to why I had a right to know the truth about Pa. Had she known all the time that he was alive? Did she know where he had been all these years? Many such questions ran through my mind. I hurried and ate my food. Curiosity was burdening me almost more than I could bear. I went outside and found Ma washin' some clothes on the porch.

"Ben, sit down. I think we need to talk about your father."

I wanted nothing more, so I quickly took a seat, facing Ma.

"He'll have to go, you know, as soon as he's able. He can't stay here with us. He's not welcome."

"He'll have to stay until he's well enough to ride, won't he?"

"He's likely to never see that day, but as soon as Doc Adair says he is well enough to move, I'm gonna see if Jay and Maggie can take him in."

"Why do you hate him so much?"

"He betrayed and disgraced me, you, and the whole family. Isn't that reason enough ta hate a man? The only reason he's in our home, now, is because he is deathly wounded and I would do the same for a wild animal. My conscience wouldn't allow me ta turn him away."

Ma was bitter. I hated to ask, but I wanted to know.

"Did you ever love him?"

"I think we have talked enough. I don't find Jacob Allen Brady a pleasant subject at all."

I was frustrated. I felt I had a right to know about my Pa. "Nobody around here does! But, he is my father, and I think I have a right ta know why my Ma, Grandpa, and half the town, or better, hates his guts."

There was a long silence, and tears welled up in Ma's eyes. I was ashamed I had spoken so hard to her.

"I'm sorry Ma."

"No, Son, you're right. You do have a right ta know, and I should be the one ta tell ya." She wiped her tears away.

"Yes, I did love him once, and that Jake Brady I shall always love, I suppose. It's like another lifetime, before the war. I remember when I met him. He was only seventeen. His blue eyes pierced through my very being. He was the most handsome man I'd ever seen. He walked as a man with authority, and seemed very sure of himself."

Her face softened. She walked over and sat down.

"Come sit by me, Ben."

She smiled and looked at me. It was obvious that she had indeed loved Pa once.

"His mother died when he was born, and his father was killed in an accident when he was six years old. His grandparents, on his father's side, raised him. His grandfather, "Pappy" he used to call him, was a Methodist minister. A good man, although I only had the pleasure of meetin' him on three occasions. The first two were during our courtship, when he took me over to Franklin to meet him. And the third was the day he married us. Pappy died two weeks after our marriage. Rebecca, Pappy's wife, had died some years before."

"Jacob Allen Brady courted me for six weeks before we were married on that beautiful summer day of June 23, 1850. We built a small house on some land that Jake had bought outside of Franklin. He worked there as an apprentice in a blacksmith shop owned by Jay's father, Delbert Thompson. We stayed there for two and a half years. Then Jay and Jake decided to move to Clayton and start their own blacksmith shop. There wasn't one here, and they felt they'd do purdy well. So we sold our property in Franklin, and with the help of Delbert, they set up the first blacksmith shop in Clayton. We did well enough to get by, and even managed to save some money. Those were happy times for us. It looked as though Jake and I weren't going to be able to have any children, until you came along in January of 1853. When the war broke out, everybody in these parts was ready to fight. They started to summon volunteers. Most of the men went immediately. Some lagged behind, but eventually went."

Ma's voice became more stern and resentful. "It was during this excitement of gettin' volunteers that your pa made his announcement at Grandpa's house, that the cause of the North was just, and that if he were to fight in this war, his conscience would allow him to fight for none other. There was a big argument that followed, and your pa was asked to leave. I went with him to our house, and we argued half the night. Or, I should say, I argued. He just sat and listened without sayin' much at all. The news got out shortly of his statement, and we began to be persecuted. Our business at the blacksmith shop had all but stopped."

Ma was uncomfortable. Her voice had begun to break up a little. "By that time, the war was goin' strong. Jake wouldn't listen to your Grandpa Beck or me. He is the most stubborn man on earth. He calmly told me one evenin', that he must go. I cried and begged him ta stay, and tried to change his mind. But he would have no part of it. He sold our half of the blacksmith shop to Jay, and made arrangements for the money ta be given ta us, and then he left. Nothin' I or Jay, or anybody could say would persuade him ta do otherwise." Ma paused, and looked over at me, "So now you've heard it."

Ma got up and walked to the edge of the porch. She looked out at our barn, and then at the pasture. She stood in silence. I could tell that she wasn't seein' anything in the pasture, just memories in her mind. She suddenly turned around.

"I need ta change the bandages. Go and get the cow in. We need ta milk, and I need ta make some butter and have ya take it over ta Grandpa.

"Yes, Ma'am." I answered, and started towards the pasture. Ma had finally broken down and actually talked about Pa. My mind was full. I had plenty to think about.

CHAPTER 3

I took my time walkin' through the pasture. I yelled a couple of times for ol' Nelly and then kneeled down by the trunk of the large oak tree that sat just outside of our corral gate. I knew ol' Nelly would find her way to the corral, soon enough.

Ma tried hard to hide it, but I could tell that she had not only once loved Pa, though she'd never admit it, she still did. Ma had never in my whole life said that much about Pa at one time. All I'd ever get was, "he's dead," or, " Son, some things are better left in the closet." Lots of short, but never to the point, statements. It was clear to me, now, she had always been afraid that her true feelings might show through her bitterness. No doubt she hated what Jake Brady did. But I saw somethin' in ma's eyes, as she spoke about him, which told me she didn't hate him.

What made him leave ma and me? I started rehashing things I had gone over at least a thousand times before. What was the use? He had to live. He had to! I'd heard from Grandpa Beck, I'd heard from Jay, I'd heard from everyone; everyone but Jake Brady. Oh God, let him live. I needed a reason, somethin' to go on. Somethin' that would allow me to take my own stand, and be my own judge of this man. If he should die and go ta hell, then at least I wanted God to let me live knowin' why.

I could hear Nelly comin'. She was better than most people I knew. At least she was predictable. A couple of yells and, no doubt about it, she was goin' to either come to the corral for feed, or you best go hunt for her dead body. I wished people were so predictable. One thing was for certain; when Grandpa Beck finds out Pa is back, his reaction will be purdy predictable.

I shut the gate and went on into the barn. Nelly followed me up to her stall. I threw her some hay and grabbed the milk pail and

19

began milkin'. I wanted to hurry and get back in the house but I knew that if I did, Ma would likely send me to bed just to keep me away from Jake. I'd just drag my feet a little and tell her the truth. I had some thinkin' to do, after all she had told me. She'd have to understand that and besides, she's got to know that I'm not goin' to be able to sleep tonight anyway. The milk splashed off from the sides of the pail. Why did Jay stay so loyal to Pa after all these years? Should I show this man any respect?

I heard a noise outside the barn in the back yard. It sounded like an animal of some kind. I set the pail aside and looked out the barn door. It was Pa's horse! In all the excitement I guess Ma and I just forgot him. He must have gotten tired of standin' there at the hitchin' post and broke loose, or more likely, he wasn't tied at all. This would kill a little more time. I figured I had better pull the saddle off and give him some feed. I caught him up and led him into the barn. He was all gaunt and drawn up in the flanks. He needed water more than he needed feed. As I pulled the saddle off, I couldn't help but notice the saddlebags were heavy and full. I was curious but I'd been raised better than to pilfer into another man's property.

Suddenly I heard a horse runnin'! It couldn't be Jay and Doc Adair, there's no way Jay could have even gotten to Blue Ridge, much less had time to get back. I ran to the barn door to see who it was. There was a man knockin' at our door. Ma answered the door and quickly stepped outside. I couldn't hear anything they were sayin' except I could tell the man was talkin' loud and fast. I figured I better get up there as quick as I could. I just kicked the gate open for Nelly and Pa's horse to get out to the pasture and headed toward the house. By the time I got there, I could see the man was Uncle Newt, and he was mountin' up to leave. As he turned his horse to ride away, he yelled back to Ma and said, " We'll keep lookin'. You remember; blood's thicker'n water, little sister. Don't you forget what that dang traitor put you, and the whole dern family through."

Ma wasn't cryin', but tears had welled up in her eyes. It was obvious why she hadn't let Uncle Newt in the house.

"Let's get inside, right now!" she said.

"I left the milk down at the barn," I answered.

"Go on back and get it then, but get right back up here."

"I turned Pa's horse loose in the pasture. He looked awful thirsty."

"Oh dear, I forgot. Where did you put his saddle?"

"It's just layin' by the stall."

"Put it back by the grain barrel and cover it up with hay. No questions, just do as you're told. I've got some cleanin' up ta do in the house. Don't waste any time, just get back here to the house as quick as you can."

"Yes, ma'am."

As Ma walked in the house, the tears began to flow freely down her cheeks. Uncle Newt was looking for Pa! How did he know he was back? Why didn't Ma let him know where Pa was? My mind raced as fast as my legs, as I ran to the barn. Pa's horse was still standin' in the barn eatin' when I got back. I figured if Ma wanted Pa's saddle hid, she sure didn't want his horse out in our pasture come daylight. I caught his horse up again. I led him down our fence line about one hundred feet to the gate that went into the Wilkerson ranch. Their ranch was big, and had plenty of feed and water. They wouldn't mind a stray for a few days. I hid the saddle, and latched up the pail of milk, and headed for the house. As I opened the door Ma said, frantically, "Hurry up and set that milk on the table, Ben, I need your help over here!"

She was still cryin' and strugglin' to move Pa, but he was obviously too much for her to handle alone.

"What do ya want me ta do, Ma?"

"Just grab the corner of that blanket. We're gonna move him down here on the floor, then drag him back into the bedroom."

The bedroom was the one that Ma and Pa used to share, but when Pa left, Ma moved to the loft bed and used this room for guests only.

"Should we move him?"

"Just do what I tell ya!"

"Yes, ma'am."

Pa wasn't movin' at all.

"Is he dead?"

"No! Just pull on the blanket. Ready, one, two, three."

Pa hit the floor hard. It was plain he wasn't dead. He moaned and tried to get up. Ma pushed his forehead back down.

"Be still! Be still, else you'll start bleedin' again. I'll never get this mess cleaned up."

It took all we had to drag him into the bedroom. We couldn't lift him onto the bed so we just left him lying beside it. Ma told me to go out and start cleanin' up the blood and rags and she'd finish takin' care of Pa. In a few minutes, she came out. Her face was red and blotchy, but she had quit cryin'.

"I'll finish cleanin' up, you get on up in your bed and try an' get some sleep."

I knew she was in no mood for comments, questions, or conversation. I went straight up the ladder to the loft and got into my bed. There would be no sleepin' for me tonight!

I spent the next few hours alternatin' between listening to Ma pacin' the floor below and openin' the front door, to tryin' to make sense of all that had happened. I, too, kept hopin' that Jay and Doc Adair would hurry up and get here.

I heard the sound of horses' hooves. I had dozed off. Three, maybe four hours had passed. Someone's boots hit the wooden porch. Then the knock came at the door. Ma was already waitin' to open the door. I crawled closer to the edge of the loft, so I could see and hear better.

"Ma'am, I am Lieutenant Riverton of the United States Cavalry. I, and the soldiers with me, were dispatched late this evening after a Mr. Jay Thompson informed Captain Samuel Roundy that Colonel Jacob Brady had been shot and needed security and medical attention, immediately."

"Where's Jay? Where's Doc Adair?" Ma questioned.

"Mr Thompson said he would continue on to find Doctor Adair, but asked that we do all we could. We have with us the finest doctor in our regiment. If we may, ma'am, I'd like to send him in right away to attend to the Colonel."

"Why yes, yes, of course. He's in the bedroom. I'm afraid ya may be too late, he's lost a lot of blood."

Without hesitation, the Yankee doctor went right past Ma and into the bedroom. I heard him say somethin' to himself that I couldn't make out and then he came out and said,"Lieutenant, I need two men, immediately, and have someone bring in the cloth wrapping out of my saddlebags."

The lieutenant responded quickly to his request. Then he walked over by Ma in the kitchen.

"Ma'am, do you have any idea who did this?"

"No! He just showed up this way. There's a lot of folks in these parts that don't like him."

"We'll be posting guards around the perimeters of your home.

22

No one will be allowed in without an escort and knowledge of who they are and what their business is here."

"This is my home, and not a jail to be guarded by Yankees!"

"Yes, ma'am and we'll be very respectful to the fact that it is your home, but I have my orders to protect Colonel Brady and see that everything possible is done to preserve his life, and that, ma'am, is what I will do."

The lieutenant politely excused himself and went outside as another soldier entered the house carryin' the cloth-wrapped bag. I could hear soldiers yellin' outside, it sounded like several of them. I could hear them everywhere!

I could hear sounds comin' from the bedroom, too. Ma stayed outside the bedroom door in the rockin' chair. It seemed like almost an hour had past. Then another knock came at the front door. It was the lieutenant again.

"Ma'am, Mr. Thompson and the doctor have arrived. Do you mind if I show them to the bedroom?"

"No, that's quite alright. Jay, when you get a minute."

"I'll be right back out. Let me check on Jake. I'll just be a minute."

"Doc Adair, thanks for comin'."

"I brought him into this world, I guess I have an obligation ta try an keep him in it. Besides, I think Jay might'a shot me if I hadn't come."

They both went in the bedroom. They stayed in there for what seemed like forever. I didn't know if that was good or bad. Jay said he'd be right out. Finally, after about thirty minutes, Jay came back out. Ma walked towards the bedroom door to meet him.

"Not so good, huh?"

"Well, I've seen worse that lived and some not as bad that didn't. But we are dealing with Jacob Allen Brady here, and my money says he'll make it."

"Well, I've never seen or heard of anyone gut-shot that made it!"

"That's the good news! Both the docs agree that it missed most of his vitals. The biggest problem seems to be the blood loss and makin' sure he don't lose anymore."

"How long is he gonna have ta stay here?"

"Now, Lizzie, that's liable ta be awhile. You're just gonna have ta get used to the idea, and the sooner the better. It'll just make things rough on everyone involved if you're not hospitable. Besides, it seems Jake was some kinda Yankee war hero. They're not movin' him anywhere until it's safe ta do it. I'll tell ya somethin' else. I'd hate ta be in the shoes of the man that did this. Sounds like they won't leave one stone unturned until he's found, and pays up."

"He sure ain't no hero around here. Has Jake said anything yet?"

"Nope, just mumbles a little now and then, nothin' you can understand. The Yankee doctor has him purdy sedated. I don't think he'll say much of anything for awhile."

"Do ya think I can go back and sit with him?"

"I'm sure ya can. They're purdy well done in there for tonight. I'll be checkin' back as soon as I get my chores tended to at the house."

Ma thanked Jay and opened the bedroom door, slowly, as Jay went out the front door.

Jay told me right! Leastwise, he told me Pa wasn't bad. Now, I had somethin' to hang my hat on. My dad was a war Hero!

CHAPTER 4

The sun was high in the sky when I awoke the next mornin'. I rose to the sound of men talkin' outside and the smell of food cookin' in the kitchen. I had to take a moment to reflect on what had happened in the last forty-eight hours. I realized my life had changed forever. The man I thought to be dead, the man I was told was dead, wasn't dead at all. My father was here in my house. I had been lied to! Was it to protect me? What was next? So many questions had been answered and yet for every question that had been answered, two seemed to take its place. All I could go on was what I felt inside, and it wasn't a bad feelin'. It was a feelin' of relief, but also anxiety about the future. God had answered my prayers and given me my father to judge for myself. I thanked God for this opportunity. I couldn't explain why or where the feelin's came from, but I had always believed that I not only had a right, but also a responsibility, to form my own opinions. Now I could. Was he a coward, a traitor, or a hero? Time would tell. One thing was for certain, whatever he was, he was here and I was glad. A knock came at the front door.

"Ma'am, Mr. Thompson is here and would like to visit Colonel Brady."

As Jay shoved past the Yankee soldier, he said, "Ah shoot, I knew these folks when you were still draggin' on your mama's tit. I don't need an introduction."

Ma got a smurk on her face. "Now, Jay, you're just gonna have ta get used to the idea, and the sooner the better. These folks will be here awhile."

Ma put her hands on her hips and tilted her head sideways after mockin' Jay.

"Yeah, guess I oughta take my own dad-blamed advice, huh? It seems a little early to be eatin' crow. What else ya got cookin'?"

"You never change, do ya, Jay? Always jokin' and always hungry."

"Most folks don't like me the way I am. I figure if I change, I risk losin' the friends I got."

"Sit down, breakfast is just about ready."

"How's he doin', Lizzie?"

"Not good. Ben, come on down for breakfast."

I had been pullin' my clothes on and was just about ready to come down anyway, but I wanted to listen to Jay and Ma talk as much as I could.

"Good mornin', Ben, or is it afternoon? Hasn't anyone ever told ya that ninety percent of the people that die in this world die in bed."

"Yes, sir, I believe you've told Kenneth and me both that a time or two."

"Long night, huh?"

"Yes, sir."

I took my usual seat at the table. Jay just sat there for a moment twirlin' a fork around in his hand. I could tell he wanted to say somethin', but either thought it was bad timing or hadn't figured out how to say it.

"Lizzie, I think ya oughta..."

"Breakfast is ready, let's eat now and we can figure out all the ought to's later."

Jay raised his eyebrows and tightened his lips together as he made eye contact with Ma.

"Yeah--Yeah, I reckon you're right. If ya don't mind I'd like ta check in on Jake just for a moment."

"No, not at all, but don't take too long. If this gets cold, you might prefer the crow."

Jay smiled and got up and walked into the bedroom. The Yankee doctor came out within a few minutes of Jay going in.

"Ma'am, Colonel Brady is awake now. The bleeding has stopped, but we're not out of the woods yet. Not by a long shot! We're gonna need ta boil these bandages that I've got here. I've used all I brought with me. Main thing now is fever. We'll need ta keep an eye on him real close."

"Isn't that your job? Ta keep an eye on him. I'm no doctor. Did you say he's awake and talkin?!"

"Yes, ma'am."

26

Though she tried to hide it from me, I could see a panicked look in Ma's eyes.

"I'll check back on him in a bit. Doctor Adair said he'd try and get by sometime this evening, but didn't know for sure. I'll just be right outside here if ya need me."

"Fine, pull the door tight. It's swelled a little and don't shut well."

Ma walked over by the bedroom door as the doctor left. She paused for a moment, and then as she opened the bedroom door said, " Jay, we're waitin' on ya ta say grace out here."

"I'll...I'll be right there, Lizzie."

Ma turned slowly and came back toward the kitchen table, leaving the bedroom door cracked open a little. She sat down at the table and then noticed that I was watchin' her. Without saying a word she turned her head as though to be lookin' out the window at somethin'. It was plain to see she was stricken with emotion. I didn't know what to say, so I just sat there and acted like I didn't notice. Within a couple of minutes, Jay emerged from the bedroom. He pulled the bedroom door tight.

"Well, are ya finally ready ta eat. Probably ain't worth eatin', now that ya let it get cold."

I could see that Jay was dealing with emotions of his own as he sat down at the table. His face was red and I could see that tears had welled up in his eyes.

"I'll tell you what. I'll eat anything that ol' Ben, here, will ask the good Lord ta bless."

Ma turned back again toward the table. Then she quickly bowed her head.

"Ben, would you say grace, please?"

"Yes, Ma'am."

I had said grace a thousand times but this time was different. I always had said the same blessing on the food when Ma asked me. I'd always asked for the same things and been thankful for the same things. But this time I wanted to be thankful for somethin' and ask for somethin' that I knew Ma didn't want. I paused a little.

"Ben," Ma said.

"Ah...Yes, ma'am. God, we're thankful for all the good things that you've given us, for our land, house and livestock, for the food that's been prepared. We ask that it make us healthy and strong. We're thankful for our good friend, Jay, and his family. God, we ask that Pa's wounds heal up proper. In the name of Jesus, Amen."

As I raised my head, a teardrop fell from Jay's eye. Ma turned away and got up.

"I better pull this curtain so we can eat our breakfast without these Yankee soldiers lookin' in on us."

"Yeah, that'd be plumb torture fer them ta see us in here eatin' this fine food and them out there in a chuck line." Jay chuckled a little.

"I wasn't worried about them!" Ma snapped back.

Jays' chuckle broke and he smiled and looked over at me. "That was a fine prayer, Ben. God loves kids. Don't he, Lizzie?"

Ma spun around and gave a sharp glare toward Jay, but he just grinned a little and looked down at his plate. Ma loved Jay like a brother, but it was obvious she was bitin' her tongue. Finally, Jay broke the silence.

"Lizzie, you cook better'n any woman in these parts." He paused, " And, Ben, if I want my Maggie ta know that little piece a information, then I'll tell her myself!"

I chuckled a little.

"Yes, sir."

Ma smiled a little and sat back down at the table. Jay sure knew how to lighten the mood. A knock came at the door. Jay got up and answered it. It was the Yankee lieutenant.

"Mr. Thompson, Mrs. Brady, I'm sorry to disturb your breakfast. I can come back later if it would be best."

"No, what is it you need?" Ma asked.

"Well, ma'am, I'd like to have a private word with you if I could."

"Mr. Thompson is like family. Anything you got ta say to me he can hear."

"Well, ma'am, I think it proper that we keep this among the adults, if you don't mind, ma'am."

"And what if I do?"

Jay looked over at me. Then back at Ma.

"Ben, ain't you been taught ta feed your stock before ya feed yourself?"

"Yes, sir."

I'd got up so late and with all that had gone on, Jay was right, I hadn't done my chores yet. I didn't want to go against Ma or Jay. I was caught between, so I just sat there.

"Ma?"

"Go do your chores."

I got my hat and reached for the door.

"Don't be talkin' to those Yankee soldiers, and make sure they're not feedin' their horses out of our barn."

"Yes, ma'am."

Part of me wanted to be in that house and part of me couldn't get out quick enough. I raised my head up as I closed the door. There were two wagons down by the barn with at least ten Yankee soldiers standing around them talkin'. They had set up four large tents just to the side of the wagons. I walked slowly toward the barn. I passed a soldier standin' at the corner of the house.

"Good mornin' Son."

Without thinking, I replied back, "Mornin'."

As I got closer to the barn I stopped and turned around and glanced back at the house. There was a soldier at every corner of our house. There were also two soldiers at the front gate to our yard. They were standin' as still as statues, each holdin' the barrel end of their rifle with the stock on the ground. When I turned back around, one of the other soldiers had walked from the wagons almost up to me.

"Well, you must be Ben Brady, the colonel's son."

I didn't say anything. Fact was, I was scared. Everything I had heard about Yankees was bad. Not to mention the fact that Ma had just told me not ta talk ta any of them; now I was surrounded by them. The soldier stuck out his hand.

"I'd like ta shake the hand of the son of the finest man I've ever had the pleasure of knowin'."

I just stood there. Ma would not only be mad but disappointed if she saw me shake his hand. But she also raised me to respect my elders. Besides, I couldn't help but be a little bit proud of what he had just said. I shook his hand.

"If you're headin' down ta do chores, we already fed your horse. I couldn't help but recognize ol' Scout, the colonel's, I mean your father's horse, whinnyin' and runnin' up and down that fence line. So I found a gate up the way there and turned him in where I could feed him, too."

I still didn't say anything. I just started walkin' toward the barn again. The soldier started walkin' beside me.

"Can I help ya do somethin' else?"

29

"Nope!"

"You don't say much do ya? You don't need ta be afraid, son. I know ya ain't used ta havin' a bunch a Yankee soldiers around your house. But look at it this way, you're probably the most protected kid in the history of Georgia. Why, if anything happened ta you, Colonel Brady would have us all shot. Are ya sure there's not some more chores I could help ya with?"

"I gotta milk the cow."

"She's already penned and waitin' on ya. I would've milked her myself but I didn't know if your ma was ready fer the milk."

I was still nervous, but this soldier seemed awfully nice.

"I'll let ya do your chores. If you need any help there, you just give a yell."

He walked back over to the wagons with the rest of the soldiers. I was relieved. Nelly was already in her stall eatin'. I got the pail and started milkin'. My thoughts drifted back to the lieutenant in the house. What were they talkin' about in there? Were they going to take Pa and leave? How long were these soldiers goin' to stay here? But the most important question was, would Pa live?

As I finished milkin' and headed out of the barn, I noticed the doctor comin' out from one of the tents. He started toward the house. He turned and saw me. He stopped and waited between the house and the barn.

"I was just headed up to check on the colonel. Would ya like me to carry that milk for you?"

"No, sir. I'm fine."

"How's your ma holdin' up? She didn't sleep a wink last night."

"She's fine, too."

"Well, she won't be, if she doesn't get some rest."

As we approached the yard gate, the two soldiers saluted the doctor and said, "Sir." As we were headin' up the steps, the front door to the house came open and the lieutenant walked out with Jay right behind him.

"There's certainly enough evidence to investigate it, anyway. If you think Colonel Brady doesn't want us to proceed, then I'm going to have to hear that from him."

"Well, why don't we cross each bridge as we get to it. Let's worry about gettin' Jake back up on his feet. Then we'll worry about crossin' that other bridge."

"Mr. Thompson, Colonel Brady, himself, told the captain his plans and if he had not told the captain, specifically, that you were a man to be trusted, we would have taken action, immediately."

"Well, trust me on this, then, the best thing ta do is let Jake Brady make the bed that Jake Brady's gonna have ta sleep in. I've known him all my life and this is a decision he would want ta make. I've seen him sleep on some awful rocky beds, but he made every one of 'em. When he's up to it, he'll make this one. I'll warn ya right now, though, when he does make his decision it will be based on truth, facts, and what's right in the long run for everyone involved."

"Yes, sir, I'd have to agree with you on that. It sounds like he's been the same man all his life. I wouldn't expect that to change now."

"Oh, Ben! Got Nelly milked already, huh? Why don't you just set that milk in on the table there and tell your mother I asked ya to ride on over to my house and see what kinda trouble you and Kenneth can get into."

"Yes, sir."

I walked on in the house with the doctor. He went straight into the bedroom. I walked over to the table and sat the milk pail down. Ma was sittin' at the table. She was cryin'. As I sat the pail down, she looked up at me. This time she didn't turn away. She reached out her arms for me. I gave her a hug as she held me tight.

"Ben, oh, Ben."

She held me tight as she stood up. I began to cry, too. I didn't know why but I knew my mother was hurtin deeply, to the point of sobbing.

"I'm so confused, Ben. I've always tried to do what I thought was right. To be a good mother and teach you right. At least what I thought was right. Now I don't know, anymore, what's right or what's wrong."

She stopped talkin'. We held each other for several minutes. The lieutenant must have asked her to let Pa stay longer than she wanted. What were Jay and the lieutenant talkin' about? As we held each other, the doctor came back out of the bedroom and walked to the front door. He paused briefly. "He's doing better, much better."

"Good, that's good."

Good? I thought she hated his guts! I thought she wanted him out of the house. Now he's doin' better and that's good? And she said it in a compassionate way.

"Ma, Jay wants me ta go see Kenneth."

"Why don't you do that. It will be good for you to get away from all this for awhile. But be home in time to do the chores."

Ma put her hands on my cheeks.

"Oh, I'll bet you think that's all I want you around here for sometimes, don't you."

"No Ma, I don't think that at all."

"Thank you, Son. My whole world revolves around you. You're all I've got. Now go on over to Kenneth's house and have a good time."

"Ma...I love you."

I walked out the front door probably more confused than Ma. Jay slapped me on the back.

"Everything will be just fine, Ben. Don't you worry about anything around here. Oh, Ben, tell Maggie I'll be a little late tonight. Kenneth will need ta do all the chores."

"Yes, sir. Jay...Ma's-"

"Don't you worry about your Ma. You'll see, everything's gonna be all right."

"Thanks, Jay."

My mind was jumpin' from thought to thought and my heart, from emotion to emotion. I was leavin' Ma cryin', but somewhere deep inside of me, I knew Jay was right. Everything was going to be all right, different, but all right.

CHAPTER 5

Kenneth and I have been friends since before I can remember. I guess we're probably like Pa and Jay were when they were growin' up. Some folks say they were joined at the hip.

Normally, when we hadn't seen each other for awhile, the first thing we would do was wrestle. I guess this time Kenneth could see I needed to just talk. He told his mother that we were going huntin' and wasted no time gettin' gone from the house. I was glad to have him to talk to and even happier that he knew what I needed to do...

"We better be headin' back to the house. Especially since I gotta do all the chores tonight. Did Pa say how late he would be over ta your house?"

"No, just said he'd be late enough you had ta do the chores."

Kenneth and I began walkin' back through the pecan trees to his house. We'd been out for about three hours. We hadn't got much huntin' done. We spent most of the time doin' just what I needed, sittin' on an old piece of dead-fall log talkin'. Mostly speculatin' on what the future would bring with Pa back in town. Kenneth stopped walkin'.

"Ya know, I sure hope your Pa gets better real quick. I can see where this, 'Kenneth, do the chores,' could get ta be a bad habit."

"Yeah, I see what ya mean. Maybe he'll get well enough ta do my chores."

We both laughed a little and started walkin'. Kenneth was just like his father. He was shorter and stocky-built like Jay and he always tried to keep the mood light and find a way to laugh when it didn't seem like there was anything to laugh at. It was good for me to come and spend some time with him. It was good to just plain get away and think things out.

"Hey, we better hook up, I still gotta ride home and do my chores."

Kenneth looked at me and rolled his eyes.

"Oh, I'm sure that's the real reason, too."

He was right. I wanted to get home to check on Pa! I wanted to see how Ma was doin'. It was also kind of interesting to me to have all those Yankee soldiers around the house. I wanted to watch them, maybe even talk to them. After all, they were really friendly to me, and they knew a lot more about Pa than I did.

"Boy, ain't we the hunters. Gone three hours and come back with two empty sacks. Hope Ma ain't gonna make us live on what we shot fer supper tonight." Kenneth laughed again.

"Heck, if I had ta live on what I could shoot fer supper I'd shrivel up and die."

I'd no sooner gotten the words out of my mouth than I realized that just the other mornin' I was plannin' to give a go at doin' just that. Boy, was I glad Jay stopped me.

As we climbed over the fence into Kenneth's yard, I looked up and noticed Jay's horse tied to the corral fence by the barn.

"Hey, I thought you said Pa wouldn't be home till late!"

"Well, that's what he told me."

Curious, we both hit a trot to the barn. My heart was poundin'. All I could think was the worst. Did Pa die? As we hit the lane that led to the barn door, Jay stepped out of the barn.

"Slow down there, young'uns, ya might fall down and blow your leg off. Or worse yet, ya might blow mine off."

Jay laughed. I knew Pa wasn't dead. Jay seemed to be too jovial for that. We slowed to a walk and he met us in the lane.

"Well, let's see the kill."

We both laughed.

"Pa it's like this, we shot a lot, but we ain't got nothin' ta show fer it."

"Are ya that bad a shots?"

"No, Pa, what we shot a lot of, was bull."

We all laughed and Kenneth slapped his leg.

"Dang, I crack myself up."

"Yeah, you're funny alright, it may not be so funny when you get to the house and find your ma lookin' through your sacks fer supper tonight."

Jay paused for a minute, " Kenneth, why don't ya head on up to the house and let me have a little chat with ol' Ben here."

"Yes, sir. See ya, Ben. Thanks fer comin' over."

"Yeah, thanks for goin' huntin' with me."

Jay chuckled.

"Huntin', is that what you two call it?"

Kenneth headed on in the house. I had no idea what to expect from Jay. All of a sudden, he seemed to get more serious. That bothered me. Maybe -- Naw, he's not that serious.

"Ben, plop yourself down on that ol' crate right there. I'd like ta visit with ya a little. Seems like you and I just got done havin' a man ta man talk the other day. Looks like we get ta have another one."

"Is he dead? Did he die?"

"No! No! Heck, he's doin' fine. I said my money was on Jake Brady makin' it, and I only make sucker bets. No, he'll be fine."

My mind was relieved. I figured I could handle any other thing that Jay had to tell me, but that would have been more than I was ready for.

"No, see, Ben, your mother and I were talkin', and things bein' what they are and all around your place... I mean, havin' ta take care of Jake and put up with those soldiers and all....well, your mother and I kinda think maybe ya ought'a stay over here with us a few days. What do ya think of that?"

I didn't say anything. I didn't want to. I wanted to be home. I wanted to see Pa. Maybe even get to talk to him. He may die and I may never get a chance to talk to him. I didn't know how to express all this to Jay.

"Who'll do the chores?"

"Well, now, it seems those Yankee boys like Jake purdy good. When I mentioned that to the lieutenant, he just jumped all over it; went and grabbed one of his little soldier boys and had your ma tell him just exactly what ta do, night and mornin'."

"Ma's gonna let a Yankee do our chores?"

"I know it don't sound like your ma, but there's a whole lot more ta this story than meets the eye. I figure when your folks want ya ta know the whole story, then they'll tell ya."

"Jay, I...I really wanted ta go home and maybe get a chance ta talk to him."

"You'll get a chance ta talk to him. They just need some time ta talk a few things out amongst themselves. Ya know, your ma ain't seen Jake in four and half years and didn't ever expect ta see him again. Things came on a little sudden fer her, too, ya know. What do ya say we give 'em a few days."

I sat again in silence. It was plain I wasn't goin' to win. I wasn't goin' home tonight. If history was any lesson, I guess I was better off to listen to Jay, anyway. He'd never led me wrong yet. I guess maybe there was the hope that Ma and Pa could work things out. That would be worth the wait by itself. After all, Ma did act like she wanted Pa to get better.

"I'll tell you what I'll do, Ben! If ol' Jake up and dies on us before ya get a chance ta chew his ear a little, I'll give ya that long-eared mule right there in the corral. You can name him Jay, just ta remind ya what a mule-headed jackass I was! What do ya say?"

I couldn't help but laugh a little. Jay was so dang funny sometimes.

"It's a deal. I'll stay."

Jay slapped me on the back and we headed up toward the house.

"Now, just so you don't think I'm tryin' ta cheat ya, I wanna tell ya straight out. That ol' mule there, he ain't worth a dang. But, you know what they say, 'one man's junk is another man's treasure.' Why you might just make a fine mount out of him."

Jay laughed again. I thought to myself, I don't want the mule, but if I do end up with him, I think I will name him Jay. Then maybe he'll get a taste of what it's like to feel like you're the product of a well bred horse crossed with a jackass and have the whole county look at you that way.

Jay spent the next two weeks goin' back and forth between his house, the blacksmith shop, and my house. Every evenin' when he came in he'd say to me, "Still looks like I'm gonna have ta keep that ol' mule."

He never went into a lot of detail with me. I knew it was because he was dog-tired, but he did take just a minute each night to pull me aside and tell me that Ma was doin' well and Pa was gettin' better. But for the whole two weeks, he never mentioned me goin' home.

Jay came in that night smilin' a little more than usual. "Maggie, tomorrow night put a little extra grub on the table, I think we might have a guest."

Kenneth and I both spent the whole next day speculatin': Was it Ma? Was he gonna bring Ma over? Surely it wasn't Pa! There's no way he could travel anywhere, yet. Maybe it wasn't anything to do with me at all. Maybe it was some of their kinfolk comin' in. Toward evenin' Kenneth and I made sure that we stayed within viewing distance of the long lane that led up to their house.

"Look! I don't think Ma made near enough food!"

I turned and looked into the golden-orange sunset. I could see at least twenty horses and riders comin' up the lane. Kenneth got a scared look on his face.

"Looks like Yankees, I'm gonna run tell Ma!"

He was right. It was Yankees, riding in pairs. As they drew closer I could tell the first pair wasn't soldiers. One of them was Jay. I walked across the yard closer to the edge of the lane. Could it be? It kind of looked like him! They rode right up to me. Behind them rode the lieutenant that had been at our house. The lieutenant slowly raised up his right arm.

"Company, Halt!"

"Ben, I guess I'll be keepin' that ol' mule."

Jay's voice began to break a little.

"I'd like ya to meet... Ben, this is your father."

I was speechless! He looked majestic! He looked dignified sittin' on his horse. It was obvious he commanded the respect of those in his presence. He and Jay swung down from their saddles at the same time. Jay reached and took the reins of his horse. As Pa walked toward me, he towered over me. When he got up to me, he knelt down slowly. Even kneeling he could almost look me in the eye. He reached out his hand. It was obvious from the way he moved that he was still in pain.

"Son."

I was filled with emotion! I was eye to eye with the man I had both loved and hated, and yet had never really known. I slowly reached my hand out and put it in his outstreched hand. He placed his other hand on my shoulder and looked me straight in the eye. Then he pulled me close up against him and hugged me tight.

"Ben Brady. My little boy...my little man."

Jay yelled out.

"You Yankee boys put your horses in that corral over there." Jay motioned with his hand. "Go on, now, right over there."

Jay took the two horses, wiped a tear from his cheek and led them into the barn. The lieutenant yelled out something and the soldiers all began to dismount or ride toward the corral.

I didn't know what to say, but I couldn't help but feel the love that this stranger had for me. Almost instinctively, I hugged him back. He stood up and placed his hand on my shoulder. Both of us, wipin' the tears from our faces, started walkin' across the yard.

"Your mother sends her love." He paused. "Ben Brady, there's a lot ta talk about and a whole lot of understandin' that needs to happen. Most of all, I guess, a whole lot of forgivin'. I know things have been rough for ya here. I knew when I left that they would be, but I also knew you'd be fine and I'd be back. I'd like ta make you a suggestion if I could, Son."

"A suggestion?"

"A proposition. Would that be alright with you?"

"Yes, sir."

"I'd like ta propose that we go in and let Maggie feed us some of her fine home cookin'. Somethin' I did without, a whole lot of, these past few years. Then I'd propose that we enjoy the evening' with our fine friends, the Thompsons. With a promise that you and I will sit down here in the near future and answer all the questions we have about each other. What do ya think?"

"Yes, sir, I'd like that. I'd like that a lot."

"Good, then we've got a deal."

"Sir?"

"Yes Son."

"Before we make our deal, can I ask just one question?"

"I suppose so. What would you like ta know?"

"Are you gonna take me home with ya?"

He stopped walkin', put a hand on each of my shoulders, and stood for a moment in silence.

"Yes Son. From now on, wherever I go, you can go, too. We'll ride for home at first light."

CHAPTER 6

The bedroom door swung open.

"Up and at'em, boys! The menfolk done ate and are already saddlin' the horses."

It was Maggie. She could stand toe to toe with anybody when it came to bein' tough. Except when it came to Jay. Then I would have to say she always stood side by side with him. I never remember them arguing much. I wished many times that I had a Ma and Pa that got along like Maggie and Jay.

"Ben, if you want somethin' ta eat, ya best get on in here, cause unless your Pa's changed a whole bunch, he won't let no grass grow under your feet. Judgin' from last night's conversation, he ain't changed a lick."

My Pa; it seemed so funny hearing that. I can only remember Pa a little before the war. I remember he was never home much. He was always workin', either at the blacksmith shop with Jay, or down helpin' Jay's Pa, Delbert, at his shop. When he'd go down there, he'd be gone two or three weeks at a time. Seein' him now, I could just catch glimpses of my memories of him when I was younger. He looked different now, older, yet more dignified.

It was fun to listen to Jay and Pa tell stories about the past. Kenneth and I sat there and listened and laughed for hours. Pa would laugh so hard sometimes, he'd have to reach down and hold his side, where he'd been shot. The subject of the war seldom came up in the conversation. Jay said once, " Just look at ya, Jake! Ya left out'a here a dirt-poor blacksmith - couldn't even afford ta shaw your own horse. Now, here ya are a war hero and got people standin' around sayin' "Yes, sir" to ya and beggin' to just hold your horse." Pa just chuckled and said; " Well, I'm still dirt-poor and as for bein' a hero, I gave orders to a lot of men that could wear that title better 'n me."

I always knew Jay and my Pa were close, but last night, for the first time, I realized how close. It was plain just watchin' them talk that they had mutual admiration and respect for each other. It was also plain that Maggie enjoyed watchin' these two dear friends spend the night reminiscin' days gone by. Now and then, between the laughter, she would chime in with a, "Remember when..." and that would get them started again on another story. Once after they got through tellin' about some pranks they had pulled when they were kids, Jay spoke up and said, " Now, you boys don't get no ideas, we ain't raisin' no kids like us." And then he laughed and went right into another story. The night just flew by. It was late when we finally retired to bed, and that was short-lived. I felt like I had only been in bed long enough to get a short nap.

Maggie looked out the window and then walked back to the table. "Better jam it down your throat and chew it later, Ben. Looks like your Pa's already saddled both your horse and his. He's walkin'up ta the house, right now."

"Yes, ma'am. Thank you for the breakfast. See ya later, Kenneth."

I grabbed a biscuit and headed for the door. They must have gotten up at four o'clock; the sun was just now barely coming up. I met Pa halfway across the yard.

"How are ya this mornin' Son? Did ya get enough sleep?"

"Yes, sir"

"I saddled your horse for ya. Are you ready ta go?"

"Sorry, sir."

"Sorry fer what?"

"Sleepin' in, so as you had ta saddle my horse."

"Why, that's nothin' ta be sorry for. I was glad ta do it. I hadn't got ta saddle a horse for ya in a long time. I enjoyed it."

"Well...thank you, sir."

"Let's talk about this 'Sir' business, too. I was raised to respect my elders and I expect that of you, too, but..."

Pa pointed over at the soldiers.

"Do you see all those soldiers over there?"

"Yes, sir."

"They and a lot of men like them have called me "Sir" for the last three years. They did it because it was their duty, and I suppose they did it out of respect, too. But, to be honest with you, I place my son just a notch or two above the best one of those men. How about throwin' in a 'Pa' now and then for me instead of 'sir'? I haven't heard that in a long time."

It made me feel good to hear him say that. I seemed to be drawn to this man. He seemed so honest and sincere. The hatred that I had for him was beginnin' to drift into the distant shadows of my mind.

"Yes, sir.... I mean, Pa."

He grinned a kind of half-cocked grin.

"I guess it'll take a little time. That's one thing we're gonna have a lot of, now that we've got that damnedable war...." He paused, "now that I'm home. Why don't you head on down there and get mounted while I go thank Maggie for her hospitality."

I headed on down to the barn where our horses were tied to the corral fence. As I mounted up, Jay handed me the reins to Pa's horse.

"Why don't ya lead your Pa's' horse up to him."

I started to ride away.

"And, Ben, remember I told ya everything would be all right?"

"Yes, sir."

"Well, a lot of that "all right stuff,"comes from inside yourself. I've always told ya your Pa was a good man. Now that he's here, give him a chance. He'll prove me right. I'm sure you won't be disappointed."

"I'll give him a chance, Jay."

Jay smiled as I led Pa's horse up to the edge of the yard fence. He hugged Maggie and, walking toward me, looked back at her and said, "I know she does, if I can just get her to remember."

He turned back and picked up his pace. The Yankee soldiers were already in formation and ready to go. Pa took the reins from my hand.

"Thank you, Son."

He stepped up on his horse with ease and waited while I pulled myself on my Dungeon.

"You ride beside me Son."

The procession started down the lane again. This time goin' the other direction. And this time, instead of Jay ridin' beside Pa in the front, I was. I couldn't help but feel a little important.

"Is our deal over yet?"

He smiled.

"What do you have on your mind, son?"

"Are you their boss? I mean, are you still a soldier?"

"Well, technically, yes. That is, I'm still a soldier. I've never really considered myself anybody's boss. As for these men, some of them have served with me, some of them not. Right now, they're under the command of Colonel Billings."

"If you're still a soldier, does that mean you have ta go back? Does it mean you'll be leavin' again."

"No, I won't be leavin' again. I'm on what's called "leave," it means time off. The more you serve, the more days you build up. I've got enough built up ta last me until I fulfill my obligation to the Cavalry, which ends in about four more weeks."

"Then you won't be a soldier, anymore?"

"That's right. Then I won't be a soldier, anymore."

"How come these soldiers still follow you around everywhere?"

"Well, because that's what they've been ordered ta do."

"Why?"

"Oh, Colonel Billings and I are long time friends, and when he got wind that I'd been... been hurt, well he thought I needed these boys ta look after me until I got better."

"Aren't ya better enough now, so that ya don't need 'em?"

"Yeah, I suppose so. But they've got their orders and until I can get a chance to talk with Colonel Billings, I guess we're just gonna have a lot of company. What do ya say I ask you a question or two?"

"Sure, what do ya have on your mind?"

He laughed at me, mimicking him.

"Good, that's good, I like a sense of humor. Son, do you feel like you're happy enough here?"

I didn't know how to answer him. I wasn't sure what he meant.

"I suppose so. I don't know no different."

"Have you ever thought about leavin'?"

"Yeah, once."

I knew Jay had probably told him what I had planned to do, so I had just as well tell him the truth.

"Where were you thinkin' about goin'?"

I was startin' to get uncomfortable. I didn't want to rehearse to him my whole stupid plan. I didn't want to look dumb. Finally, I responded.

"What do ya say I ask you a question or two."

He laughed again.

"I can see you've been spendin' way too much time around Jay. He's as quick-witted a man as I know, but you're not far behind him. Fair enough, how can I help you?"

"Do you know who shot you?"

He pulled his horse to a halt, without even lookin' my way. The lieutenant, behind, quickly yelled, "Company, Halt!" He sat in silence for what seemed like forever. I was certain that I'd made him mad at me. Then he turned back toward the lieutenant.

"Lieutenant?"

"Yes, sir"

"Why don't you give my son and me a little room here for a minute."

"But, sir, Captain Roundy said when you were out of doors I was to-"

"Lieutenant! Do you see Captain Roundy? As a matter of fact, do you see anything but that oak tree for a mile?"

"No, sir."

"Then give me some room!"

"Yes, sir."

We rode ahead a little bit before the lieutenant began to follow us again.

"Son, it's not always wise ta reveal all ya know. It is true, that the truth will set you free, but if you're already free, then tellin' all you know about somethin' has no real benefit or use to ya and could have the potential ta harm someone else. I know that sounds a little complicated, but if you can make sense of it, it will serve you well through your life. Do you understand why I'm not going ta discuss who shot me?"

"Yes, sir."

I didn't really understand all he said, but it was plain enough to me that he was not willin' to talk about who had shot him. I could tell he was tryin' to be patient, and talk to me in a way I could understand. What I did understand plainly was, he did know who shot him. What I didn't understand was why he wouldn't tell me; why he didn't want the lieutenant to hear what he said to me.

It wasn't far now to our house. I was ready to get home. Ready to see Ma. I was curious as to how my folks were getting along; how they would act toward each other. I had no idea what the future held for me, for Ma, or for Pa.

"I didn't make you sore, did I?"

"No, sir."

"Good, sometimes I come across soundin' a little different than I mean to."

We rode the short distance on to the house without askin' anymore questions. I just listened, while Pa, pointed out things around us that he remembered and talked about the past.

The sun had taken the dew from the grass by the time we rode into the yard. I could see Ma on the porch. As we got closer I could tell Ma looked different. She looked younger. She had her hair fixed up like we were goin' to prayer meetin' on Sunday mornin'. Her appearance had changed. It was bright and she seemed to glow as she came off the porch. I could smell food cookin'.

"You two boys hungry?"

Pa smiled at Ma, glanced over at me, then looked back at Ma.

"Well... I bet between the two of us we could eat a horse."

Then Pa turned to me and said under his breath, "I believe the better part of valor, here, says we don't mention that we've already eaten."

I laughed.

"Yes, sir, I know what ya mean."

It was obvious that Ma had been waitin' for us to get home. It was also obvious that she was tryin' to be more than a mother. Two weeks of them bein' together must have paid off. At least I sure wasn't seein' any open hostility. Then Ma gave me a reality check.

"I didn't fix enough for any of them Yankees."

"Lizzie, them Yankees aren't here because they wanna be here. As far as I know, they haven't eaten any food from this house, yet. I'm not sure I see any call ta be unpleasant to 'em."

Ma stopped where she was, then slowly turned around and headed back toward the house. Pa looked down and shook his head.

"I'll be in the house when you're ready ta eat."

"We'll be right in."

It wasn't like Ma to not give me a hug or somethin' after being gone even one night, much less two weeks. She was a strong-willed woman and I could tell, my folks had a long way to go before things would be right between them. I wondered if things ever could be right again. There was a lot of hatred, at least on the part of Ma and I guess I had some things to get over, myself. I'd spent four and a half years without a father. Ma and I had to work hard just to survive. Pa and I dismounted and one of the soldiers took our horses.

"Son, do you mind if I go in first and have a word with your Ma."

"No...Are ya gonna fight?"

"You don't know me very well, yet, Son." He paused and looked in the direction of the house. "No, we're not gonna fight, just talk. You come on in the house in a few minutes. Why don't you help put the horses up and that'll be about right."

"Yes, sir."

I hurried down to the barn to help put the horses up.

"Your ma sure don't like us much, does she, boy?"

"Nope, I reckon not."

"Ah, I can't blame her much. Fact is, I guess there ain't too many in these parts that do."

He was right, it wasn't just my Ma. Nobody liked the Yankees being around. Since the war had been over, some of the townsfolk said we didn't have any rights, "We're under Yankee rule." I didn't really care about all that. I just cared about what was happenin' in the house and wanted to hurry up. I quickly tended to my horse and ran as fast as I could, back to the house. I paused to catch my breath a little before I opened the door.

"Come on in. Let's eat. I'm starvin'. How about you, Ben?"

"Ah, yes, sir, I'm hungry as I can be."

The table was set and Ma and Pa were seated across from each other. I took my seat. We all just sat in silence.

"Jake, I believe it's your place ta..."

"Oh, yes, thank you, Lizzie. I'll say grace if you don't mind."

We all bowed our heads.

"God of heaven and earth, we thank you for the food we are about to eat. We thank you for the hands that prepared it. We're thankful to be together, as a family again. Bless us with understandin'. In the name of Jesus, amen."

Before I could hardly raise my head, Ma looked at me.

"Ben, I was wrong out there. There's seldom any call for open rudeness like that. I'm sorry."

"That's okay, Ma."

"No, it's not okay, and you need to know it."

We all started eatin'. It was a little tense. Was it ever goin' to be peaceful? Would our home ever be like Jay and Maggie's? Why didn't those Yankee soldiers just go away? We didn't need them around here, anyway.

"I notice there's a few things that need fixin' up around here. Ben, what do you say you and I put those soldiers out there ta good use right after breakfast. I think if they're gonna use our land ta camp on, they ought'a earn their keep, a little. The roof on both the house and the barn could use some work and it looks like some of those posts in the corral are rottin' off at the ground. That's no surprise. I guess it's been four, no...it's been about six years ago that I built that corral. Time's just flown by."

Ma looked up sharply at Pa.

"For some folks, I guess. For others, it drug along purdy slow."

She noticed I was watchin' her. I looked down and started eatin' again. Ma did the same.

"Yeah, you're right, it does drag on sometimes. I reckon it just depends on how you spend it."

We all finished our breakfast. We got up and started to clean up the table.

"Ben, you've been gone near two weeks and you haven't even given me a hug."

I smiled and gave Ma a big hug.

"Ben," Pa looked at me with that half cocked grin and then looked up at Ma and winked. "Let's go put those "blue bellies" to work!"

Ma smiled, then turned her head so I couldn't see her.

"You do that, but you'd better yell at me about a half hour before your 'Brady bellies' start ta get empty and I'll get ya some lunch."

Pa laughed. "We'll do that."

We picked up our hats and headed out the door. Ma was fightin' an inner battle. I could tell that her emotions went from love to hate to somewhere in between. It was easy to recognize because I was fightin' the same battle, just not as hard as Ma. I guess Ma's battle was from a different angle than mine. I missed not having a father and she had always had hers. But it was certain we both had felt betrayed, in our own way. Pa and I walked out the door.

"Lieutenant."

"Yes, sir."

The lieutenant had been standin' by a couple of other soldiers. He immediately turned and came toward us.

"Looks like your men are gettin' fat."

"Sir?"

"Maybe a little work would trim them up and make them better soldiers."

The lieutenant looked back over his shoulder at the soldiers. He looked back at Pa and grinned.

"Yes, sir, I'm sure it would. What did you have in mind, sir?"

"Well, if it were my outfit, not that it is, you understand, but if it were."

"Yes, sir."

"And I was stayin' as a guest on someone else's place, I believe I'd take the opportunity ta teach my men how ta patch a roof on a house, and a barn, and set fence posts around corrals. Maybe clear a little unsightly brush from around a house. Don't you think these are all things that a good soldier ought'a know how ta do?"

"Yes, sir I do! I believe I'd like to be excused so I can go start the training immediately, sir."

"Good, I thought you'd see the benefit in such trainin'. I'll take care of startin' to train my son and you're excused to go and train your soldiers."

"Yes, sir, thank you for the suggestion, sir."

"Anytime, Lieutenant, anytime."

Pa grinned and the lieutenant chuckled as he walked away and began shoutin' orders to his men.

"Ya see, Son, your trainin' has already begun. Never try ta do the work of ten men when you've got ten men sittin' around on their butts."

I thought, this is going to be great. All these men working and Pa and I givin' orders. I thought wrong. I never worked so hard in all my life. By three o'clock I felt like I had done the work of ten men.

"Jake! Jake!"

I heard the voice of my mother yellin' from the porch. Pa and I were workin', clearin' brush along the pasture fence. Pa didn't hear her.

"Sir?...Pa?"

"That's more like it. What, Son?"

"Ma's hollerin' at ya."

"Oh."

He turned toward the house.

"What do you need, Lizzie?"

By that time Ma had come off the porch and was halfway to us.

"He's only a boy! You've got ta feed him, now and then, or he'll never get ta be a man."

Was I glad to hear that! Pa turned toward me.

"Are you hungry?"

Hungry! I was starvin' to death, my feet hurt, and I thought I was goin' to die of thirst.

"Yeah, I could eat."

"Well, I guess those two breakfasts I had, lasted me longer than I thought. Let's go eat a bite."

I watched Ma as she turned around. She saw all the soldiers workin'. I could tell she was surprised at all that had been done. So was I. The weeds and brush around the house and barn were cleared. The corral fence was standin' up straight again and there were soldiers on the roof of the house and the barn. I guess I had been workin' so hard to keep up with Pa, to just plain stay alive, that I hadn't paid any attention to what the soldiers had done. Ma turned back around.

"We might wanna keep these Yankee boys another day or two."

Pa smiled, "I figured that might build a little morale around here."

He put his hand on my shoulder and we followed Ma to the house.

"You ain't tired are ya Son?"

"Just a little."

"You'll feel better after ya eat. Then we'll go check with the lieutenant and see if he's finished trainin' his soldiers yet."

He laughed. I knew I was as trained as I wanted to be. The only thing I figured I could be trainin' for was slavery, and I thought the war did away with all that.

"By the way Son, did you pick up on that second little piece of trainin' I gave ya?"

"What's that, sir?"

"Never ask a man ta do somethin' that you're not willin' ta do yourself or haven't already done sometime in your past. That's why

48

we got out here and worked beside these men. It builds respect. Not just from those around you, but most important, it builds self respect."

After today, I ought to be well-respected. He was right though, I did think purdy highly of myself after all that work. Mainly, just because I survived it!

CHAPTER 7

The next few days we worked like dogs. Pa never missed the sun comin' up. I was almost certain that he went down every mornin' to the chicken coop and kicked the roosters out of bed. Now and then, a sharp word; now and then, an apology. Things seemed to be gettin' less tense. The distance between confrontations seemed to be gettin' longer and longer.

It was Saturday evenin'; my folks, and I were sittin' on the porch chairs after a hard-day's work. The Yankee soldiers had already eaten their supper and some of them had gathered around a campfire. They were laughin'. Then they'd sing a song or two and then laugh again.

"Do we have ta listen ta them sing them Yankee songs all night?"

"Why no, Lizzie, we could plug our ears."

Pa laughed. Ma looked at him. Her face was expressionless.

"Don't get mad, now, I'm just funnin' ya. What would you like them ta sing? Tomorrow's Sunday, I'll bet they know a few old gospel hymns, or as a matter of fact, I bet they know a few Johnny Reb songs. They heard enough of them this last year from prisoners. Let me slip down there and see if I can change their tune a little."

"Oh, you don't have ta do that. I'm just gripin'. Let'em sing what they want, I'll ignore it."

"I'll be right back."

Pa sprang to his feet and trotted off the porch down to the soldiers.

"That man is stubborn as a mule, sometimes. He will do what he wants ta do, no matter what anybody thinks."

"He's doin' it fer you, Ma."

She looked surprised. I could tell she thought I was taking his side, against her.

"I mean, he's just tryin' ta please ya.

"I know. You're right, I know."

"Ma, do you think things will ever be normal for us? I mean, will we ever be a close family?"

Ma stood up and put both hands on her hips, then she walked out to the edge of the porch and looked up at the evenin' star.

"I'm not gonna lie ta ya, Son. We've got a long way ta go ta be what I would call a close family. Fact is, I don't know if we ever can be, livin' here."

"Why?"

"Too much bad blood. Too much water under the bridge. Even if your Pa and I start ta see eye ta eye, the folks around here will never treat us like a normal family. I could be wrong, that's just my opinion."

She stood silently and then slowly walked back to where I was sittin'.

"And that ain't fair ta you."

"Then let's leave! Go somewhere that nobody knows us."

"But, this...this is our home! You don't just up and leave your home. You don't leave what you've worked so hard ta get."

Pa came runnin' up the steps.

"I believe those boys are gonna change their tune."

Pa had no sooner sat down then a group of the Yankee soldiers walked up and stood in the yard, in front of the porch. One of them stepped forward.

"Ma'am, the colonel...Ma'am, we'd sure be honored if you'd allow us ta serenade ya with some of the songs we've learned."

The soldier just stood there.

"Well, Lizzie, the boys want ta sing to ya a little."

"Yes, yes, that would be nice, thank you."

The soldier still just stood there. Pa smiled at Ma and then looked back at the soldiers and raised his eyebrows.

"Are ya gonna sing, or just stand there like statues?"

"Oh, yes, sir, and a... thank ya, ma'am."

He slightly bowed his head and backed up and took his place with the other soldiers. I could tell he was kind of embarrassed. The soldiers sang several songs to us. They had very good voices and I could tell Ma was enjoyin' it. They even sang Dixie.

In the middle of one of their songs, Pa stood up, suddenly.

"Hold up, boys!"

They stopped singin'. We could hear the sound of a horse runnin' fast on the hardpan road that led up to our house.

"Rider comin'!"

In just a few moments, we could see a horse and rider appear in the moonlight as he streaked between the trees beside the road. He was runnin' wide open.

"He's alone." Pa said.

A soldier yelled down to the lieutenant.

"Rider comin', Lieutenant!"

The group of soldiers around the campfire immediately jumped up, got their rifles, and started runnin' to the house. They got to the house just ahead of the rider and took position at the front gate to our yard. The rider pulled his horse to a halt and dismounted, quickly.

"Halt!"

"Don't shoot me, dad blame it!"

It was Jay Thompson. Pa walked out in the yard to meet him.

"Let him through, men. He's friendly."

"I may be, but they sure as heck ain't."

Jay pointed off into the distance. About a mile away, we could see the flickerin' of several torches moving down the road that led to our house. My heart started to race.

"Who is it?" Pa asked.

"It's that dang knucklehead, Newt, and a bunch of the men from around these parts. I've been keepin' my eyes and ears open just like you asked me ta do. It seems that Colonel Billings has made an arrest, if you know what I mean."

"On what grounds?"

"Well, Jake, the dang fool couldn't keep his mouth shut. Went ta braggin' ta everyone. Said he was gonna finish the job. Since the arrest, Newt's been drinkin' and stirrin' up everyone he could. He's done a good job of it, too. There's sure a good bunch of 'em."

"How many?"

"I'd say at least thirty, maybe forty men."

Jay noticed Ma and me standin' behind Pa.

"Sorry, Lizzie."

Ma didn't say anything to Jay.

"What are we gonna do, Jake?"

"You take Ben and go in the house."

"Don't kill him, Jake! Please don't kill him!"

"There won't be any killin' tonight, if I can help it. Now do as I said, go on in the house."

Ma latched onto my arm and took me in the house. The window shutters were open and Ma and I both stood close enough to hear what was being said. Ma noticed I was tryin' to listen, too.

"You get on up ta the loft."

"Ma, let me stay. Let me stay by ya, Ma!"

"Okay, but if trouble starts, you get up in that loft."

"Yes, ma'am."

I could tell she wanted to listen to the conversation outside worse than she wanted to argue with me.

"Well, Lieutenant, what's your plan?"

"Sir, I've never held off a mob before, just fought Rebs. I'm wide open to suggestion."

"Have five of your men flanked on the right and five on the left, out of sight. Put two at the back corners of the house. Get the remainder of them right out front, here. Lined up close enough where they can hear you plainly, except one. Who's your best shot?"

"That would be O'Reilly, sir."

"Have him standin' right by this post here on the porch. Then take a seat here beside Jay and me. Oh, and Lieutenant, tell your men if they hear a shot, not to start shootin'. Hold their fire until ordered. Why don't ya bring me a sidearm, just in case."

"Yes, sir."

The lieutenant immediately left the porch and called his men together. We could hear the running, of soldiers. Ma took a couple of steps toward the window and looked out.

"Are they gettin' closer?"

"Yes, they're at the end of the cow pasture."

"Can I look?"

"No!"

"Please, Ma, let me look."

"Okay, take a peek, then get back."

They were about a quarter of a mile away. Jay said there were only thirty or forty, but it looked more like a hundred. I'd never been so scared in all my life. Pa seemed so calm and under control. He was just sittin' next to Jay on the porch. The soldiers had all gotten to their positions. All was quiet, except for the lieutenant walkin' across our wooden porch toward Pa and Jay. He handed Pa a pistol and then took a seat beside him. Ma tugged at my shoulder.

"That's enough. Now get back."

I moved out of the window, but stayed closer than I had been before. Ma was right next to me. She was tense. She leaned forward grippin' the window frame.

"Lizzie?"

"Yes, Jake."

"You stay in the house. No matter what happens. Ya hear?"

"Yes."

The yard began to light up from the torches, the men were carrying. We could hear them talkin', but we could barely understand what they were sayin'.

"Well, would ya looky there. That blue-bellied traitor is just sittin' out on the porch waitin' ta die."

It was Uncle Newt's voice.

"Boys, this may be a little easier than I thought. Lessin' any a you other 'blue bellies' got a hankerin' ta die tonight, why don't ya just lower those rifles down real easy like and step aside. We're just interested in the traitor, tonight. Right, boys!"

Ma and I couldn't stand it. We had to look out the window. We both moved closer. She looked out one corner and I looked out the other. The lieutenant started to stand up. Pa put his hand on the lieutenants leg and pushed him back down.

"Lieutenant."

"Yes, sir"

"Shoot his horse!"

"His horse, sir?"

"Have your man there, shoot his horse!"

"Kill him?"

"Right in the head, Lieutenant!"

"O'Reilly, did you hear the colonel?"

"Yes, sir."

"Then carry on, O'Reilly."

"Well, what's it gonna be? You Yank's gonna give up the coward or - "

The rifle fired and Uncle Newt's sorrel horse dropped stone dead. Uncle Newt dropped his rifle and fell out to the side of the horse, and rolled a good ten feet. Pa jumped up and yelled, "Hold your fire. Nobody needs ta get hurt here."

Two soldiers that were flanked out to the side, rushed in and grabbed Uncle Newt. The rest of the soldiers stepped out on both sides of the men.

"Now, Newt's had a little too much ta drink and it cost him his ride home tonight. Most of you men know me. Fact is, I grew up around most of ya. I know ya don't agree with the decision I made, and that's just fine. I would gladly fight and die ta protect your right ta think the way you'd like to, and I am also willing ta die to protect my right ta think the way I like. Those of ya that know me know I mean what I say and I'll do what I say. Now, unless you all feel like walkin' home tonight, or worse yet, never seein' home again, I suggest ya holster those weapons and go on home ta your families."

"What about Newt?," one of the men yelled. "We ain't leavin' Newt."

"Newt will be taken care of. The only one that's gonna get Newt hurt, is Newt. You have my word on that. But you are leavin', without Newt!"

One of the men rode forward a little. It was Mr. Johnson.

"You killed my sons!"

"No sir, I didn't kill your sons. This war killed a lot of mothers' sons on both sides. As for your sons, Mr. Johnson, I didn't kill them. But I can tell you where one is buried, cause I buried him myself. If you'd like to know, I'll draw you a map. You'll find a marker at his head that reads, "Tim Johnson, my friend, died bravely in battle Oct. 12, 1863."

Mr. Johnson was overcome with emotion. He dropped the torch he was carrying, turned his horse, and started ridin' down the lane.

"Men, I've seen enough killin' ta last me a lifetime. Good men, some wearin' blue, some wearin' grey, but all good men. If you've got differences with me, I'm acceptable ta sittin' down with any, or all of ya, and workin' out a peaceable solution. Tonight, we've only lost a horse, and knowin' the way young Newt, there, judges horse flesh, it probably wasn't a good horse at that. Why don't y'all follow Mr. Johnson's lead, and go on home ta your families. We'll all feel better in the mornin'."

Only moments after Pa stopped talkin', the mob of men, one by one, began to turn their horses and leave. Uncle Newt was kickin' and tryin' to yell, but the two soldiers held him tight and had stuffed a kerchief in his mouth.

Jay got up and slapped Pa on the back.

"Ya handled that like a colonel, Jake."

"Many thanks, Jay, we'd have been in real trouble if ya hadn't warned us."

"No problem."

The lieutenant stepped forward and shook Jays' hand.

"Yes, sir, thank you very much."

Jay looked at the lieutenant and nodded his head, then looked back at Pa.

"Jake, I...I think this is far from over. I best be gettin' home."

"I know."

Jay walked back out the front gate and mounted his horse.

"Jay, ya might hold back a little and give those boys ahead of ya, there, a little room."

"I'll be all right, Jake. They weren't at my house a tryin' ta get me. You watch yourself, Jake."

Jay reined his horse around and slowly disappeared down the lane.

"Sir?"

"Yes, Lieutenant."

"What would you have us do with this man?"

He pointed at Uncle Newt.

"Take him out in the brush and shoot him."

"Sir?"

"I'm jokin', Lieutenant. He's hardly a man. Men don't act that way. Make sure he's disarmed, then tie him up in the barn with a twenty-four-hour guard on him. I'll deal with Newt in the mornin'."

Pa paused for a moment and rubbed his beard.

"Lieutenant?"

"Yes, sir."

"Get me a rider. I need ta dispatch a message ta Colonel Billings."

"Yes, sir."

Pa turned and came in the house.

"Thank you, Jake."

Ma had a look of relief on her face.

"I would never harm any man when it could be avoided, much less your brother, Lizzie."

"What are we gonna do?"

"I need ta find out a little more information. I'm writin' a note ta Colonel Billings. I expect I'll hear back from him in a few days.

Until then we don't do anything. Just wait."

"Will they come back?"

"Maybe. I'll see if I can't get Newt to understand that he's just gonna make matters worse by stirrin' folks up."

"Are you gonna let him go?"

"Yes, fact is, I really don't know if I've got a legal right ta hold him. I think the best thing, maybe, is ta have the lieutenant escort him back ta Captain Roundy, and let him make that decision."

Pa sat down at the table and dipped his pen into the inkwell and began to write a note. He had no sooner laid the pen down when a knock came at the door. Ma opened it.

"Ma'am, I was sent up ta see the colonel."

"Yes, he's right.... Ah, come on in."

"Colonel, the lieutenant asked that I come see ya."

"Yes, soldier, I'd like ya ta take this message directly to Colonel Billings. Wait for his reply, and bring it back to me, immediately."

"Yes, sir."

"Soldier, leave out, the back way. Cross over the little knoll here behind the house, then double back. I'm afraid ya might have trouble this other way. Go slow until ya get at least three miles from the house, then sink spur. You understand?"

"Yes sir."

The soldier took the message, walked out and shut the door.

"Are you gonna talk ta Newt, tonight?"

"Nope, in the mornin'."

"You're not gonna leave him out there tied up in the barn all night like a caged animal, are ya?"

Ma was startin' to get angry again.

"I won't bandy words with a drunkin' fool, Lizzie. Tonight, his behavior was like an animal. He got off light. I'll deal with Newt in the mornin'."

Pa didn't raise his voice, but spoke with an unmistakable firmness. He had made his decision and nothin' would change his mind. I could tell, Ma didn't like it much, but somehow she knew he was right. I didn't know what to think. Part of me was proud of Pa, and the way he handled the armed mob. The other part of me was thinkin' about my Uncle Newt, tied up, and being guarded by Yankee soldiers. Even I knew that Pa was right, and what Uncle Newt had tried to do, could not be justified. Still, I was confused.

Uncle Newt was family.

CHAPTER 8

Pa had slept in the bedroom, Ma in my bed in the front room, and I had slept in the loft since Pa had been here. I heard noise comin' from the bedroom. Pa was awake. I wanted to get up with him this mornin'. I wanted to see Uncle Newt. I wanted to see what Pa was going to do to him, or with him.

I thought about Uncle Newt a lot last night before I fell asleep. He was only eighteen years old. He was always talkin' about goin' and fightin' in the war but somehow never did. I guess by the time he was old enough, the war was about over. Uncle Newt had always been a big talker. He was a small man and I think, because he was small, he felt like he had to continually do things to be noticed.

I hurried and put my clothes on and was comin' down from the loft when Pa came out of the bedroom.

"Up early this morning, huh, Ben?"

"Yes, sir, I didn't sleep real good."

"Well, it's no wonder, with all that ruckus last night. Grab your hat and let's go feed."

Ma sat up in her bed and startled both of us.

"He doesn't need ta go down there!"

"Lizzie, you almost stopped my heart! What do you mean he doesn't need ta go down there?"

"With Newt and all, he doesn't need ta see all that."

"After last night's little performance by Newt, I'm not sure what more he could do, ta tarnish his image in the boy's eyes."

"That's not the point! Newt doesn't know when to keep his mouth shut and you know it."

"Yeah, I see where you're comin' from now, Lizzie."

Pa walked over and sat down at the kitchen table. He put one elbow on the table and rested his chin in his hand. Ma was puttin' on her robe and gettin' up. I figured I'd best stay busy, so I started puttin' wood in the stove.

"How old are you now, Ben?"

"Turned thirteen this last January, sir."

Pa folded his arms and leaned back in the chair.

"Lizzie, I believe Ben and I will go feed. Shouldn't take us long, if you wouldn't mind fixin' us breakfast we'd appreciate it."

Ma stopped dead in her tracks.

"Jake, no!" Ma paused, "Please Jake."

Ma wasn't as stern. She was almost pleading. I wanted to go bad, but I felt caught in between. Normally, I guess I would have spoken up and said I'd just stay at the house if it would be all right, just to avoid the contention. But, I couldn't make myself do it. I wanted to go. I wanted to know. I knew there were things that I wasn't being told, and I wanted to find out as much as I could.

"Ben?"

"Yes, sir?"

"You go huntin' much?"

"Yes, sir."

"Do ya know the difference between a squirrel and a skunk?"

I laughed a little.

"Yes sir."

"What's the difference, Ben?"

I didn't know what he meant or wanted me to say, so I just figured I'd tell him what came to mind.

"Well, sir, ya hunt squirrels ta eat, they're smaller than a skunk and they're brown or grey. A skunk's black and white, you don't eat 'em and they stink."

"How do ya know they stink?"

"I've been sprayed by 'em before."

"So if ya see a skunk, do you stay far enough back, now that you've been sprayed, so ya don't get sprayed again?"

"Yes, sir, I sure do."

"If I pointed at a small animal movin' in the brush, say six hundred yards away, would ya be able ta tell me if it was a squirrel or a skunk?"

"No, sir, I doubt it."

"If you were huntin', would ya try ta get a little closer. Close enough ta see if it was a squirrel, but not so close you'd get sprayed if it were a skunk?"

"Yes, sir, I'd say so."

"Lizzie, that's why Ben needs ta go down with me ta feed. Ya see, men are the same way. Ben will come back from that barn either proud of what he's found or sprayed by a skunk. I'd like the boy ta learn the difference so when he goes out huntin' for friends, he won't come home with skunks."

Ma walked over and sat down at the table. I could tell she was angry, but she held her tongue.

"Don't worry, if a skunk starts sprayin' down there in the barn, I'll send Ben ta the house before he gets ta smellin' too bad. Ben, ya ready ta go feed?"

"Yes, sir."

"Well, lets go. Who knows, Lizzie, we might just bring back a squirrel for breakfast, heck it wouldn't be the first time I've seen whiskey turn a squirrel into a skunk."

Ma got up and walked to the door with us. We put on our hats and started out the door.

"You hurry back, Ben. Far as I'm concerned, we've had several skunks hangin' around our barn, lately."

Pa laughed.

"See, that's the problem with ya, Lizzie, ya haven't been out huntin' enough."

Pa pulled the door shut. I knew, full well, what he was talkin' about, now. It made me feel good that he trusted me enough to make my own mind. Since Pa had been back, I had to admit I hadn't really ever disagreed with his behavior or much of what he said. The things he said and did, always seemed to make sense to me. As we stepped off the porch, he chuckled.

"You make sense out of any of that?"

"Yes, sir."

"Good... good, I thought ya might. Let's go lookin' for a squirrel, but don't be surprised if you get sprayed by a skunk."

"Yes sir."

As we approached the barn, the Yankee soldiers were already up and eatin' breakfast. The lieutenant stepped away from the men, and walked toward us.

"Good morning, sir."

"Good morning. How's our boy?"

"I think he's comin 'to, a little bit, sir."

"How'd things go last night?"

"From what I understand, not so good for awhile. He kept

thrashin' around and sayin' lots of bad things about ya, sir. Then, from what I was told, about midnight he stumbled and hit his head on the butt of Corporal Nelsons' rifle and slept like a baby after that."

Pa smiled.

"Have you fed, yet?"

"Why, yes, sir, we always feed our stock before we feed ourselves. You taught us that, sir."

"Did you happen to feed my stock?"

"Yes, sir, everything but the ol' milk cow and you've been feedin' her as you milked her. We can, though, if you'd like, and milk her, too."

"No, I'll tend to the cow. You're gonna make me plumb lazy."

We started into the barn. Pa stopped and looked back at the lieutenant.

"Where's he at?"

"Just inside the door to the right. Ya can't miss him. Just shine your lantern until you find the one with a knot on his head."

We walked on through the door. Pa held the lantern up. There were two soldiers standing on each side of Uncle Newt. He was sittin' on the ground, leanin' back against the barn wall.

"How is he, Corporal?"

Before the corpral could reply, Uncle Newt began to thrash around.

"None of your business, turncoat!"

"Has he been fed?"

"No, sir."

"Get him some food."

"I don't want nothin' cooked by a Yankee!"

"Would ya prefer your sister cooked it?"

"Got no use fer her, either. She'd see her own kinfolk shot, just so she could shack up with a coward."

"Colonel, I think he's about ta hit his head again."

"Let him talk. So ya think I'm a coward?"

"No, I know you're a coward and a traitor."

"Now, Newt, I believe that if I would have wanted to gun you down, I wouldn't have brought a mob with me ta do it. I believe I would have worked that out between you and me. By the way, Newt, which side of the war, did you fight on? I seen lots of sixteen-year-old Rebs in that war but I don't recall runnin' in ta you."

Pa put his hand on his chin and thoughtfully rubbed his cheek with his finger.

"A traitor and a coward, hmmm. While Ben and I go milk this cow, why don't ya see if ya can't come up with some answers to those questions."

We turned to walk away.

"Good, get on out of here. I'm tired of lookin' at ya and your bastard kid, anyway!"

Pa stopped.

"He's startin' to spray a little son, are ya alright?"

"Yes, sir."

I was deeply hurt. Uncle Newt had never been overly friendly to me, but he had taken me out huntin' a time or two. I had never done anything wrong to him in my life, yet he was attacking Ma, and me. I could understand him hatin' Pa and turnin' on him, but Ma and I were flesh and blood. Pa shined the lantern on my face and looked at me. I couldn't help it; tears had streamed down my face.

"Corporal! Smells like a skunk's in my barn. Why don't ya see if ya can't throw him out, so my son and I can get a little fresh air."

"Yes, sir. My pleasure, sir."

The two soldiers jerked Newt to his feet and started pullin' him out the door.

"You ain't nothin' but a low down - "

I heard a slight groan so I turned to look back at Uncle Newt.

"He hit his head again, sir!"

Newt fell limp and they drug him out the door.

"Sorry Son, sometimes people that ya love will disappoint ya. I've come to the conclusion that it's a God-given right for a man ta be able ta make his own choices in this world. I also believe that we're all a product of our past choices. When people choose ta be skunks, about the only right we have is ta see that they don't stink up our house and barn."

Pa didn't say anymore. He didn't have to. He slapped me on the back and we went over and milked ol' Nelly. As we left the barn Uncle Newt was nowhere to be seen. We went on in the house and sat the milk on the table. Ma walked away from the washtub dryin' her hands.

"How's Newt?"

"He's gettin' a little fresh air."

"Is he hungry?"

"No, I believe it'll just be the three of us for breakfast."

I guess Ma got the hint that things didn't go so well. She didn't say anymore and started puttin' breakfast on the table. I was still in shock. Though I was deeply wounded by what Newt had said, I was glad that Pa took me with him.

All through breakfast I pondered on what had taken place in my life, so suddenly. Nobody spoke at all. I thought about the barn, the mob, and all I'd been told about Jacob Allen Brady. I could see that I didn't agree with all I had been told. So far, all I could see was a well-humored man who was the same man every day. A man that had obviously earned the respect and loyalty of those he had been around. I thought of Uncle Newt and Grandpa Beck. I honestly couldn't remember anyone ever braggin' about them to me.

"Stack your plates in the tub, there. You didn't answer my question, Jake!"

"What's that, Lizzie?"

"How's Newt?"

"Lizzie, ya knew the answer ta that question before we ever went ta the barn."

"So, he's not gonna need me ta fix him a plate?"

"Not unless you've figured out how ta feed a skunk without him stinkin' up your house."

Ma threw her apron down on the table and walked out slammin' the door. I could see her on the porch. She was walkin' back and forth, cryin'.

"Guess this may have been one of those times that it would have been smart not ta reveal all the truth. That remark could have been left unsaid."

I didn't say anything. Pa got up and went outside. Within a few minutes they were sittin' down talkin'. I didn't even care to listen to what they had to say to each other. I had enough on my mind. I just had to keep goin' back to what Jay had told me weeks ago, "Everything will be all right." I know I wanted it to be all right, and I had to have faith that it would be. I just wasn't sure what all right was. I went up to the loft and layed on the bed.

The door opened. Ma and Pa walked in together.

"Ben?"

"Yes, Ma, up here."

"I'd like ya ta get your copy of the Good Book and come on

down here. Jake...your father and I, have some things we'd like ta talk with ya about."

"Yes, ma'am."

I dug around in the loft and finally found my Bible underneath some paper and books I had gotten from grammar school. I hadn't had Ma read anything out of the Good Book to me in a long time, much less try and read it myself. I dusted it off and climbed down from the loft.

"Would ya look at that! That's Pappys' old Bible, ain't it?"

"Yes, it is."

"Thank you, Lizzie, thanks for keeping'it. You don't know how much that old Bible means to me. If I had a dollar for every hour Pappy read ta me out of that Bible, I'd be a rich man."

Pa reached out for me to hand him the Bible. He took it and began to thumb through the pages. The room was quiet. Pa had tears in his eyes. It was as though a peace had come into the room that hadn't been there before. The contention was gone, at least for now.

"Had I the choice to make, I'd gladly turn down the dollars and keep what I gained from Pappy and this old Bible."

"Ben, we were talkin' outside and today bein' Sunday and with all the problems, we...."

"Ben, what your mother is tryin' ta say, is that we decided that if there was gonna be peace in our home, we needed the Lord's help. It seems ta us, that tryin' ta go ta any worship service might just cause more contention. So we thought it might be nice ta read from the Good Book and see if we can maybe have our own worship service here at home."

A knock came at the door. Pa turned and opened it. It was the lieutenant.

"Sir, I felt that it might be appropriate for me ta have four soldiers escort Mr. Beck back ta the fort and turn him over ta the custody of Captain Roundy."

"Yes, Lieutenant, yes, that would be fine. Have them tell Captain Roundy that it is my wish that Newt, or Mr. Beck, receive some stern fatherly sort of advice and then be released."

"Released sir? Ya know, sir, if he's released he'll –"

"Lieutenant, how well do ya know Captain Roundy?"

"Well, sir, I've served with him for eight months, now."

"Eight months, huh? Lieutenant, I've not only served with

him, I've fought with him, lived with him, sweat with him and helped him bury a lot of our friends. I have every confidence in his ability ta deal with young Newt. If there's a failure, it won't be mine, or the captain's; it'll be Newt's and, ultimately, Newt'll be the one ta pay up. Send my wishes and my regards ta the captain, Lieutenant."

"Yes, sir"

"And, Lieutenant?"

"Sir?"

"My family and I would like ta not be disturbed anymore today if at all possible. Today is Sunday and it's been a long time since I've.... Well, since I've...."

"I understand, sir. I'll see to it."

"Thank ya, Lieutenant...thank ya. Oh, and, Lieutenant, tell your soldiers to see that ol' Newt don't fall and hit his head anymore."

The lieutenant smiled.

"Yes, sir, I'll see to that, too."

The lieutenant pulled the door shut.

"What do ya say we all sit down here at the table and start this service. Lizzie, do we have another Bible or do we all need to share this one?"

"No, I'm afraid that's the only one I've...we've got."

"Not a problem; matter a fact I believe the Book itself teaches us that we ought ta share with each other."

We all sat down at the table. Pa began to both reminisce and read, from the Book of Matthew in the New Testament. We all read in turn. Neither Ma nor I could read nearly as well as Pa, but we all took our turn. I didn't understand, half of what we read. One thing that I did understand and I could never deny, was we hadn't had this kind of feelin' in our home, before. If we could keep this peaceful feelin' in our home, then Jay would be right for sure. Everything would be all right. It's a day I'll never forget.

CHAPTER 9

We spent the next few days workin' around the house. Somehow, I began to feel like we were prisoners in our own home. We didn't dare go into town, we didn't dare go anywhere for fear of havin' trouble. I knew that folks wouldn't harm Ma or me, but after knowin' how Uncle Newt had turned on us, I wasn't sure of anything, anymore.

The Yankee soldiers worked right along beside us, and our place was lookin' real good. I could tell by the conversations that Ma and Pa had been havin' that there was a lot of uncertainty in the future. They would talk one minute like we were going to be here forever, and the next minute one of them would say something like, " You know we can't stay here." I just kept on thinkin' about what Jay had told me, "Everything will be all right." Somehow I knew it would, but I still felt like a prisoner. I wanted to go see Kenneth. I was told it wasn't safe. I wanted to go squirrel huntin' and I was told only if a Yankee soldier was with me. Somehow my routine life had become a helpless victim to circumstances beyond my control. I was becoming frustrated. I needed to talk to Ma about it but it seemed that she became upset at the littlest things and would start cryin'. I didn't know if I could talk to Pa or not, I just didn't know how he would react. I used to be able to go over to Kenneth's house and talk to Jay when I had problems, but now I couldn't even do that. I decided that I had to talk with Pa. After all, he was my father, and Jay trusted him. I decided that after supper, I would ask if I could speak with him privately.

We began gatherin' up the dishes and puttin' the scraps in a bucket to feed to the hog.

"Pa...um..., I was wonderin' if I...."

"What Son? Spit it out."

"Well, sir, I'd like ta have a private word with ya tonight if I could."

Ma immediately looked up.

"Ben, there ain't nothin' you can't say in front of me."

I didn't know what to say. I had wanted to talk about it with Ma but I knew it would just cause her grief and now because I had chosen not to, it was hurting her anyway. Thankfully, Pa broke the silence.

"Sometimes, Lizzie, a boy needs ta talk man to man with his Pa. I know, Pappy and I used ta have those kind'a conversations a lot. What do ya say, Ben and I go out and feed these scraps ta the hog and you dip us up some of that cherry cobbler you've been hidin' all day."

"Oh, you've been diggin' around my kitchen, huh?"

"No, but my nose ain't forgot the smell of your cherry cobbler. We'll be back as quick as Ben and I agree he's got me lined up like a row a corn."

Pa grabbed the bucket and we both put our hats on. The Yankee soldiers were at their usual stations. The ones that weren't guardin' our house were already gettin' in bed. Since the mob had been to the house, the Yankee soldiers seemed to start takin' their job a lot more seriously. That was the problem, everything seemed like a life and death situation.

"What did ya have on your mind, Son?"

"Well, sir, I think I'd like ta slop the hog, and then find some place that we can sit and talk for awhile."

"Oh, I see, ya think it might take ya awhile ta get me staightened out."

"No, more likely the other way around, sir."

We slopped the hog and then went on through the barn out to the corral. Pa leaned against the corral fence and I climbed up on a corner post where I had spent many hours before, thinkin' about things.

"What a beautiful night. Would ya look at that moon! God sure made a great place for us ta live, didn't he, Ben?"

"Yes, sir, he did."

"I always loved a full moon with a million stars around it. Well, I'm sure ya didn't want ta talk ta me about the night sky. What is it I can help ya with?"

"Well, sir, it's about that great place we live. Ya see, it hasn't been so great here, lately."

"Yes, Son I know, it probably hasn't been too great for you. Tell me what ya think the biggest problems are, and how ya figure we can fix 'em."

"I guess my biggest problem is that I feel like a prisoner in my own house. I've kind'a felt like I was alone for a long time because...well, ta be honest with ya, I don't have a lot of friends except Kenneth. After you left us, I became purdy much an outcast. But now that you're back, it seems like I'm even more restricted. I feel like our house is a jail."

"Are you upset that I'm back?"

"Oh, no, sir, that's not it at all."

"You can and should, speak your mind, Son. I won't hold anything ya say against ya. I realize that my sudden return has put a cramp in a lot of people's lives."

I knew the only way I was ever going to be satisfied was to ask the questions that had haunted me for so long. I felt some of the emotions of the past, swell up inside me.

"Why did ya ever leave? How could ya leave Ma and me and be gone so long?"

"That's a fair question, Son. I'll answer ya as straightforward as I know how. Ya see, it became obvious that war was gonna break out. It also became obvious that most of the men would be expected ta go and fight in the war. I was raised by my Pappy, my Pa's father. He was a God-fearin' man that taught me ta always make my own choices, because I would not only have ta live with them, here, but, someday, I would stand before the judgment bar of God Almighty and be held accountable for those choices. He taught me, that often the right choice wasn't the most popular choice. He said that if I were ta maintain my integrity, I would have ta follow the dictates of my own conscience, make my own stand, and live with it. When I began ta study this war, and the issues that were the cause of the war, it became clear ta me, that I couldn't allow my birthplace ta be the sole determining factor for my decision. Ya see Son, I was destined to leave you and your mother and fight in the war. Whether I went to the North or to the South, you and your mother were gonna be left without a husband and a father for a long time. For all I knew, I might not ever come back. A lot of good men didn't. I wanted ta be sure I could live and die with my decision. Don't get me wrong, Son, I believe that wherever you're born, or whatever country ya live in, ya have an obligation ta fight ta defend the liberty of the people in that country. But I was born in the United States of America and I believed in my heart that I had the right to choose to defend it, or ta rebel against it. I chose ta defend it. Does that help you understand any better?"

"Yeah, it does. But what do we do, now? People around here hate ya and because of your decision, they hate me and now probably Ma."

"I realize that Son. Do ya have a solution ta this problem?"

"I think we're gonna have ta leave, to ever be happy."

"Well, Son, you may very well be right. But convincin' your mother may be the most difficult part of that solution. Your mother and I have discussed that possibility. She won't have any part of going north, and I can't blame her for that. She doesn't want ta give up her home and leave her family, and I can't blame her for that either. I'd say let's give it a little more time and see if somethin' falls into place. I believe that the good Lord wants this family ta be together and I think if we're patient, he'll help make it possible, in a way that everyone can live with."

"What do we do in the meantime? Live in a prison?"

"No, I think we can do a little better than that. Why don't we invite the Thompsons over here for dinner one evenin' and maybe Kenneth can stay the night."

"That would help. I'd like that."

"Consider it done. I'll dispatch a soldier, immediately, ta go invite our friends over. We'll have a big feast and maybe you and ol' Kenneth can get up early and go kill us a squirrel for breakfast."

"Thanks for talking ta me Pa."

"Pa.... I like that, Son. You're welcome. We better get back in there before your Ma thinks ya took a rope to me and gave me the whopin' of my life."

We both laughed a little and we headed back to the house with his hand on my shoulder. I felt much better. Not that we had solved any problems, but that we were able to talk about them and at least make some plans to help get by for awhile. I was glad he shared with me, why he made the decision that he made about the war. Pa had a way of makin' everything make sense. As we approached the door to the house, Pa stopped.

"Ben, thanks for talkin' ta me. It did me a lot of good ta be able to tell ya all that."

"You're welcome."

It had done me a lot of good, too. We opened the door and Ma was sittin' at the table with three dishes of cobbler.

"There you are. I was beginnin' ta think that I was gonna have ta eat this cobbler all by myself."

"I told Ben we'd better hurry, or all we'd find is an empty pan a sittin' by a fat woman."

"I noticed you've put on a little weight, yourself, since you've been grazin' around here."

"By-George, I think you're right. It's all this home cookin'."

Pa paused for a moment.

"Lizzie, I didn't just miss the cookin', I missed home."

Ma just looked at him for a minute. I didn't know what she was goin' to say to him. I hoped it was good.

"We missed you, too, Jacob Brady."

They walked towards each other. Pa reached out both hands and Ma slowly did the same. They just stood there and looked at each other for what seemed like ten minutes.

"What ya say we eat that cobbler before Ben here has ta watch a grown man cry."

"Only after ya promise you'll never leave this grown woman ta cry again."

Pa pulled Ma up against his chest and embraced her with both arms.

"Oh, Lizzie, with God as my witness, I never wanted to hurt you."

I noticed a tear run down Pa's face. He stepped back from her and looked her right in the eye.

"Lizzie, I can't promise that I'll never make ya cry again. I am a fool-headed man, at times, with a stubborn streak in me a mile wide. But I can promise that I will love ya for the rest of my born days and I will give everything I have ta makin' a happy home for ya."

Now Ma was cryin' and they hugged again. I was caught completely by surprise. Though I was a little embarrassed, I was happy. There was love in our home.

"Let's eat that cobbler. If Ben would've known what he was gonna have ta go through ta get his cobbler, he may have just stayed out with the hog."

"No, Jake, I don't think so, you've been gone a long time."

Ma was right, I would have given up all the cobbler I had ever eaten, just to have both a mother and a father that loved each other. We all sat down and began to eat our cobbler. A knock came at the door. Pa got up to answer it. It was the lieutenant.

"Sir, I'm sorry ta bother ya so late, but I thought you'd want this, immediately."

He handed Pa a telegraph message.

"What is it, Jake?"

Pa looked up at Ma.

"It's from Colonel Billings."

Pa looked back at the lieutenant.

"Lieutenant, could ya have a rider leave early in the mornin' ta go over to the Thompson home. We'd like ta have 'em over ta our home tomorrow night for supper. Would ya have your soldier extend that invitation for me, with an apology, that I can't be there myself ta make the invitation. I'm sure Jay will understand."

"Yes, sir, I'll have two men ride at first light. Is there anything else, sir?"

"No, not right now. Thank you, Lieutenant."

"You're welcome, sir. Good evening, ma'am."

The lieutenant excused himself.

"I hope you don't mind, Lizzie, I was feelin' a little cooped up and thought it would be nice ta have some friends over."

"No, I don't mind. I just don't know what I'm gonna feed 'em. We seem ta be runnin' out of everything around here. I'm sure I can patch some sort of meal together."

"Ben, run in under my bed and get my saddlebags."

Pa went to the door and opened it up. He leaned out the doorway.

"Lieutenant!"

In a moment I heard footsteps on the porch.

"Yes, sir."

"Would you mind waitin' here for just a minute? I have one more little errand I'd like ya ta do for me, if ya don't mind."

"Oh, no sir, not at all sir."

Pa shut the door. The saddlebags; I'd forgotten about them. I had wondered what was in them, and now it looked like I was goin' to find out. I drug them out from under the bed. They were heavy. As I came out of the bedroom, Pa reached over and took the saddlebags out of my hands.

"Purdy heavy load, huh, Ben?"

"Yes, sir. What's in them?"

"Well, Ben, it's either the stuff dreams are made of, or the stuff nightmares are made of, dependin' on whether you have it or not, and how ya use it, if ya do have it."

He took the saddlebags over to the table and opened them up, one side at a time.

"Come on over here, Lizzie. You too, Ben."

We both walked over toward the table. Ma had a bewildered look on her face. I could tell she didn't know what to expect, either. We both looked in the saddlebags. There was more gold in there than I had ever seen in my life.

"Jake!"

Ma put her hand over her mouth.

"Jake, where did you get all this money?"

"United States Cavalry, mostly. Some, I got from things I invested in."

"How much is there?"

"Near two thousand dollars. Do ya think that'll buy some grub for our friends ta eat? Ben, take these five gold pieces and give them to the lieutenant out there. Tell him we need supplies, and we'd be obliged if he would send a couple of men into town in the mornin' to fill your Ma's grocery list."

"Well, I don't have a list."

Pa looked at Ma and smiled.

"Ben, just tell the lieutenant ta stop by the house and pick up some money and a grocery list in the mornin'."

I went to the door and told the lieutenant what Pa asked me to. I hurried back to the table. By the time I got back in, Ma was sittin' down at the table cryin'. She looked up.

"Why didn't you tell me?"

"I guess I wanted that hug, first."

"Are we rich?"

"Yes, Ben, we're rich, but it ain't got nothin' ta do with what's in them saddlebags. It's things like family, love, good health, and good friends that make ya rich. The money in those saddlebags can make ya poor, if ya don't use it to help your friends and those ya love and if it makes ya too lazy to work. Yes, Son, I'd say...I'm rich. I've got you and your Ma. I've got my health back. We're invitin' some good friends over ta share a wonderful meal with us. Yep, I reckon that makes us all rich."

"What was the telegraph about?"

"It looks like we'll be havin' some visitors in a few days, Lizzie."

"Who?"

"Oh, just some more 'blue bellies.' Let's don't worry about that, right now. Let's just cross that bridge when we get to it."

It was plain that Pa didn't want to talk about what was in the telegraph, though I knew Ma wanted to know.

"Ben, just keep this money to yourself. Men have been killed for a lot less than this."

"Yes, sir."

"I'd say it's about time ta hit the hay wouldn't you?"

"Yes, ah... Ben, why don't ya go on up ta the loft, and go ta bed. I want ta talk ta your Pa a little more."

"Yes, ma'am."

I hurried up to the loft. My mind was racing. I couldn't believe all that money. I could hear Ma and Pa talkin', but I didn't pay any attention to what they were sayin'. My mind was occupied with what the future had in store for us. We had always been poor and now we were rich. I knew Pa was right though; we were rich in more ways than one. But it sure was nice to have all that money.

CHAPTER 10

The next day was filled with conversation about the future. What should we do? What shouldn't we do? Ma had been in a good mood. I had to admit, since Pa had returned, things had gotten drastically better; though at times it didn't seem like it. I think it was because we all tended to focus on the past, instead of takin' each new day and lookin' forward. I came to the conclusion that no matter how many times I thought about the past and tried to figure out what went wrong, or why this person did this or that, it still would not change the past. The only thing that I had any ability to change was the present and the future. It seemed to me that my future looked brighter than it had in a long time and if I were to be honest with myself, it was thanks to Jacob Allen Brady, my Pa. I may never completely understand why he left. I think I can accept that, now. I was just glad he was back, and I didn't want the past to make him think that he should leave in the future. I guess, I was startin' that forgivin' that he was talkin' about when I first got to talk to him over at Jay's house.

Kenneth would be over tonight. I couldn't wait to hear what all he had heard from the folks around town, about Pa, the mob, and Uncle Newt.

"Ben, why don't ya jump down off from that corner post there. I'd like ta sit on it and see if it helps me think any better." It was Pa.

"Oh, sir, you scared my inards out'a me."

"I got used to sneakin' up on people in the war. Bad habit, I guess. You sure aren't too tough ta find. If ya show up missin', just come down ta the corral and look on your old roostin' post."

"Yes, sir, I come down here a lot, I guess."

"Well, I'm sure it does take a lot of trainin'."

"What do you mean, trainin', sir?"

"Ta be a rooster, Son. I'm not sure why you'd want ta be a

rooster. Maybe it's just a phase you're goin' through. I guess I won't start worryin' about ya until I find ya down here crowin'.'"

I laughed a little. Sometimes he reminded me of Jay. "I don't wanna be a rooster."

"Oh now, Son, I wouldn't give up on yourself so soon. As I was walkin' up here and saw you sittin' on that post, why you looked right dignified with both hands down by your side, holdin' onto the post, and your face, with almost the perfect angle, lookin' up at the sky. If you keep practicin', you might make a fine rooster."

I laughed even harder and jumped down off the post. "Well, I guess I'm all done trainin' for today, since you broke my concentration and all."

We both laughed together. He put his hand on my shoulder and we headed back through the barn.

"That's good. Tit-for-tat, that's good. I guess you have been hangin' around Jay Thompson. Since you're done with your rooster trainin', ya ought ta head up to the house and help your Ma. I think she's got some chores she'd like ya ta do. She wants everything ta be just right. She hasn't been able ta entertain guests in awhile. Let's try ta make it a pleasant evenin' for her."

"Yes, sir."

I headed up to the house and Pa turned and went over to talk with the Yankee soldiers. As I got to the porch, I turned back to look at him standin' down there with the soldiers. Somehow, I couldn't picture him in one of those blue uniforms. All I could see was an ordinary man with an extraordinary presence about him.

"Oh, Ben, there you are. Could you take these old rugs out and take a stick ta beat some of the dirt out of 'em? They've seen a lot of feet, lately. When ya finish that, I'd like ya to sweep off the porch and then come back in here. I'll need some more help straightenin' up, inside."

"Yes, ma'am."

Pa was right, this was important to Ma. I thought this was all for me. I could see now, I wasn't the only one feelin' caged in. We finally finished all our chores and the three of us sat on the porch, talkin'.

"Looks like it might rain, tonight, Lizzie. Clouds are buildin' up in the west."

"I hope not, that would make an awful trip back for Jay and Maggie."

"Well, if it gets too bad, they can just stay here."

"Where will they sleep?"

"In the house with us. We'll make room. It wouldn't hurt ta crowd us up a bit, anyway. Matter of fact, now that I think about it, I think I'd like ta excuse myself and slip in the house here...ah... ta pray for a little rain."

Ma's face turned red, and then she smiled a little. Pa got up and chuckled a little, then turned toward the door.

"Lieutenant! Lieutenant!"

The lieutenant jogged up toward the house.

"Sir?"

"What time did you say those soldiers would have the Thompsons over here?"

"Four o'clock, sir."

"Good. I'll pray for the flood to hit about six."

"Sir?"

"Never mind, Lieutenant, just see that their horses get fed and stalled. I've got a lot'a faith that it's gonna rain tonight."

"Yes, sir, is there anything else, sir?"

"Not unless your soldiers know a good rain dance."

"Well, sir, I can find out, and if they do, we'll start the dance about five thirty for you, sir."

"Thank you, Lieutenant, you do that."

Pa turned back toward Ma and me.

"Ben, this place is full of funny people, ain't it?"

I just laughed a little and Pa went on in the house. The lieutenant just shook his head, chuckled a little to himself, and turned and walked back toward the group of soldiers. I heard him yell. "Any of you know how to do a rain dance?"

I looked at Ma. She had her right hand coverin' her face and her left hand cradlin' her right elbow. For a minute I thought she was cryin'. There had been a lot of that around our house, lately. She moved her hand off from her face a little, when she turned toward me. She was laughin' almost uncontrollably. What a relief! It was the first time I'd seen Ma laugh like that in a long time.

"He still thinks he's funny. Just ignore him, Ben."

"He must be funny, you're laughin', Ma."

"He is, but don't tell him. It just makes him worse."

I was laughin' with Ma now. I think, more, because she was laughin' so hard, than anything else.

"Riders comin'!" The lieutenant walked back up to the porch. "Looks like your guests are about here, ma'am."

"Thank you, I'll go tell Jake."

Ma turned toward me and, with a sneaky grin, she asked, "Do you think I should interrupt his prayer?" She was still laughin' as she went on in the house.

I ran out to the end of the lane and waited for them, there. I couldn't wait to talk to Kenneth. As they approached, I could hear Jay singing'. He loved to sing. He didn't have a great voice for it, but he never let that stop him.

"Ben, how the heck are ya?"

"Just fine, Jay."

"I've been a serenadin' these fine Yankee soldiers, a little. I figured it was the least I could do, with 'em givin' me such a fine escort over here." Jay stepped down from his horse and rubbed the top of my head. Kenneth got off from his horse, as well.

"Why, it's been a month of Sundays since I serenaded you. Should I sing ya a little tune?"

Before I even had time to answer, Jay broke into song.

> "Well, I'll sing ya a song,
> And it won't take long.
> I'll sing ya a song about murder.
> I pushed a big fat dog
> Right off from my log,
> And the song don't go no further."

Jay laughed at himself. "Maggie, let me help ya down off from that fine steed you're ridin', there, and let's have these younguns' take care of our horses while we go up ta the house and chew the fat with Jake and Lizzie."

Maggie smiled. "Knowin' how Lizzie cooks, I'll bet we get a little somethin' better than just fat ta chew."

Jay helped Maggie down and Kenneth and I led the horses toward the barn. The soldiers, that rode in with the Thompsons, had already ridden on over and joined the other men at the barn.

"Boy, am I glad to see you, Kenneth. I didn't know if I was ever gonna see anybody again. Have ya seen Tom or Larry?"

About that time, the Yankee lieutenant walked up to us. "Why don't you boys let us take care of those horses for you?"

"That's okay, we can do it."

"Oh, I know you can do it, and normally I'd let you. But you heard your Pa give me a direct order, to see that these horses were stalled and fed. Now, you wouldn't want me to disobey a direct order, would you?"

"No, sir."

"All right then, you boys go have a little fun and we'll tend to the horses. Besides, it looks like your Pa's prayers are working; I just felt a raindrop. You better hook up if you're going to do much of anything outside."

The lieutenant and another soldier took the horses and headed on into the barn.

"What did he mean, your Pa's prayer?"

"Oh, nothin'! Pa was just wantin' it ta rain so y'all would have ta stay the night."

"Sounds good ta me! I've only seen Tom. I ain't seen Larry at all. But Tom had a whole lot ta say."

"About what?"

"You promise not ta say I told ya any of this? Pa didn't want me talkin' about it."

"Yeah, I promise. What'd he say?"

"Well, he said his Pa was down at the train depot, and there were a bunch of men down there talkin'. Seems like most of the folks around here don't want your Pa in these parts. He said he heard at least three men say they'd shoot him on sight."

My heart sank a little. I guess Kenneth could tell it. He hadn't realized that I was growin' closer to Pa.

"Don't worry, though. Tom said his Pa told him, even if they wanted ta do it, most of 'em were a bunch of cowards that would turn tail and run at the thought of facin' Jake Brady."

"Did ya hear about the mob of men that came to the house?"

"Yeah, I overheard Pa tellin' Ma about it. I guess your Pa had 'em all scared for their lives."

"Have ya heard who shot Pa?"

"Just rumors."

"Who are they sayin' did it?"

"Oh, it could'a been anybody."

I could tell that Kenneth was avoidin' givin' me a straight answer. He and I had been friends for a long time. I had thought that he would never keep anything from me.

"I know it could'a been anybody, but who are folks sayin' it is?"

"Can't say."

"Can't say? Why?"

"I made a promise ta Pa. He made me promise that I wouldn't say anything to ya about who was arrested or anything."

"They arrested somebody for shootin' Pa?"

"Dad blame it, Ben, I wasn't suppose ta say anything about any of that. You're gonna get my tail tanned. Besides, I never broke my word ta Pa."

I was frustrated. I wanted to know more, yet I knew that it wasn't right for me to ask Kenneth to break his word.

"Did your Pa say when you could tell me?"

"Oh, I figure it won't be long until ya find out. He said that it was somethin' your Pa needed ta tell ya. It was a family matter and needed ta be handled by your family."

"A family matter? Was it Uncle Newt?"

"No, it wasn't Newt. Pa said he was scared of his own shadow, much less Jake Brady. Pa said there ain't too many in these parts that would even consider takin' on Jake Brady in a heads-up fair fight. He said your Pa was tougher'n rawhide."

That made me feel a little proud. I guess he was purdy strong. He did get shot in the gut and was up workin' faster than most men would have been.

"Ya know, things ain't been so good over our way, either."

"What do ya mean?"

"Well 'cause Pa is friends with your Pa, he's been hearin' a lot of comments in town and he said the only reason some folks still come ta get work done at the shop, is because they can't get it done elsewhere."

"What kinda things are people sayin' to him?"

"Nobody is sayin' stuff right ta his face, but he hears it around. Things like, he's a 'Yankee sympathizer' or 'friend of a turn-coat' or 'traitor', just stupid stuff."

"What does your Pa say about it?"

"He said some folks are like a cow pie. After awhile, they crust over and ya can't smell 'em, but all ya gotta do is stir 'em up a little and they go right back ta stinkin' as bad as ever."

"Sounds like somethin' he'd say."

We both laughed a little. It had started to rain a light mist. Kenneth and I got up. We had been sittin' down at the pond in the bottom of our cow pasture. We started walkin' back to the barn.

"Do ya like him?"

"Pa?"

"Yeah, are you startin' ta like him?"

I had to think about that for a second. I hadn't even asked myself that question, yet.

"Yeah, I reckon I do. He hasn't done anything ta not like, except work me half ta death."

"Pa said, 'ol' Ben's days of sleepin' in will come to a halt.' I guess he was right."

"That's for certain! Pa don't like ta lay in bed much."

Suddenly, we heard someone yellin'. It was Ma and Maggie. We couldn't hear what they were sayin' but it was obvious by the way they were wavin' their arms that they wanted us to come to the house. We both waved back at them and started trottin' toward the house. Talkin' with Kenneth was good for me.

"You boys are soakin' wet! Ben, get on up ta the loft and see if you can find dry clothes for both you and Kenneth. Mercy! You boys."

"Yes, ma'am."

"Lizzie, they're just like their fathers; always in ta somethin' or schemin' about somethin'."

We hurried on in the house. Ma and Maggie stayed outside on the porch. Pa and Jay were sittin' at the table. Both of them were laughin'. Tonight was going to be just like over at Kenneth's house a couple of weeks ago. Pa and Jay were goin' to stay up half the night tellin' stories. I couldn't wait to hear them!

"You two boys look like a couple a drowned rats."

"Yeah, I guess your prayers worked. It's startin' ta rain hard out there. We'll change and be right back down."

"You been prayin' fer rain, Jake?"

"Ya might say. About like I prayed we'd win every battle in the war. Didn't care that much about the battles, I just wanted the war ta end. A little rain might just help ta end a war. I figure with the weather bein' what it is, you and Maggie just as well stay over here tonight."

"Oh, that's all right, Jake. We've rode in the rain before. We don't need ta impose on ya."

"No, Jay, you don't understand. We've got plenty of room. You and Maggie can sleep downstairs here. The boys can sleep up in the loft, and Lizzie and I can sleep in our bedroom."

"Oh, I see. Kinda like when yer horse showed up lame and you couldn't ride back ta Clayton with Maggie and me that night."

"Ya might say."

"Mmm, boy, I do owe ya."

We finished changin' as quickly as we could. We were both starting to get hungry after comin' in the house and smellin' Ma's cookin'.

"You boys feel a little better, now?" Pa looked us up and down.

"Yes, sir, we sure do."

"Why don't ya slip out to the porch there, and tell your Ma that there's a couple of old dogs and two nursin' pups in here that could use some food."

I just shook my head and grinned a little.

"Yes, sir."

I went out and told Ma exactly what Pa had said.

"I'll not ask which is which," was her reply.

We all ate until we couldn't eat anymore. I couldn't remember when we'd had so much food at one meal. Ma had gone all out. As I thought, we spent another night listenin' to Pa and Jay tell stories. The difference, this time, was, Ma was there and she laughed as hard as anyone. The evenin' flew by. Before I knew it, Kenneth and I were both about to fall asleep in our chairs.

"Lizzie, Jake, thanks so much for the wonderful meal and good evenin'. I reckon it's time ta call it a night."

"Jay, why don't y'all just bunk over here tonight? The rain's slowed a little, but it's still awful muddy out and I know you're tired."

"Maggie, what do ya say?"

"Oh, we really better get on back to the house. We got our chores in the mornin' and I really don't wanta impose."

"Oh, them chores'll keep. These folks have been nice enough to feed us a good meal. Besides, Jake and Lizzie are just like family. It ain't like we've wore out our welcome. Why, this is the first time we've got together in years. Lizzie would be happy ta find us a bed. Ain't that right, Lizzie?"

"Ah, why certainly. We could...."

"Boys, why don't you head on up to the loft. Jay, you and Maggie just make yourself at home right out here and Lizzie and I will go to our bedroom."

"Yes... ah, that would be fine."

Ma gathered some of her things from around the bed in the front room. Then she hugged Maggie and Jay and told them, "good night." As she headed for the bedroom, Pa reached out and touched her shoulder.

"Aren't ya forgettin' some?"

He looked over toward Kenneth and me.

"Oh, yes. Good night, boys."

She came over and gave us both hugs. Then she turned and went into the bedroom.

"Good night, boys, Maggie...Jay."

We all said good night and retired to our beds. What a day! We worked all day and played half the night. I was tired, but things were better, much better. Although, I knew that there were still many problems ahead for us, I felt like at least we would be fightin' the battles together now and besides, what else mattered; we had each other. Yep, Jay was right. Everything was all right!

CHAPTER 11

A shot rang out! Kenneth and I sat straight up in bed!

"What was that?"

"Sounded like gunfire!"

We both crawled over to the edge of the loft. Ma and Maggie were standin' at the front door. Jay came runnin' down the porch and in the door.

"Get back in the house!"

As soon as Jay cleared the front door, there were three more shots fired. Jay slammed the door behind him.

"Where's Jake? Who's shootin'?"

"Jake ran toward the barn. Don't know who's shootin'. Lizzie, I need a gun. Get me a gun!"

"Ben! Ben, where's your gun?"

"Leanin' by the door, Ma!"

"You and Kenneth get down here, now, and lay on the floor!"

Ma grabbed my rifle and handed it to Jay. Kenneth and I hurried down from the loft and hunkered down by the stove. Jay peeked out the window. We could hear the soldiers yellin' outside but couldn't hear what they were sayin'.

"Ya got any cartridges? I need cartridges!"

"Ben, where's your..."

"In the trunk at the foot of the bed!"

Mom hurried over to the trunk and got the cloth sack that I kept my cartridges in and gave it to Jay. We heard someone yell, "Up there behind the house." Several shots were fired. Jay moved from the window to the door; he cracked it open about a foot.

"You're not goin' out..."

Suddenly, a bullet hit the door right by Jay's hand. Wood splinters flew across the room. The door flew wide open.

"Dad dang! Stay back! Get over in the corner and stay down!

84

Don't they know there's women and kids in here?"

Jay jumped across the doorway and slammed the door closed again. Ma, Maggie, Kenneth and I were all lying down in front of the kitchen cupboards. Jay moved across the room to the window that looked out along the ridge behind the house.

"There's Jake!"

"Where?" Ma asked, anxiously.

"He's up in the trees along the top of the ridge. He's got a pistol in his hand and he's crawlin' on all fours."

Jay moved back to the window by the front door.

"The Yank's are all scattered out in the trees along the lane. They're all lookin' up toward the ridge in front of Jake. There they are! There's two of 'em!"

Jay moved over by the door again.

"You're not goin' out there!"

Maggie gave Jay a stern look.

"No, I'm not. Least wise not yet. I'm just gonna open this door a little ta see if I can draw a little fire. That'll help them other boys draw a bead on 'em."

"Yeah, and get us shot."

"No, you'll be fine. Just get behind that potbellied stove there."

We all got as close as we could, behind the stove. My heart was about to beat out of my chest. Kenneth's eyes were bugged out so far you could scrape them off with a stick. Jay took his hat and put it on the end of my gun. He pushed the door open, slightly. We were all braced for more gunfire, but nothin' happened. Jay put his hat back on his head and moved back to the window by the door.

"Looks like I was too late. Ol' Jake's got 'em both up there. He's marchin 'em down out'a the trees."

Ma and Maggie started to get up.

"Wait just a minute!"

Jay motioned for them to get back down.

"Are there more of 'em?"

"Hold on, Maggie, I want ta take a better look, here. Well, I'll be... Lizzie, Maggie, I want you ta promise me that you'll stay put with these boys right where you're at till I come back."

"What is it, Jay?"

"Just you never mind. Trust me on this one, Lizzie, this is somethin' ya don't want the boys ta see."

"Is it safe for ya?"

"Yeah, it's safe, Maggie. I'll be back shortly. You just don't be lookin' out these windows."

Jay took my rifle and headed out the door. He shut it tight behind him. My mind was racing. What was it that he didn't want us to see?

"Well, he said it was safe enough. I guess we don't have ta stay jammed up behind this stove. I'm gonna ring that man's neck when we get home. Draw fire!"

We all moved out from behind the stove. Ma had Kenneth and me sit with our backs against the bedroom wall. She and Maggie leaned up against the bed. We could barely hear voices in the background, and they were too faint for us to make out what was being said.

"What do ya think it is, Ma?"

"I don't know, Son, maybe one of the soldiers got shot."

"I saw Pa when he was shot."

"There wasn't much choice in that. If ya got a choice, it's better not ta put that in your mind."

"Your ma's right, Ben. Jay wouldn't have said what he did unless he had good reason."

I could see that I was goin' nowhere quick with this conversation. I decided to be quiet, and see if I could hear anything. We waited for fifteen minutes or so, but it seemed like an hour. The voices started gettin' louder. They were walkin' up toward the house. I could hear horses' hooves down by the barn. Finally, I heard the sound of boots on the porch.

"I know, I know, you've got your orders, Lieutenant. Just do what ya have to, but you take care of her and get him off my land! Tell Colonel Billings I'll ride at first light ta talk ta him about those orders."

Jay had the door half open.

"Come on in, Jake. You could talk to that lieutenant for hours and he ain't changin' his mind."

"I know, that's the problem with the Cavalry; sometimes orders overrule common sense."

"I'm afraid, this time I agree with the lieutenant, Jake. I don't really see another option."

"Jay, ya know that ain't gonna help anything. It'll just cause deeper wounds."

"Jake, he's bent on killin' ya and that ain't gonna help anything, either. Just let the man do his job and you do yours. Stay alive. Your family needs ya."

The door came completely open. Jay walked in. Pa came to the doorway, then turned and looked down toward the lane and shook his head. I could hear the sound of several horses drift into the distance. Pa turned around, came in, and shut the door.

"Who was it?"

"A fool that can't shoot."

"You're bleedin'!"

"Not as bad as I could've been if that fool could shoot."

"Where are ya hit?"

"Just grazed on the shoulder. It'll heal in a day or so."

Ma hurried over to look at Pa's shoulder.

"Really, Lizzie, it's just a scratch."

"What happened?"

"Well, Jay and I had just finished the chores and he was up havin' a cup with the soldiers. I was standin' out in front of the barn lookin' over the place, when all of a sudden, I felt a sting on my shoulder and then the shot rang out right behind it. I yelled at Jay ta get to the house and I darted back into the barn. It caught us all off guard. The lieutenant threw me a pistol through the barn door. As I reached out ta get it, they fired again. The lieutenant's men returned a couple of rounds. I could see where the shots were comin' from, so I told the lieutenant ta cover some of his men while they ran from behind the wagons and down to the trees by the lane, just under where the shots came from. While they did that, I slipped out the back of the barn and got up on the ridge and came in behind them."

Pa stopped for a minute. He looked at the door where the bullet had splintered the edge of it.

"He shot at the house?"

"Yeah, Jake, that hate must run awful deep."

"Who? Who was it, Jake?"

"We'll talk later, Lizzie. Jay, I appreciate ya helpin' out. I'm awful sorry for this mess. Seems like you're gettin' hurt, too."

"Jake, we all have things we're willin' ta fight for, I'd hate ta think I wouldn't stand by my friends through good and bad. Jake...ah... it may be none of my business, but as a friend, I'm gonna tell ya, anyway. This thing is gettin' bigger than just you. If it were me, I think that maybe I'd want ta be the one ta tell certain things ta a few folks around here, rather than have them find out by chance."

Pa looked up at Jay, then over at Ma. He cleared his throat and looked down at the floor.

"Yeah, I reckon you're right."

Pa looked over at Kenneth and me.

"Ben, would you and Kenneth mind steppin' outside for a few minutes and let me talk ta Maggie, Jay, and your Ma a bit? We'll yell at y'all when breakfast is ready, okay?"

"Sure, Pa."

I went out the door with Kenneth right behind me. Both of us were anxious to talk to each other.

"What do ya think they're talkin' about?"

"I don't know. I guess about who's been tryin' ta kill you're Pa."

We walked down to the lane and looked up on the ridge. I lightly hit Kenneth on his arm, with the back of my hand.

"Let's go up and see if we can see where they were shootin' from."

"Do ya think your folks would mind?"

"Naw, they're busy, anyway. What do ya think your Pa meant when he told my Pa that 'this thing is gettin' bigger than just you?'"

"I think he figures that your Pa is gonna have ta tell ya about the stuff that's been goin' on in town."

I hoped Kenneth was right. We climbed up the muddy hillside lookin' for tracks. It didn't take us long to find where three sets of tracks had come down. We followed them up until we found the one set of tracks that met the other two. Pa had come down the ridge, and got them from behind.

"This must be where they were shootin' from."

We looked around to find where we thought they had been sittin'. Finally, we found an old, dead-fall tree where the mud was full of tracks and you could see where someone had been sitting. We sat and talked about the events of the mornin'. We both agreed that Pa was right about them being a poor shot. We figured, either one of us could hit a skunk standin' at the barn door from here.

"Look! A knife!"

Kenneth pulled a knife out of the side of the dead-fall limb.

"One of them must have stuck it here before Pa slipped up and got 'em."

"Let me see that!"

Kenneth handed me the knife. My heart sank. I recognized it!

"What's wrong? You look like you've seen a ghost."

"Nothin'."

"Boys? ...Boys?"

It was Pa on the front porch, yellin' for us. Kenneth yelled back.

"Up here."

"Come on in, breakfast is ready."

"I'm keepin' the knife if ya don't mind."

"Sure, I got lots of knives."

We headed down the slippery hillside. As I walked to the house, I wondered what I should do with the knife. I felt it was time for Pa and I to have another man to man talk. I was confused, hurt and afraid, except not just for myself, now. I was afraid of what was goin' to happen in the future. What was goin' to happen to our family? How could things be all right, now? We took off our muddy boots on the porch and went on in the house.

"What were you boys doin' up there?"

"Just lookin' around."

"Did you do any findin' or was it all just lookin'?"

"Yeah, we found where Jake came up on those guys and marched them down the hill. While we was sittin' there, I found a knife stuck in a log."

"A knife?"

"Yeah, Ben's got it."

"Let's see it, Ben."

Ma didn't know what she was askin'. I didn't want to pull it out of my pocket. I knew Ma would recognize the knife, too; I hesitated.

"Pa, can I see ya for a minute in private?"

"Sure Son."

I walked out on the porch and Pa followed me. As he shut the door behind him, I pulled the knife out of my pocket.

"Here's the knife."

He took the knife and looked at it for a moment.

"Why don't I put this in my pocket and you and I will talk about it as soon as the Thompsons leave? I think they'll be leavin' shortly after breakfast."

"Yes, sir."

We went back inside. Everyone had already started eatin'. Nothin' more was said about the knife. I didn't feel much like eating but stayed at the table and ate a little out of good manners. My mind was racin' in thought, while my heart was burdened with grief.

CHAPTER 12

As we watched the Thompson family ride out of sight, I turned and walked in the house. My folks stayed on the porch. I could hear them talkin', but couldn't make out what they were sayin'. As I sat down at the table, the front door closed. Their voices got a little louder. I saw Ma walk past the window. She was cryin'. Then she turned and walked back. Things got quiet for awhile. I began to focus again on the knife. It was an easy knife to recognize. I had seen it many times over at Grandpa Beck's house. He had made it himself. The handle was made from the antler of a white-tailed buck that he had killed. Long as I could remember, that knife had hung in the corner of Grandpa's bedroom. It was the same corner where he leaned his rifle. Every time one hand reached for the rifle the other would reach for the knife.

The door slowly opened. Pa had his hand on Ma's back. She was tryin' to hide the fact that she had been cryin'. Ma came over to the table and sat down. Pa closed the door. He turned and pulled the knife out of his pocket.

"I guess, it's time we had a talk, Son."

He walked over to the table and sat the knife in the middle of it. Then he took a seat.

"I was hopin' that we would never have this conversation, but thanks to some mule-headed people that can't leave well enough alone, we do. What I'm fixin' ta tell ya may not be too easy ta swallow, Son."

He didn't have to say anymore. I had already figured out who had shot him. It was Grandpa Beck. Now the soldiers had taken him away for tryin' to do it again.

"It was Grandpa Beck that shot ya, wasn't it?"

"No Son, it wasn't. Although the Cavalry thinks he did. That telegraph I got from Colonel Billings, was him tellin' me that your grandpa had been arrested and had confessed ta shootin' me. I spoke with Lieutenant Riverton about it. He said that your grandpa had been braggin' about doin' it."

"Why? Why would he brag about doin' it, if he didn't?" I paused, "Who did do it?"

"Son, I haven't figured out a lot of things about why people do this or that, but what I figured out is, right or wrong, they have their reasons."

"Why would he lie?"

"Some folks have the idea that it's okay ta lie if they think it's for a good cause. All I've ever seen it cause is a passel of grief and trouble ta follow it."

"If Grandpa's in jail, then who was on the ridge? What are they gonna do with Grandpa?"

The questions were comin' to my mind faster than I could get them answered.

Ma got up and left the table. She walked over to the window and leaned against the frame.

"Let's take one thing at a time, here. Colonel Billings said he would be over ta talk with me about what they were gonna do with Grandpa Beck. He should be here this mornin'. I'll see that he got my telegram and knows that your grandpa didn't shoot me. I expect he may run onto the lieutenant's men on his way over here and they'll have told him about this mornin'."

"Will they let him go?"

"Yes, they'll have to. The only crime he's committed is lyin'. The kinda lie he's been tellin' is more of a crime against him and God, than anyone else. If they started lockin' up all the men who committed that crime, they'd have ta lock up the better half of the population."

"Will he have ta go on trial?"

"Well, that's what I'm gonna talk with Colonel Billings about. Ya see, your grandpa probably doesn't know it, but it is a crime ta lie in a courtroom. It's perjury, and they will lock a man up for that. That's the kind'a lie that ya have ta lock men up for or it would be impossible ta have any integrity and justice in our laws. That's why I need ta talk with Colonel Billings, so we can get the truth out and maybe then we won't be havin' any trials."

Ma turned and walked back toward the table.

"Son, your father has promised me for a long time that he would do everything possible ta help...ta help fix this whole mess."

Ma started cryin' again.

"In all the years I've known your father, I've never known him ta lie. He'll fix it."

Pa rested his hand on Ma's shoulder.

"Thanks, Lizzie, I appreciate ya sayin' that. I always used ta tell the men I was given command over, 'It's better ta be trusted than ta be loved.' I'm a lucky man, I've got both."

Ma smiled a little at Pa and then turned and went back toward the window. I was confused. Why would Grandpa say he did somethin' he didn't do?

"Was it Newt? Did Newt shoot ya?"

"You remember me talkin' to ya about it not bein' wise ta reveal all truth unless it was gonna be beneficial?"

"Yes, sir."

"Well, this is one of those times when I feel inclined ta reveal a little of what I know, because it might help ya sleep a little better at night. Ta answer you're question, truthfully, I'd have ta say, yes, Newt did shoot me. However, lucky for me he can't shoot worth a darn and he only grazed me."

"So, it was Newt up on the ridge."

"Yes, it was."

"Was he the one that shot ya in the belly?"

"No, he wasn't."

"Who did?"

"Now, we're back to a 'need ta know' basis, and whether or not to reveal all truth. It wouldn't do you any good or benefit you in any way right now, and maybe never, ta know the answer ta that question. I think ya know all that ya need ta know for now. You'll just have ta join your mother and trust that I'll do everything within my power ta help Grandpa Beck and ol' Newt."

"How big a trouble is Newt in, for shootin' at ya this mornin'?"

"Well, Son it'll be viewed as a federal crime, because I'm a commissioned officer in the United States Cavalry. He could be charged with attempted murder of a federal officer. That's a serious crime ta be convicted of."

Ma quickly turned and came back over by the table.

"But, your Pa's gonna help him!"

"What would they do ta Newt if he got convicted of that?"

"Well, he'd fer sure go ta prison, but, Son, I think that there's a good chance this may never even go ta court. I think we've talked enough about this for now. Your mother and I just felt it was time ta share a little of the truth about this matter with ya. Why don't ya go saddle up that ol' pony of mine and ride over ta Kenneth's house?"

"I can go over ta Kenneth's by myself?"

"Yes, Son, I think all the shootin' is over around here. If ya hurry, ya may get there in time ta help them do their chores."

"Jake, are you sure he should go alone?"

"Well, all the folks that's been doin' the shootin' ain't in no position ta hurt anybody, and as soon as I talk ta Colonel Billings, we can probably get rid of these 'blue bellies', too."

"You needn't call them that for my sake, Jake. They've actually been quite a help and I know they're your friends."

Ma turned and walked over to the door. She opened it and stood in the doorway. She held her hand above her eyes to block the mornin' sun.

"Well, it looks like your colonel is comin' and he's bringin' the whole Yankee Cavalry with him."

Pa got up and stepped quickly to the door. He had a curious look on his face. I could tell he didn't understand what he was seein'.

"Ya know, Jake, my family may not be the only ones wantin' ta do some shootin'. I'd feel better if Ben stays home."

"Ben...ah maybe your mother's right. Do ya think you can stay caged in a little while longer? Just until we get this all sorted out?"

"Yes, sir."

I walked over to the door with Ma. I could see the soldiers comin' down our lane. They were ridin' in pairs and it looked like they were at least a mile long. There had to be over a hundred of them.

"We ain't got enough hay in our barn fer all those horses. This Colonel Billings must think he's purdy important ta have all them soldiers followin' him around," Ma said, disgustedly.

Pa walked out on the porch.

"No, that's what's odd. He don't normally have more than fifteen or twenty men ridin' with him. Lizzie, you remember, you can make my job a whole lot easier if you'll be hospitable to Jim. He's a good man and he carries a lot of clout with General

Haywood. If anyone can help me clean up this mess, it's Jim Billings."

"I will, Jake. I made you a promise three weeks ago and I'll keep my promise. I'll do whatever I can ta help."

"Thanks, Lizzie. Ben, go on down to the barn, there, and see that the stalls are empty. If the cows or any horses are in 'em, just push 'em out into the pasture. I'll have the lieutenant stall the colonel's horse for him."

"How long will he be here?"

"As long as it takes, Lizzie. As long as it takes."

I squeezed between Ma and Pa. It was plain the way Pa was starin' out at the soldiers, that he hadn't figured out why Colonel Billings had brought so many with him. The lead men were about to the end of the lane. I jumped off the end of the porch and headed down to the barn. The lieutenant had all of his men lined up in formation, standin' in front of the wagons. He only had about half of the men that he had when he first came to our house. I figured most of them must have left to take Uncle Newt into the fort this mornin'. I hurried and checked all the stalls. Pa's horse was the only one in the barn. I ran him out in the pasture and shut the gate to the barn so he wouldn't come back in. By the time I got back to the front of the barn, our whole yard was full of horses and Yankee soldiers. I passed two soldiers, each leadin' a horse into the barn. I hurried back up to the house. Ma was on the porch and Pa was just steppin' off the porch to meet two soldiers who were walkin' towards him.

"Jake, good to see you're still kickin'."

"General Haywood, sir! I wasn't expectin' you. I thought...."

"You're in civilian clothes, now, let's dispense with the formalities, Jake. Call me Ron, that's my name. Ol' Jim, here, thought that I could be of some assistance."

Colonel Billings stepped forward and reached out to shake Pa's hand.

"Jake, when I spoke with Ron, about your situation, he felt he'd like ta come down himself and see what needed ta be done."

The general gently slapped Colonel Billings on his back with his ridin' gloves.

"I figured ol' Jim wouldn't leave me alone until you were out'a the woods, anyway."

The general looked up at Ma and me.

"I guess Jake's been off to war, so long, that he's forgot his manners, ma'am."

"Oh, I'm sorry! Ron, Jim, this is my wife, Lizzie, and my son, Ben."

"Pleased to meet you, ma'am. Young man, you come from mighty fine stock. I'm sure glad you got your mother's looks, though." The general laughed at himself. "Jake, I understand there was a little more excitement around here this mornin'?"

"Yes, sir, a little. Nothin' we couldn't deal with."

"Well, I guess I made a damn fool mistake."

The general apologetically looked up at Ma.

"Oh, pardon me, ma'am. I guess I must have lost some of my manners, too."

Ma smiled and nodded her head, to let the general know that his apology had been accepted. Pa was watchin' Ma, then he turned back to the general.

"How's that, sir?"

"In the matter of Mr. Beck."

"Oh, it was an honest mistake, Ron. If I'd been in your shoes, I'd have probably had him arrested too."

"That's not the mistake, Jake. The mistake I made was orderin' him to be released this mornin'. With the 'cargo' those soldiers passed me with, from your little episode this mornin', I'm afraid he's gonna be none too happy. I'd have been better off just to leave him where he was, until I spoke with you."

"Why don't you two come on into our house, and maybe you can figure a way ta dig me out'a this mess." Pa opened the door.

"After you, dear."

Ma and I went into the house. Pa followed General Haywood and Colonel Billings inside. The door closed shut. I could hardly wait to hear these men talk. I hoped they might reveal a little more than Pa had this mornin'. The three men all took seats at the table and Ma went over to the washtub. I hurried up into the loft. I was afraid that Pa would notice me listenin' to their conversation and find an excuse for me to leave. I climbed up on the edge of the loft and sat down; I was all ears. The three men sat silent for a few moments. Finally, the general leaned forward.

"Jake, this is about as awkward of a situation as I believe I've ever seen. What's your recommendation?"

"Well, sir, I'd like ta see it all just go away. Let bygones be bygones."

"The problem with that, Jake, is it takes everyone involved to feel the same way, before that can happen. Right now, I wouldn't give odds on that plan workin'.."

"Maybe if I rode back with you and talked to them, maybe they would come around."

"Maybe. Maybe not. Then what? You know these folks purdy well. Can you honestly tell me that you think they can overcome their hatred for you, at least enough to not kill you?"

"I can't say, sir."

"Can't or won't?"

Pa looked up sharply.

"Can't, sir! It's not my place ta speak the heart of other folks. They're bitter, right now. I understand that. That doesn't mean they can't change."

"I'm not talkin' about forgivin' Jake. I'm talkin' about character. Do they have good character? Is their word any good?"

"I'm willing ta risk it."

"If it's a risk, then there must be some question in your mind about it. I'm not sure I'm willin' to risk it."

"With all due respect, sir, it's my life that's being risked here!"

"No, Jake, it's bigger than just you. You're not the only southern boy that came north and fought for the Union army. If we allow you to be killed, then it might just give folks the idea that killin' boys that fought for the North is a good thing. No, it's bigger than just you, Jake."

The general leaned back in his chair a little and grabbed his chin. Ma walked over to the table.

"Can I get you men anything?"

"No, ma'am, I've had more than my share, already."

The general chuckled and patted his potbelly. He sat in thought for a moment. Then he leaned forward and glanced up at Ma, then back over at Pa.

"Jake, would you mind if I asked your wife a question or two?"

"No, sir, not at all. I know she wants this mess cleared up more than anybody."

Pa looked up at Ma. I could tell by the look on his face, he was hopin' she would be polite and answer the general's questions.

"Lizzie, do you mind?"

"No, not at all."

"Ma'am, we managed to get this man through a war without gettin' him killed. He served well, and through it all, somehow, we all came to like him. I don't want him dead, even if he doesn't mind the risk. I consider him my friend, and I do mind the risk. My question to you, ma'am, is, what is your commitment to my friend? Are you willin' to stand by this good man?"

Ma walked over by Pa and put her hand on his shoulder.

"I never stopped lovin' my husband, General! I stayed true ta him the whole time he was fightin' in that war. Yes, General, I married him until 'death do us part' and I will stand by him."

"Well ma'am, it's that "death do us part" that I'm worried about. Are you willin' to do whatever it takes to keep him alive? Before you answer that, I want you to know that it may mean a lot of sacrifice."

"If you're talkin' about him goin' away with you again and me not havin' my husband for years on end, then the answer is NO! I'd sooner take a gun and shoot ya on the spot than ta give up havin' my husband and me together."

Colonel Billings had been silent until now. He laughed a little. "I'm sorry, ma'am. I'm not laughin' at ya. I was just thinkin' it might be worth kidnappin' ol' Jake here, if you'd really shoot Ron." He paused a moment. "She sounds purdy committed, ta me, Ron."

All three of the men laughed, and Ma smiled at Colonel Billings.

"I take it that you're givin' me your word then, ma'am?"

Ma stopped smilin' and got a serious look on her face. "Yes, General, you have my word."

"Jake, how much leave do you have left?"

"About another week, sir."

"Good... good. Colonel, step outside and tell the lieutenant, that he is to take about half of those men out there and go find Mr. Beck. I want him arrested on the spot and taken to the fort with the other two." The general stood up and faced Pa. "Colonel Brady, I'm canceling your leave. You are to report to me in front of this house in one hour. Your assignment is to bring your wife and son with Colonel Billings and me, back to the fort. Have them prepare for about four days. If I need to, I will extend your active duty to accomplish our task. We'll cross that bridge when we get to it. I'll expect you in full uniform." He looked at Ma. "Ma'am, I'll hold you to your word, and I'll give you my word that I will do everything within my power to keep our mutual friend alive so that you can spend many more years with him before we have to worry about that 'death do you part' stuff."

The general excused himself and walked out the front door. Colonel Billings was right behind him.

"Jim... I don't have..."

"I brought your uniform. I even brought all those medals. I figured if ya didn't want 'em, maybe your son would. I'll bring 'em in."

"Jim." Pa walked over toward the door and stuck out his hand. Colonel Billings shook his hand. "Thanks."

"Anytime, Jake, but you'd better wait ta thank me. I have no idea what he's plannin' next. He just said, 'get his uniform' and so I did." Colonel Billings put his hat on and stepped out the doorway. He reached back and shut the door behind him.

Pa turned around and looked at Ma. "It's a start. Let's get our things together, an hour ain't much time."

"Can we trust him, Jake?"

"I've put my life in his hands more times than I care ta count and I'm still here. Yeah, we can trust him, Lizzie." Pa looked up at me in the loft. He waved his hand. "Well, hurry up, Son, looks like you and I get ta ride together."

"Yes, sir."

I started grabbin' clothes and puttin' them in my clothes sack, I used, when I went over to stay at Kenneth's house. Boy, was I glad I didn't leave and ride over to Kenneth's. I'd have been left out of this, for sure!

CHAPTER 13

He came out of the bedroom. I couldn't help but stare at him. He was dressed in full uniform. His boots shined like he had polished them for hours. The shiny, brass buttons stood out against the crisp, blue cloth of his coat. He paused a moment to straighten his cuffs. I couldn't help but admire him. He had a softness about him, yet gave off a distinct feelin' of bein' in control. I could tell that he was not a man who demanded respect; he was a man who had earned it. It was obvious that he had not only earned the respect of the men that served under him, but also those that had served with him and over him.

"Oh, I best not leave those saddlebags in there."

He turned and walked back into the bedroom.

"I should say not!"

Ma walked on past me and followed him in the bedroom.

"Ben, are you ready ta go?"

"Yes, ma'am."

I stood by the front door with my clothes sack in one hand and my rifle in the other. A knock came at the front door. I reached over and opened it.

"Well, son, you're just the man I was lookin' for."

It was Colonel Billings. He was carryin' a small, leather pouch.

"Your Pa said he didn't want these when he left ta come back here, but I hung onto 'em for some reason, and now I'm glad I did. Your Pa ain't one ta brag, at least not on himself, so if ya wanna know how he earned each one of these medals, I'll set down with ya someday and tell ya."

He handed me the small pouch. It was purdy heavy for its size. I opened it up and looked inside. It had at least ten or fifteen medals, some gold but mostly silver.

"Why don't ya throw 'em in your clothes sack there and I might get time ta set with ya at the fort. Oh, tell your Pa that we've got his horse saddled, and we hitched up a wagon for your Ma ta ride in. We figured she might want ta take more things than we could carry on horseback. I hope ya don't mind, but I saddled your horse, too. I thought ya might wanta ride alongside your father."

"Thank you, sir. I'll tell him."

Colonel Billings excused himself and I shut the door. I looked at the medals for a minute, and then proudly put them in my clothes sack. My Pa really was a war hero. It was plain that Colonel Billings had great respect for him. I went into the bedroom and told my folks what the colonel had said.

"That's good. Ya see, Lizzie, I told ya he was a good man. Go ahead and gather up what ya think we might need. I hope we're back in a few days, but it's a thirty-five-mile ride back, so if we don't have it we'll just have to do without it. It's better ta be safe than sorry. Oh, Lizzie, would you grab Pappys' ol' Bible, I might get a chance ta read it, a little. Ben, help your Ma carry things out ta the wagon. I'm gonna go on out ta see that things are in order in the barn and talk to the general."

He had his ridin' gloves in one hand, and the saddlebags in the other. He effortlessly slung the saddlebags over his shoulder and went out the door. Ma had me get the blankets off of the beds, then we wrapped some of them around dishes and some of them around some bottled venison. We loaded the blankets into four old, wood crates. I put my clothes sack on top of one of the crates, picked it up, and carried it out, while Ma held the door for me. As I started down the porch, two soldiers came joggin' up to me.

"Oh, let me get that fer ya, boy."

"No, that's okay. I can get it."

"Are ya sure?"

"Yes, sir."

"Just put it down there in the wagon, yonder. Is there more in the house?"

"Yes, sir."

The two soldiers went on up the porch steps and met Ma at the doorway. I looked down toward the wagon. The soldiers were all mounted and in formation. Pa was over talkin' with the general and Colonel Billings under the pecan tree at the end of our lane. Ol' Dungeon and Pa's horse were tied to the wagon. I pushed the crate into the back of the wagon. The two soldiers were right behind me with the other three crates. Ma closed the door behind her and walked out on the porch. Pa excused himself and walked up to Ma. He took her by the arm and walked her down to the wagon.

"Lizzie, General Haywood has asked that I ride with him in the lead, and that Ben and Colonel Billings ride behind us. Do ya mind if Sergeant O'Reilly handles the lines on the wagon? They've made a sort of makeshift seat for ya in the back there, Lizzie, but it looks like it will be comfortable."

"No, that'll be fine. How long of a trip is it?"

"Oh, with the wagon, I'd say we'll see the fort after the moon's shinin' bright. I'd guess about six or eight hours, dependin' on how much we stop. If ya need anything, anything at all, this man will be ridin' right here beside the wagon; just tell him and he'll either get it or get me."

Pa helped Ma up into the wagon. Then he turned toward me.

"Mount up, Son! The general has requested that you help lead this bunch of hooligans."

I untied my reins and pulled myself up on Dungeon. Dad gracefully stepped up on his grey gelding. Together we rode to the front of the procession. The general and Colonel billings were already mounted and waitin' at the front. The general turned to me.

"Ben, why don't you ride along side ol' Jim and let me visit with your Pa, up front, here awhile."

"Yes, sir."

"Oh, Ben, don't hurt his feelin's any. If he tells ya some big yarn that's hard ta believe, just smile and play along. Your Pa can tell you the straight of it, later."

I laughed a little.

"Yes, sir."

"That's a good boy, Jake. Got good sense."

The general raised his arm up high and then dropped it in a forward motion.

"Let's move out!"

I felt like royalty! I could see that the general was goin' out of his way to treat Ma and me good. I knew why, too. It was plain that being the son of Jake Brady finally meant somethin'. At least it did with these men, and it felt good. We started down the lane. Pa looked over at the general.

"How long ago did the lieutenant leave?"

"About thirty minutes."

The general turned back toward us.

"Wouldn't ya say, Jim?"

"Yeah, about that."

He looked back at Pa.

"I told them to go straight to the Beck place, first, and if there wasn't any sign of him, ta ride on into town and see what they could scare up. Do ya think they'll have any trouble, Jake?"

"Could! I've known that old man for years, and he's as stubborn as the day I met him."

"Whatever possessed you to go over there, anyway?"

"I knew I had it ta face and I knew if I could get things right with them, then everyone else would fall in."

"They been around these parts awhile?"

"They're rooted purdy good, about three or four generations, I guess."

"So, they're well respected?"

"I'd say, influential would be a better word."

"I see."

The general cocked sideways in his saddle and started lookin' out through our pasture and back at our house.

"You have a nice place here, Jake. How many acres is it?"

"We've got a...what is it, Ben?" Pa glanced back toward me. "About a hundred and seventy five acres?"

"Yes, sir, not includin' the twenty acres of woods behind the house."

"Oh, that's right."

Pa turned back straight in his saddle.

"That's a nice-sized place, Jake."

"Yeah, but it's still not big enough ta make a livin' on. That's why I've decided ta buy back my interest in the blacksmith shop. I spoke with my old friend and partner, Jay Thompson, the other day, and he said he'd sell it back to me for just what he bought it for."

Pa turned back again.

"How's that sound ta you, Ben? That'll give you and Kenneth somethin' ta do in a few years. Jay and I can just sit on the porch in our rockin' chairs and let you boys pull our slack for awhile. What do ya say about that son."

"Sounds good ta me, Pa."

We rode for a couple of hours without sayin' much. The afternoon sun was hot.

"Sir, I'm gonna break ranks and go back ta check on Lizzie."

The general nodded his head. As Pa reined his horse to the right and rode back down the line of soldiers, the general moved his horse over to the center of the front of the formation.

"Ben, has your Pa ever told ya about the battle of Turkey Creek?" Colonel Billings asked.

"No, sir."

"Watch your leg, Ben. Ol' Jim will pull it purdy hard, if you're not careful." The general chuckled a little and shook his head.

"Well, Ben, we were afoot. We had been in a scrape with some Rebs the evenin' before. Our horses broke their reins and got away from us. We had walked all night and most of the next day. We were about ta choke, plumb ta death, not ta mention the fact that we were so hungry that our big gut was about ta eat our little gut. Anyway, we spotted this creek that ran over some sandstone rock and then dropped off into a thick grove of trees. We were still concerned about there bein' some Rebs in them trees, but we knew we had ta have some water. We had ta risk it. As we got closer, we could see that it was a live spring comin' up through the rocks. I couldn't contain myself anymore. I about ran clear over top of your Pa and started headin' for the water. As I passed him your dad tackled me. He said, "Ya dang fool, are ya tryin' ta get us killed?" Of course I was supposed ta listen to him, 'cause I was still a captain at that time and he was a full-blown colonel. As we both lay on the ground arguing, your Pa said, "What's that noise? It sounds like a Reb whistle." We both got real quiet. See, all that was there was your Pa and me. We peeked through the grass, and saw movement down in the trees. We crawled on our bellies with our sidearms in our hands. We got about twenty feet from the trees, when all of a sudden we heard a voice say, "You Yanks don't turn around. Lose them horse pistols." My heart was in my throat. I thought we were dead fer sure. Then the voice said, "Now, get up and turn around toward me, nice and easy." Well, naturally we did. Heck, we didn't have much choice. As we turned around, there he was; had us dead ta rights. He said, "You boys have two choices: You can stand there and I'll shoot you both so I don't have ta worry about you shootin' me while I'm eatin' my supper. Your second choice is, you can surrender to me, pick up your pistols and holster them, and I'll take ya down here in the trees and fill ya full of good, cold, spring water. Then I'll stuff ya full of a turkey I shot. After that, we'll sit around and talk about anything but this war. Then we'll go ta bed and I'll release ya in the mornin' with a handshake." Your Pa showed a yellow streak, a mile wide that day. I stood firm, waitin fer his order ta attack this Reb and kill him with my bare hands. But no, your dad went and surrendered. Yeah, the Rebs won that battle. Thanks ta your Pa."

Colonel Billings had a straight face, but the general burst into a deep laugh. Then Colonel Billings and I joined in. About that time, Pa rode back up and joined us.

"What's so funny up here?"

"Jim was just tellin' Ben about the battle of Turkey Creek."

"Did he tell ya how I almost shot him for turnin' yellow, Son?"

"No."

The general laughed again.

"I think you're gonna have to tell him your version of that story someday Jake. Jim may have told it from his perspective." The general's laugh softened to a smile. "How's she doin'?"

"She's fine. Probably could use a break, in a bit."

"We've been at it about three hours. I could use a break, myself. Since they stationed me up in Washington, I havn't ridden hard, much. At least until I heard about this mess."

"Sir, I appreciate ya comin' down ta help."

"Jake, you were the best soldier that ever served under me. I'd have rode to the California gold mines, if I thought I could help you."

The general sat erect in the saddle and faced forward. His voice deepened a little.

"Jake, you know, friend or no friend, I'll have to do what I think is right. The President has authorized me to take whatever action I deem necessary to rectify this type of problem. We've had several other little blowups, and he doesn't want any chain reactions to cause an all-out war, again."

"I understand, sir."

"There's a shady, little grove of trees. Why don't we stretch our legs, a little."

The general spurred his horse and rode off the road ahead of us. He rode over to the grove of trees and dismounted. Colonel Billings raised his right hand.

"Company, halt!"

All the soldiers immediately pulled their horses to a stop. Pa rode back to Ma. In a moment, he came ridin' back with the wagon following. The soldiers moved aside as the wagon passed them. After parkin' the wagon, the soldier that was drivin', helped Ma down, while Pa tied his horse. I stayed beside Colonel Billings.

"Company, dismount!"

We got off, found a place to tie our horses and loosened our cinches. I felt like a soldier. I was fine, but I could tell that some of the older soldiers were glad to have the chance to get off and walk around.

We hadn't been there long, when one of the men yelled, "Rider comin', sir! And he ain't sparin' his horse any!"

We all got up to look. It was a Yankee soldier. He was comin' from behind us. He was leanin' forward in the saddle spurrin' his horse every time the front hooves hit the ground. As he approached us and began to pull his horse to a halt, I could see that the horse was lathered up. He had been ridin' hard for a long time. The soldier dismounted as his horse was still stoppin'. He ran straight over to where the general was standin'.

"He's dead, sir!"

My heart came up in my throat.

"Who's dead, Private?"

"The lieutenant, sir!"

"What happened private?"

"He never had a chance, sir!"

Then the general stepped up to the private and put his hand on his shoulder. Ma was standing by Pa with both hands over her mouth.

"What happened, private?"

"We rode into the old man's yard and the lieutenant had barely stepped down from the saddle, when the old man stepped out the front door and yelled somethin' about Yankees. Then he shot the lieutenant right in the forehead, sir."

"Did you apprehend Beck?"

"Yes, sir. Then the sergeant told me to high-tail it up here and catch you. Last I seen, he was kneelin' by the lieutenant and cussin' the old man."

"Colonel Billings, take five of these men and go meet the Sergeant. I want Beck at the fort by sunrise, if you have to ride all night to do it. Bring the lieutenant's body." The general looked back at the private. "Private, you're dismissed."

The general looked over at Pa and my Ma.

"Brady, we'll discuss this matter in private when we get to the fort, not a minute before. I need time to think on it." He shook his head, "I'm sorry, ma'am."

Ma was cryin'. Pa was holdin' her. I was in shock. I couldn't believe that my grandpa had shot the lieutenant. I couldn't believe he would shoot anybody. I knew he could be mean, sometimes, but I couldn't believe he would shoot anybody for no reason. I had never been this close to death. Tears streamed down my face, too.

"Brady, you ride with your wife." The general looked at me. "Son, you ride alongside me. I think your folks need some room." He glanced at the rest of the soldiers standin' by us, then started over to his horse. "Let's get mounted!"

Colonel Billings and the soldiers with him, were already mounted and leaving. The rest of the soldiers mounted up and got into formation. I didn't ask any questions. I just pulled myself up on my horse and followed the general. Pa tied his horse to the back of the wagon and helped Ma up in the seat by him. She was still sobbin'.

"Move out!"

We all began down the road again. The wagon fell in at the back of the procession, this time. I turned around to face forward, wipin' the tears from my cheeks. The general looked over at me as if to say something. Then he shook his head and spurred his horse from a walk to a trot.

CHAPTER 14

As we approached the fort, all was quiet except the sound of the horses' hooves striking the hardpan road. The general never slowed his horse the whole time. We had kept at a steady trot, and he had said very little to me. The four-hour ride seemed like an eternity to me. Nobody was happier to see the fort than I was. I was wondering how Ma was doing, and what would happen to Grandpa. I couldn't believe that Lieutenant Riverton was dead! My mind kept thinkin' back to all the conversations that I'd had with him. He was always polite and treated me well. I couldn't help but picture in my mind what must have happened at Grandpa's house.

"Attention!"

The guards at the front gate both saluted the general, as we rode through. It was dark, but the fort was well lit up with lanterns on every post and at every door. There was a big fire goin' in the middle of the fort and we rode over to it.

"Attention!"

The men around the fire all started to scramble around to face the general. They all stood like statues and saluted.

"Company, halt! Dismount! At ease, men."

I got off my horse with the rest of the soldiers. I looked off to my right and saw Pa gettin' out of the wagon. Ma sat up in the back. She must have been sleepin'. The fort was about a two-acre square. There were buildings along each side of the gate we had just ridden through. Along the sides, it looked like there were living quarters for the soldiers. At the back, was a corral and one lone building that had soldiers on every corner of it. I figured this was the jail where they had Uncle Newt. As a soldier from the fire walked over toward the general, he turned back and looked at the soldiers that had just gotten off their horses.

"You men tend to your horses and get something to eat."

He turned back around.

"How was your trip, sir?"

"I've had better."

"Where's the colonel, sir."

"Colonel Billings should be along in another few hours. We had a little trouble along the way. Colonel Brady is over there by the wagon with his wife. This is Colonel Brady's son, Ben. Ben, this is Captain Roundy."

The captain reached out to shake my hand.

"Pleased ta meet ya, son. I've had the pleasure of servin' with your pa, he's one of the best soldiers I know."

"Thank you,sir."

The general took his eyes from me and looked back to the captain. "Captain, does Lieutenant Riverton's wife live here at the fort?"

"Yes, sir."

"Does he have any children?"

"Yes, sir, a three-year-old son. You're not tellin' me what I think you're tellin' me, are you sir?"

"I'm afraid so, Captain. Would you personally go get Mrs. Riverton for me and bring her to Colonel Billing's office. I'll wait for you there." The captain was obviously upset.

"Yes, sir. How did it happen, sir?

"How did it happen, Captain? A fool general went against his better judgment. That's how it happened." The general turned and started to walk away. He stopped. "Oh, Captain, take another woman with you to get Mrs. Riverton. Tell her she'll need to watch the boy." The general noticed me standin' alone with my horse. "Son...ah... go on over there with your folks. Your Pa will show you where to put your horse."

I walked over to the wagon. The soldiers had already unloaded all the wooden crates and my clothes sack. They were stacked in front of an open door behind the wagon. My folks were standin' by them. All of a sudden my heart about stopped.

"I'll take care of that horse fer ya, boy." A soldier from behind me, took the reins out of my hands. "Did I scare ya, boy?" He laughed a little and led Dungeon away.

I walked over to my Ma and Pa. Two soldiers came walkin' out of the open cabin door. They had their arms full of clothes and rifles in their hands.

"Thank you, men. I appreciate ya doin' this."

"Oh, no problem, sir, we were makin' the other boys jealous, anyway."

The two soldiers walked quickly across the yard to the other side, and as another soldier pulled the wagon away,he said, "I'll tend ta the horses, sir, and leave your wagon down by the corral."

Pa just waved at him and walked on in the door.

"It ain't home, but I guess it'll have ta do for a few days. Ben, start carryin' those crates in."

I picked up the crate that had my bag of clothes on it and walked in the door. There was a small table in the front room.

"Just stack it all right there in the corner by the table. Your Ma and I will sleep back in this bedroom. You can put your bedroll out here in this room. It's a little small. You may have ta move that table out'a your way."

I sat the crate down and started back out the door. Ma stopped me. She put both hands on my shoulders and looked me right in the eye. Tears streamed down her cheeks. "I've had some time ta think on this a little Son, and I don't know how this is gonna turn out, but I want ya ta know, your father is right. No matter how ya crack it, it's never right ta shoot a man in cold blood." Mom hugged me tight. "Oh, Ben, God lets us go through problems sometimes just ta see if we'll make the right choices when the goin' gets tough. It don't get much tougher than this." Ma wiped the tears off her face and kissed my forehead, then went back into the bedroom.

I walked on out the door. Pa had already carried the other three crates into the cabin. As I got outside, I noticed Captain Roundy standin' at the door, just two cabins down. He had a woman with him. The door came open.

"Ma'am, General Haywood would like ta see ya for a moment. He asked me ta bring Miss Rita, here, ta watch your youngun'."

"What does the general want with me?"

"Ah... He's waitin' in Colonel Billing's office. I'll escort ya down there, ma'am."

"All right."

The lady stepped in the cabin and Mrs. Riverton left with the captain. I was squattin' down by our cabin door. The captain and Mrs. Riverton started walkin' in my direction. As they passed, I could see she was a young woman.

"Did my husband ride in with this group of men?"

"No, ma'am."

The captain just looked straight forward, and kept walkin'. They walked to the end building that joined our row of cabins, stepped onto the porch and went in. I felt so sorry for Mrs. Riverton. I knew what the general was goin' to tell her. I would give anything to go back in time to this mornin' and change the events of this day, if I could. Death was so final.

"What are you doin', Son?"

It was Pa. He'd stepped out of the cabin and shut the door.

"Just thinkin'."

"Yeah, been doin' a lot of that, myself."

Pa sat down and leaned up against the cabin.

"Captain Roundy just took the lieutenant's wife ta see the general. He had another lady stay with her three-year-old boy. She lives right there." I pointed to her cabin.

"That's a tough assignment. I've been there myself, many a time. If the general weren't here tonight, I'd probably be there, right now. It's always the highest rankin' officer's duty ta deliver such news, when possible. Sort of an unwritten rule. They have a little boy, huh?"

"What are they gonna do with Grandpa Beck?"

"Well, they'll bring him in tonight and put him in that makeshift jail over there. Then the general will start out first thing in the mornin', takin' statements from all the soldiers that were there, on what happened."

"Will he take a statement from Grandpa?"

"Yes, it'll be the last thing he does, probably."

"Then what?"

"There'll have ta be a trial held."

"Pa, what I'd like for ya ta tell me, is all the truth. I'd like ta know what ta expect."

"Fact is Son, I'm not a prophet and I don't know one. I can't tell you for sure what's gonna happen. All I can do is tell ya what I think might happen, and that wouldn't have anything ta do with the truth, or facts. It would just be speculation. I don't like speculatin' much, Son. I've been wrong too many times."

We heard someone cryin'. Pa and I both looked up. It was Mrs. Riverton comin' out of the general's office. Captain Roundy and the general were on each side of her. Pa stood up. He opened the door to our cabin.

"Lizzie! Lizzie, we may need a little help, here."

Ma walked to the door.

"The lieutenant's wife. The general just told her. She probably ain't in no shape ta go back to her cabin. She's got a three-year-old boy."

"Jake, I... I don't know what ta say to her."

"She won't need ya ta say much, Lizzie, just listen. Bring her in our cabin and Ben and I will leave ya alone until she calms down."

Ma was uncomfortable, but I could tell she knew the right thing ta do was go help Mrs. Riverton. "Remember what I told ya, Ben."

"What's that Ma?"

"It's about choices in tough spots."

Ma stepped out of the cabin and went up on the porch where the general and the captain were standin', tryin' to comfort Mrs. Riverton. Pa and I followed close behind her. The general moved aside and Ma put her arm around Mrs. Riverton.

"Mrs. Riverton, I'm Liz Brady, Colonel Brady's wife. Why don't you come to our cabin for a bit."

Mrs. Riverton was sobbing. She nodded her head. I was all choked up. I had a big lump in my throat. They came down the steps and walked past Pa and me.

"Jake, that takes a good woman ta do that, under the circumstances."

"She knows right from wrong, General."

"Yeah, looks like you got the cream of that crop." The general turned toward the captain. "Captain, I'd like Colonel Billings to come see me the moment he rides in. Have them lay the lieutenant in a straw-covered wagon bed down under that lean-to by the corral. Cover him up, in case it rains."

"Yes, sir."

The captain saluted the general and Pa, and excused himself.

"Jake, come on in here. You can bring Ben, there, if you don't mind me being frank in front of him." The general turned and walked in the office. He left the door standin' open.

Pa stood still for a moment. "Son, I'm gonna leave this decision ta you. If you'd like ta come in with the general and me, you are welcome. However, I'll forewarn ya, he is inclined ta predict the future and it may be hard for ya ta take."

I wanted to go in, but I was afraid. "I'd like ta go in with ya,

Pa, if ya don't mind."

"That's fine, Son, you've been invited."

We walked into the office. The general had already taken his seat behind the desk. "Sit down there, men. I say, men, on purpose, Ben, cause you've been forced to do a lot of growin' up fast, today. Jake, start at the top and tell me what happened. How did you get yourself shot?"

"Lookin' back, I guess it was a fool thing ta do, but I thought that I needed ta get things right with Lizzie's parents before I rode back ta my place. Lizzie's mother is a lot like her or I should say, Lizzie's a lot like her mother. I figured after all these years gone, hard feelin's would have died down. Ya see, Beth, Lizzie's mother, and I, have always been close. She met me out on the road before I left for the war and brought me some food. She said, 'I'll take care of him, you just stay alive and come back home.' I rode into the yard and stepped off my horse. Newt was standin' at the corner of the house. Chester was on the porch. He came off the porch and yelled, 'What in the hell do you want?' I didn't realize until he got right up next to me that he didn't recognize me. He walked right up within two feet of me and he yelled again, 'Get the heck off my land, you dang Yankee! Newt, get my gun. I may have ta kill me a Yankee.' Newt ran in the house and I said, 'Chester, it's me, Jake. The war's over.' I turned back to my horse and was movin' my rifle out of the way, so I could get the package I had brought for Beth. Just like that, I was shot. I could tell the shot came from inside the house. Out of instinct, I guess, I got back on my horse and rode away. I knew I was hit bad, so I went straight ta my place. I didn't know fer sure who'd shot me, 'til on the ridge the other mornin'."

"I guess the woman was tellin' me the truth."

"What woman, sir?"

"Beth, your mother-in-law."

"You spoke with her, sir?"

"Yes, I did. We'd barely broke camp, when we ran onto them yesterday mornin'. I tried to speak with your brother-in-law, but I don't believe that boy would tell the truth if his life depended on it. I guess he'd worked up the courage to try to kill you a couple of days ago. His mother said she couldn't talk any sense to him. He went on and on about his Pa bein' in a Yankee jail and him bein' beat by several men. He said he had to kill you for family honor. She apparently got up yesterday mornin' just in time to see him goin' in the barn to saddle a horse. She went out and convinced him to let her go with him. She told him that, 'Since she started the job, she ought to be there when it was finished.' She claimed that she didn't even know it was you she shot until her boy Newt told her after we arrested her husband for braggin' about it. She said her boy just ran in the house and yelled, 'Get the gun, there's a Yankee gonna kill Pa!' I guess the boy ran past her and went in the bedroom where the rifle was usually kept. The old man had just cleaned it, reloaded it, and left it in the corner by the front door. She grabbed it when she saw you start to pull somethin' out by your rifle; she thought it was a pistol, and she shot ya."

"Well, sir, you got more details out of her than I had time to. The lieutenant said that he had orders to arrest Newt and bring him in, immediately, if there was any more trouble out of him. When Beth told me that she was the one that had shot me, but it was an accident, Newt started throwin' a wall-eyed fit. She said she had better go with Newt back ta the fort and that way she could be with Chester, too. She asked me ta do what I could as soon as I could and she'd try and settle her menfolk down."

"You believe all that?"

"Yes, sir, I do. Beth wouldn't lie ta me."

"I do, too, Colonel."

"What I couldn't figure out, was why Chester went around braggin' about shootin' me when I knew he hadn't."

"Well, I asked her that same question. I guess it had to do with that 'family honor' stuff again. She said he was all-fired sure that you were gonna bring charges against her, so he wanted to take the fall instead of her. I guess, right after she shot you, Newt and the old man talked it over and decided that they needed to finish the job before you had time to talk. You made it to your house too quick, and I guess Lizzie wouldn't let Newt in. He and the old man got ta snoopin' around town and found out that Lizzie was hidin' you, so they all but disowned her." The general got up and walked over to the window and looked out with both arms folded. "A mistaken identity. A mistaken identity and now I've got a dead lieutenant, a cryin' widow, and an orphan on my hands."

Pa stood up. "I'm awfully sorry about this whole mess, sir. If there is-"

"No, Colonel, I've looked at your role in this. Don't apologize for a mess you had very little to do with. Trust me, if I thought you were responsible for the death of this man, I'd throw the book at you. Fact is, I'm more responsible than you." The general turned back around and raised his right hand to his chin. "You see, colonel, I rode in here and found out we had an innocent man in jail and ordered him released without findin' out the dynamics of the whole situation. That's why the lieutenant's dead. That, combined with the fact that we aren't dealin' with the most reasonable folks I've ever met. The question, now, is how do we fix this?"

The general took his seat again and motioned for Pa to sit back down. I sat as still as I could and tried not to make eye contact with the general. I didn't want him to ask me to leave. "I won't over-look cold-blooded murder. How many of these Becks are there? This mornin' you said they were influential, what did you mean?"

"Just that, sir. There's a whole bunch of them in these parts. They mostly stay to themselves, but right or wrong, they'll defend each other. Last I knew, a Wally Beck was the marshal in these parts."

"Well, Jake, you've been in this business long enough to know what I've got to do, marshal or no marshal."

"Yes, sir."

"Is there anything else I ought to know or do, in your opinion, to stop anymore senseless killing? I'd like to get this cleared up and get back to Washington City."

"Yes, sir, there is one thing we might be concerned about. That friend I was tellin' you about, Jay Thompson. I'm afraid that because he has been loyal to me, him and his family might be in harm's way."

"Will they come to the fort?"

"Yes, sir, if I ask them to."

"You're not goin' anywhere, Colonel. Write a note to them and give it to Captain Roundy with directions to their place. Have him dispatch twenty five men to go get the Thompsons. As a matter of fact, tell him I'd like for him to go, personally."

"Thank you sir."

"You're dismissed, Colonel."

We got up and headed to the door.

"Colonel! Find out from Captain Roundy where your mother-in-law is, and see that she's comfortable. Looks like she's goin' to be another victim in this mess."

"Yes, sir."

Pa told me to go on to the cabin and check on Ma. He said he would find Captain Roundy, get Granny and meet me back at our cabin. I walked back to the place. I could hear voices inside. Mrs. Riverton was still in there with Ma. I sat down by the door where I had been before. All the events of the past made sense, now, but the future was still uncertain. Why was Pa so worried about Jay? I couldn't wait to see Granny. She always had made me feel good. I was tired. This had been the longest day in my life.

CHAPTER 15

I woke to the sound of my mother's voice. "Wake up, Ben, it's time for breakfast."

I looked around; for a minute, I didn't know where I was. Then I remembered the events of yesterday. After a moment, I realized that I didn't remember comin' in the cabin.

"How did I get in here?"

"Your father carried you in last night. He found you sound asleep, wedged up against the woodpile and the cabin wall."

"I don't remember that at all."

"Your father is over at the soldier's mess kitchen. He said ta get you up and at 'em and he'd be right back with some breakfast."

"How's Mrs. Riverton?"

"About as good as could be expected."

"What's she gonna do, now?"

"She's not sure. We talked late into the night. She's a Mormon and all her folks are out in the Utah Territory."

"What's a Mormon?"

"It's a religion of some kind. I don't know that much about 'em, just that most folks don't like 'em. I guess they got run outa Illinois and went out West ta live."

"How far is it out ta the Utah Territory?"

"From here, it's halfway across the world. Ask your Pa when he comes back. It's a long ways, I know that much."

"She ain't got no kinfolk any closer?"

"No, she says not. I reckon she'll try and make her way out there as soon as she can."

"Does she know?"

"Know what?"

"Who shot the lieutenant."

"Yes. I told her and I apologized on behalf of our family. Let's not get in ta that subject right now. There's a washbasin right outside. Wash your hands and face and then go see what's keepin' your Pa."

"Yes, ma'am."

I walked out to the basin that had been set up about thirty feet from our door. There was a soldier there, washin' his hands, and as I approached, he looked up.

"Good mornin', boy."

"Mornin' sir."

He looked back into the basin.

"That your grandpappy we brung in last night, boy?"

"Yes, sir."

"Dang shame. He shot that boy in cold blood." The soldier raised up and took the rag from the side of the basin and wiped his face. He was an older man with a silver beard. He looked like a hard man that had seen a lot of death in his life. "I watched the whole thing. It was cold-blooded murder, that's fer sure." He paused and looked me in the eyes. " Sorry, boy."

He turned to walk across the yard. I started washin' my hands and face. Some of the emotions that I had felt the night before were beginnin' to surface again. I was glad to have the cool water on my face. I didn't want any tears to start. I looked up after wipin' my face and saw Pa comin' from the jail. Granny was walkin' beside him. I laid the washrag down and jogged over to them. I hadn't seen Granny in at least three months.

"There's my little Ben." Granny reached out her arms to hug me. "Why, you ain't so little, anymore. You've grown, Ben." She gave me a big hug. "Are ya alright, Benny?" Grandma squeezed me tighter.

"Yeah, Granny Beth, I'm fine"

She let go of me. I looked at her. Her eyes were all welled up with tears but none had fallen yet. I had grown, or she had shrunk; I was the same height as her, now. She had always kept her silver hair in a bun at the crown of her head and was always neat and tidy in her dress. Now her hair was half out of the bun and her hands, face and clothing were all dirty. She looked older to me than she had ever looked before. Her face had more wrinkles than I remembered.

"I thought your Granny would like ta join us for breakfast. Granny, why don't you go on in the cabin with Lizzie, while Ben and I go over here and get the baskets of food. They ought'a have 'em ready by now."

Granny looked up at Pa and nodded her head. She gave me another quick hug and walked toward our cabin door. Pa stayed right there until she had gone in and closed the door.

"Let's go see about that grub."

We walked over to the cabin, at the end of the row of cabins across from ours. It had black smoke comin' out of the chimney.

"Did Granny have ta stay in jail last night?"

"No, Son, she chose to."

"Why?"

"I went down and spoke with her after we left the general's office last night. When I told her that they were bringin' Chester...your grandpa in last night, she wanted ta stay and wait for him."

"Did you stay up and wait for him?"

"Yes, I did."

"Is he all right?"

"If you mean physically, then yes. Otherwise he's a bitter man, that let hatred cloud his judgment and wound his spirit." We walked up the steps to the cook cabin.

"Mornin, sir."

"Good mornin', Private. How's the grub?"

"Tastes as sweet an' succulent as a freshly-grilled and seasoned buffalo chip, sir. But don't tell ol' Cookie I said that or he might quit puttin' the seasonin' on it for me."

Pa chuckled a little and we went on in the door. There were three small baskets of food. One had meat, the other biscuits, and the third, some fried potatoes.

"Private Lewis said ya had some fine grub in here, Cookie."

"Lewis said that, sir?"

"Yeah, he sure did."

"I'll be danged. He's the first soldier I ever met that liked his sausage seasoned with horse manure, sir."

Pa laughed again. I couldn't help but laugh a little myself. "Well, I hope that ain't what you're feedin' me."

"Oh, no Sir. You're gettin' the top of the hog, sir. The finest cookin' between here and New York City, cept my dear sweet mother's, and there ain't no cookin' like Ma's." He looked up at Pa, "Don't worry, sir, I even washed out the pan after I got the private all fixed up."

119

Pa smiled, "When are you goin' home ta that dear sweet mother, sergeant?"

"I reckon I ain't. At least not ta stay. I signed up ta go with a company out West to the Utah Territory, sir."

"Home ain't pullin' at ya, Sergeant?"

"Some sir, but the cavalry has been home ta me for near five years now. Besides, them boys might starve plumb ta death if they didn't have a guy like me that knew how ta make a meal out'a buffalo chips."

Pa just laughed again, then turned to me. "Son, let this be a lesson to ya. Don't ever make the cook mad at ya. There ain't no tellin' what you'll be eatin'."

The sergeant looked at me. "Oh, they'll be some tellin', and it'll be the cook that does the tellin', too. After he's had the pleasure of seein' ya eat. By the way, if ya see Private Lewis out there, tell him as soon as he's swallowed that last bite of sausage, I'd like ta have a word with him." The sergeant belly-laughed and turned back to his cookin'.

Pa and I walked out the door and passed Private Lewis sittin' on the steps.

"Cookie said he'd like a word with ya, when you're through eatin', Private."

"Yes, sir, I'd like a word with him too. This is the sorriest sausage I've ever sunk my teeth into."

Pa just shook his head and kept walkin'.

"Did he really put horse manure on his sausage, Pa?"

"I don't want to know the answer to that question, Son. But if I were to speculate, knowin' ol' Cookie the way I do, I'd say the private just ate his first manure-seasoned sausage. Ol' Cookie's as nice a man as you'd want to meet, but he makes a bad enemy." Pa laughed again.

We opened the door and went into our cabin.

"Breakfast is served!"

Ma and Granny were sittin' at the small table. It was obvious they had both been cryin'.

"Ben, why don't ya help me spread this out here on the table, while these two fine women go out and wash up."

Ma and Granny walked out to the washbasin and Pa and I sat the food out on the table. They walked back in the cabin, just a few minutes later. They were both tryin' to smile. Ma looked at Pa and then me. "Thank you, gentlemen. Jake, where are we all gonna sit?"

"You and Granny Beth, take these two chairs, here, and Ben and I will just plop down on our fists and lean back on our thumbs." Pa said grace on the food and we all began to eat.

"Oh, this sausage is good, I must be hungry."

I looked up at Pa and he looked back at me. "Not a word Ben!" Ma looked puzzled, Pa glanced back at Ma, "Yeah, Ol' Cookie knows how ta cook a pig, nothin' like you, though, Lizzie."

We finished our breakfast without saying much more.

"Looks like we got a few leftovers. Jake, would ya mind if I took them down ta Mrs. Riverton and her son? I'm sure she hasn't felt like fixin' anything this mornin'."

"No, not at all, Lizzie. Let's just put it back in those baskets and you and Granny can take them over there."

Granny had been sittin' with both hands in her lap just listenin' to the conversation. She got a worried look on her face.

"Jake, I don't think I should go with Liz, under the circumstances."

"Suit yourself, Granny, but I don't think Mrs. Riverton would mind."

"Jake's right, Mama, she is a very nice, young lady. I spent several hours with her last night. Amazingly enough, she doesn't hold any of us responsible for what happened. Before I took her home, she asked if I would mind if we knelt and said a prayer before she went back to her cabin. I've never in my entire days heard such a sincere prayer. We both were cryin' when she was done."

"Well, if ya think it won't offend her. I guess I've got a lot of things ta face, I reckon this is as good a time ta start as any."

Ma and Granny gathered all the food into the baskets and walked outside, shuttin' the door behind them. Pa reached up and got his hat off the wooden peg by the door.

"Ben, no matter what anyone tries to tell ya, those are two of the finest women that ever walked the earth, and if anyone says different, they'll deal with me."

"Me too, Pa."

"Good, Son, that's good. Ya always take care of your womenfolk."

Dad opened the door and stepped out of the cabin. He looked in the direction of the front gate.

"Captain Roundy ought'a be ridin' in with Jay and his family early this afternoon. Let's go up and chew on the general's ear, a little."

I picked my hat up off the floor and followed him. As we walked up to the general's office, I looked down at the jail. I knew they had Grandpa in there. They had eight men around it, now.

"How come there are so many soldiers around the jail, Pa?"

"Oh, just a precaution, Son."

"They think Grandpa and Uncle Newt might try ta escape?"

"No, I'd say it's more for their protection than anything, Son. Ya see, a lot of these men served with the lieutenant, and they're none too happy about your Grandpa killin' him. Sometimes men get ta thinkin' it's okay ta take the law into their own hands. The general's just tellin' 'em they can't."

"Can I go see Grandpa?"

Pa stopped walkin'. He looked down at the jail and then stared at the ground.

"Not now, Son. I spoke with him last night and I think he needs some time ta cool off before he's fit ta have a conversation with anyone."

We started up the steps to the general's office. Pa knocked on the door, then walked on in. Colonel Billings and General Haywood were in the office.

"Did I interrupt somethin'?"

"No, come on in, Jake. Jim and I were just discussin' a little incident that happened to him as they were leavin' the Beck place. We can't make sense of it; maybe you can help."

"What's happened, Jim?"

"Well, when I got ta the Beck place, things - as I told you earlier - had almost gotten out'a hand. I calmed the men down. We got the lieutenant taken care of and got Mr. Beck mounted. As we were headin' back ta the main road, we hadn't gone more than a hundred yards past the house when we heard someone sing out, kinda like singin' a little ditty. They sang out a couple of times from back in the trees beside us, 'Tell the Yank, we're gonna catch a birdie,' the old man laughed out loud. I sent a few soldiers back in the trees to see if they could find who yelled, but they came up empty."

"Why didn't you say anything about this ta me last night, Jim?"

"Well...I was bushed, I guess. I just plumb forgot about it."

Pa looked alarmed. He turned to the general.

"General, when I was growin' up around here, Jay Thompson and I went everywhere together. The group we ran around with called Jay, "Birdie." When the war broke out, they all went and fought for the Rebs, except Jay and I. Jim, what time was it when you left the Becks?"

"I can't rightly say, about sundown, I reckon."

Pa looked back at the general. "Captain Roundy was probably dispatched too late, sir."

The general stood up, "Jim, how many men do we have available in this fort?

"Total men, about a hundred and sixty-five, sir, less whatever you sent with Captain Roundy."

The general walked out from behind the desk.

"I want seventy-five men ready ta ride in twenty minutes!"

"Yes, sir."

Colonel Billings got up and quickly walked out.

"I'd like ta go with them, sir."

"I'm not sure that is a wise thing to do, Jake. You do remember that it's you they want?"

"Yes, sir, but I know this country and I know these people."

"It's your choice, Colonel Brady. I'll stay here at the fort, if you feel you would be of more assistance."

"Thank you, sir."

Pa turned, immediately, to me. "Tell your mother I'll be back as soon as I can." Pa walked quickly out the door. He went straight for the corral.

I could see Colonel Billings down by the jail. I started jogging over to our cabin to tell Ma. I opened the cabin door. Ma and Granny were sittin' at the table.

"What's the matter, Ben? Where's your father?"

"He's goin' with Colonel Billings to help Jay! He said ta tell ya he'd be back as soon as he could get back."

"What's wrong with Jay? What's happened, now?"

"Nothin' for sure, but the general, Pa and Colonel Billings think that Captain Roundy may need some help."

I remembered what Pa had told me, about speculatin' and revealin' all the truth when it wouldn't help. I figured tellin' Ma and Granny what Colonel Billings had said, would just cause them to worry unnecessarily. I was worried about Jay, Maggie and Kenneth.

I kept on rememberin' what Jay had told me a few weeks ago, "Everything's gonna be all right." Ma, Granny and I stepped out of the cabin. Pa was mounted. He rode over by us.

"Ben, ya take care of the womenfolk, Son."

"Yes, sir."

"Lizzie, I'll be back when I get back. It may be nothin', but we'd better go ta be safe."

He whirled his horse around and rode back to the soldiers.

"Let's move out!"

CHAPTER 16

The fort seemed empty. Earlier this mornin' there had been soldiers everywhere, now I could only see the guards at the gate and a few soldiers walkin' around the fort. The general had a soldier that stayed by his office door. I heard the sound of metal being hit with a hammer. I looked down by the corral, and the old soldier that I had seen at the water basin, this mornin', was shoeing a horse. I noticed that they had cut the guards on the jail back to four again. I guess they thought that most of the men were gone and they didn't need as many to protect Grandpa and Uncle Newt. I got up from the woodpile in the front of our cabin and opened the cabin door.

"Ma I'm gonna walk around the fort."

"You be careful, Son and don't go down by the jail."

"When am I gonna get ta see Grandpa? Pa said it would be awhile."

Granny got up and walked to the door.

"I'm afraid your Pa is right, Bennie. Ya probably better not talk ta Grandpa right now. He's not himself, with all the problems. Why don't we wait a bit for that?"

That was what Pa had said. We should wait a bit.

"Okay. I'll just be around here."

I closed the cabin door. I wanted to talk to Grandpa. I didn't care much about talkin' with Uncle Newt or even seein' him, after what he had said over in our barn. I figured he purdy well disowned Ma and me. But I did want to talk to Grandpa. I wasn't really close to him. He had been grumpy as long as I could remember, but I'd always been able to talk to him. I hadn't always agreed with him or how he felt about people, but I learned a long time ago to just listen and not say anything. The general opened his door and walked out on the porch and said something to the soldier posted by his door. The soldier started walkin' toward me, then turned and knocked on our cabin door. Ma answered the door.

"Ma'am, the general has requested ta see ya for a moment."

"What about?"

"I don't know, ma'am. He's waitin' up there on the porch."

Ma stepped out of the cabin and started up to see the general. "Come along, Ben I'm sure this is nothin' you can't hear."

I jogged over by Ma and the soldier and walked up to the porch with them.

"Mrs.Brady, I know I'm askin' an awful lot of you, but I could sure use a little assistance."

"What is it, General?"

"Well, ma'am, with the heat and all, we need to have a funeral as soon as we possibly can. I'd like to have you help me arrange it with Mrs. Riverton. This fort hasn't been established here long enough to have a burial site. It used to be an old ammunition depot for the Confederate Army, and we just kind of moved in. I was thinkin' that down between the corral just off from the end of those cabins would be a suitable spot. If you don't mind, I'd like you to take Mrs. Riverton down there and let her pick the exact spot, so I can get a couple of men started diggin' the grave. I'd like to have the funeral right before sundown if I could. I'll have the men clean the lieutenant up as good as we can. He'll be dressed in his uniform and Mrs. Riverton and the boy can spend a few minutes alone with him if they'd like. I'm sorry to have to ask you to do this, Mrs. Brady, but I feel you would be a greater comfort to her, than this old, crusty general would."

"I understand, General. And no offense, but you're probably right. I'll see to it at once."

"Thank you, ma'am and no offense taken. Soldier, pull that wagon back behind these cabins on this other side. Make sure that you are out of sight. Get a couple of men to help you with the wagon and prepare the lieutenant's body for burial. Then report back to me."

"Yes, sir."

The soldier left at once. The general just stood on the porch and watched the soldier walk away.

"What about a grave marker? He'll need a grave marker."

"Oh, yes, he will, ma'am.... I'll walk down and see if I can get some men started on that."

Ma and I walked back to the cabin. Ma opened the door and stuck her head in the doorway.

"Granny, the general has asked that I help him with the lieutenant's funeral. He wants me ta take Mrs. Riverton down ta pick out a grave plot. I'd like ya ta go with me, if ya would."

"Yes, child, I wouldn't ask ya ta do it alone. That little girl is gonna need all the help we can give her."

Granny got up and came outside.

"Ben, you're welcome ta come along, too."

"I'd rather not, Ma. I don't think I'd be any help and I'd just as soon not be around it."

"I understand, Son. Why don't ya go check on ol' Dungeon. He's gonna think you've forgot all about him."

"Yes, ma'am."

I wanted to go down by the corral, anyway, but I'd been afraid to. It was close enough to the jail that I thought I might get a look at Grandpa or Uncle Newt. Ma and Granny went down to Mrs. Riverton's cabin, and I started walkin' down toward the corral. The general was just ahead of me. He noticed me walkin' behind him. He stopped and looked back at me. "Where are you going, son?"

He scared me. I was afraid he didn't want me goin' down there. "Down ta the corral ta check on my horse."

"Well, that's where I'm goin', too. You can walk with me." He waited for me to catch up with him. When I did, he put his arm around my neck and started walkin' with me to the corral. "Your world has kind of turned upside down, hasn't it, son."

"Yes, Sir, a little."

"A little? I'd say a lot, from my perspective."

"Yes, Sir, a lot."

"You know, son, your father is a good man, and a brave man. He didn't want anything, except to come back home to you and your mother, and get this war behind him. As far as I can see, his biggest fault in this matter was overestimating your grandmother's ability to soften your grandfather towards him. If you grow up to be half the man your father is, you'll stand tall among men, son. I've seen him do things, time and time again, that went above and beyond what normal compassion, friendship, or duty required. That's why I didn't stop him from goin' to help his friend. I would have been askin' him to go against his true character. I'd rather live with that decision, right or wrong, than to have forced him to stay here and have something happen to one of his friends that he felt responsible for. Men like him are gettin' harder to find. You understand what

I'm sayin', son?"

"Yes, sir, I think so."

"Good. You just remember that, no matter what happens in the future, your duty is to bring honor to your father. The way you do that, is by havin' the same high standards that he does."

"Yes, sir."

The general patted me on the back as we walked up to the soldier, shoein' the horses. "Sergeant!"

The soldier came to attention and saluted the general.

"Yes, sir."

"At ease, sergeant."

The sergeant relaxed his stance.

"I need a grave marker made. Can you help me with that?"

"Why, yes, sir. And I'd be proud to, sir."

"This is Colonel Brady's son. He'll run up after he checks his horse and get all the particulars from his mother. Mrs. Brady is helpin' Mrs. Riverton with the preparations. Ben, can you handle that?"

"Yes, sir."

"Which horse is yours, Ben?"

We walked over to the edge of the corral fence. The general leaned on the upper rail and I climbed up on the bottom rail so I could see over the top.

"That buckskin, over there." I pointed at Dungeon.

"That's a good lookin' pony, Son. His hooves look a little grown out. Sergeant, shoe that pony next, for me."

"Yes, sir."

"Thank you sir. Thank you, Sergeant."

I jumped down off the fence.

"I'll go check with my mother about the marker."

I could see Granny, Ma and Mrs. Riverton walkin' down toward the end of the cabins. To get to them, I had to walk about fifty feet in front of the jail. I looked at the jail as I walked by. It was dark inside and I couldn't see in very well. The guards noticed me lookin' their way, so I turned my head back around straight. I walked up and met the three of them under a large tree.

"Ma could I see ya for a minute, in private?"

Ma walked over a few feet with me and I told her what the general had asked me to do.

"I've already got that written down here for ya. It's nothin' fancy; just name, birth date, and death date. Mrs. Riverton said that would be sufficient."

Ma handed me the paper, and I went back toward the corral. I couldn't help but look toward the jail, again. I looked, and what I saw startled me. Grandpa was standin' in the doorway lookin' right at me.

"Don't worry 'bout me, Bennie, Ol' Grandpa can take care of himself."

The guards on the corners of the building started walking over to the door of the jail.

"Shut up, old man."

"See how they treat me, Ben? You'd think I shot someone important, instead of a Yankee."

One of the soldiers took the butt of his rifle and hit the bars by Grandpa's face.

"I said, shut up, old man. Boy, you skeedattle on out'a here."

I took off runnin' over to the corral and handed the piece of paper to the sergeant that was shoein' the horses. The general had started walkin' back to his office. After I handed the paper to the sergeant, I started walkin' fast back to our cabin. The general had turned around, and was walkin' back toward the jail. He must have heard the commotion and felt he needed to talk to the soldiers at the jail. I just gave him a glance as we passed; all I wanted was to get back to our cabin. I walked in and went straight back to the bedroom and layed on the bed. It was plain that Grandpa felt no remorse for killin' the lieutenant, I was deeply saddened. I was beginnin' to see where my loyalty should be placed. The rest of the day, I stayed in the bedroom. Ma and Granny thought I was asleep. Several times, Ma would look in on me, and I would close my eyes. I could hear them talkin' but I didn't pay much attention. My mind was busy reviewin' the events of the past few weeks and contemplatin' what might lie ahead. After several hours, I heard a knock at the front door.

"Ma'am, the general said ta tell ya that everything was ready for the funeral. He would appreciate it if you'd accompany Mrs. Riverton down to the grave site."

"Yes, tell him we'll be right there."

The door shut.

"Do ya think we ought'a wake Ben, or just let him sleep?"

"I think I'd just let him sleep, Lizzie. What good is it gonna do ta have him at the funeral, anyway."

"You're probably right. He's been through enough."

I wanted to go to the funeral. I knew the lieutenant, and I guess that I was curious, as well. I hadn't been to many funerals. I got off the bed and opened the bedroom door.

"Oh, Ben, you're awake. You've been asleep for a long time."

"Yeah, I guess I was tired."

"We were just gettin' ready to get Mrs. Riverton and take her down ta the grave site. You can stay here if you'd like."

"I'd like ta go, if ya don't mind."

"No, I don't mind. Are ya sure you're up to it?"

"Yes, ma'am, I can handle it."

"Okay, maybe you can help take care of little Seth. He's Mrs. Riverton's little boy. Get your hat."

Ma and Granny had both changed into clean clothes and had their hair done up in buns. We walked down to Mrs. Riverton's, and Ma knocked on the door.

"Sarah, it's time ta go down to the grave site."

"Oh, already?"

"Did ya get a chance ta spend some time with him?"

"Yes, ma'am. The general came down and got me. We had Miss Rita watch Seth. Neither of us felt it would do him any good to see his father that way. They had him dressed in his uniform and even had his cap on his head. He looked so empty, though. I know it was just his body and he wasn't there, it still brought me peace to touch his cheeks and tell him that I love him one last time."

She wiped a tear off of her face, then turned and walked back into the cabin. She came back holdin' Seth's hand in one of her hands and a piece of paper in the other.

"I wrote a short poem for him. I don't think that I can get through it. Would you read it for me, Mrs. Brady? I've asked the general if I might offer a prayer at the end of the service. I'm afraid that will be about all I can do."

"I'll try, Mrs. Riverton. I'm afraid I'm not a very good reader and I tend ta be emotional at this type of thing, but I'll do the best I can, if you'd like me to."

Mrs. Riverton handed Ma the paper.

"You'll do fine, Mrs. Brady. And thank you."

She stepped out the cabin door and we all walked down to the grave site. They had parked the wagon about ten feet from the head of the grave. In the wagon, was a newly-made wooden box with a lid on it. There were soldiers on each side of the wagon. At the foot of the grave there were five chairs set up and we walked toward them. There were two rows of soldiers behind the chairs and soldiers along each side.

"Attention!"

They all came to attention. The general walked over and met Mrs. Riverton and took her by the arm. He escorted her to her chair; Ma and Granny followed with Seth. I stopped by the soldiers. After the general seated Mrs. Riverton, he motioned to Ma and Granny to sit in the chairs beside her and Seth. He went to the head of the grave.

"We don't have a chaplain, or any type of preacher, in the fort. I'm certainly a long ways from a preacher, but I'll do the best I can. I spoke with a few of these men that served with your husband, Mrs. Riverton, and I'd like to share with you some of the comments made about Lieutenant Joseph P. Riverton." The general slowly took a piece of paper out of his pocket and unfolded it. He began to read:

"He was always fair.
I felt like I could talk to him about any problem I had.
I never knew him to tell a lie.
He worked right along beside us.
He never asked us to do anything he wouldn't do.
He never used foul language, he didn't drink or smoke.

These are all noble and great characteristics that any man would be proud to have said about him. But one sergeant that was particularly close to your husband, said something about him that I think is the greatest compliment that could be given to a man. He said, 'He loved his wife and he loved his God and was true to both of them.' Mrs. Riverton, I can't explain why bad things happen to good people. But I feel certain after talkin' to these men, that we truly lost a good soldier, a good husband, a good father and a great man. Comfort can be taken from the fact that his life will go on being an example to the men he served with and the wife he loved. I would admonish you to write down your memories of this good man and teach his son about him. I feel that this child will truly be his greatest legacy. I haven't a lot more to say. I understand that you have asked Mrs. Brady to read a poem that you wrote for your husband. After the poem is read, we'll hear the bugle and move the coffin into the grave. We'll forego the firin' of the rifles as a final salute. Mrs. Riverton and I both felt that that might upset little Seth. Mrs. Riverton has asked that she be allowed to say a prayer at the end of the service. Mrs. Brady."

Ma got up. There were tears comin' down the faces of several of the soldiers. Ma wiped the tears from her face. The general stepped to the side, as Ma approached the head of the grave.

"May I publicly say before I read this poem for Mrs. Riverton, that there is no honor in what my father has done, only disgrace. Though no apology can bring back the life of your good husband, I feel the need ta extend one. Mrs. Riverton I am truly sorry for this senseless act."

Mrs. Riverton quietly said, "Thank you," as Ma unfolded the paper with the poem on it.

Joseph, my love, you have always been true.
When I looked for a standard
The standard was you.
I've been amazed by your spirit, strength, and zeal
Your passion for honor
Your ability to feel.
Death struck, and I was lost for a course.
What should I do?
Then I remembered your source.
I prayed all night long, to God above.
By morning, the comforter came,
And filled me with love.
My hand now clinging, to the Iron Rod,
I vow to teach your child,
The words of our God.
My mission is clear, my course I now see.
To teach righteousness,
For our Posterity.
Go my love, go and continue to grow.
You serve God above,
And I'll serve him below.
One day I'll embrace you, and you'll embrace me
And together we'll walk
Into eternity.

Ma's voice was shakin' and tears streamed down her face as she finished the poem. She folded the paper up and slowly walked back to her chair. The soldiers moved the wooden coffin from the back of the wagon and lowered it down into the grave with ropes. They saluted Mrs. Riverton and stepped back two paces. A soldier walked to the head of the grave with a bugle in his hand. After he was through, Mrs. Riverton stood up and took her son, Seth, with her to the head of the grave. "General, would you mind asking these fine men to remove their hats and bow their heads, while I say the prayer?"

"No, ma'am, not at all. You men take a knee, remove your hats and bow your heads for the prayer."

The soldiers all got down on one knee, removed their caps and bowed their heads. Mrs. Riverton knelt down on both knees and sat her son beside her.

"Our Heavenly Father, we come to Thee to thank Thee for the knowledge of Thy Son Jesus Christ. We are thankful for His gospel and we ask Thee for the strength to follow thy Son, and endure the many trials, that this life hands to us. Help us to keep our eye single to Thee, Father, that we may always do Thy will. We are thankful for Joseph and ask that Thou wilt protect this grave until the morning of the Resurrection, that it will not be disturbed in any way. We ask Thee to be with the soldiers that are out away from the fort at this time that they will return in safety. We ask these things in the name of our Savior and Thy Son, Jesus Christ. Amen.

The general got up and helped Mrs. Riverton up. He took her by the arm and walked back toward her chair.

"Ma'am, I've seen a lot of funerals in my day, but never have I felt as good after a funeral as I do now. Thank you for that poem and prayer, ma'am."

"You're welcome, General."

"Would you like to sit here awhile or go back to your cabin?"

"I'm ready to go back to the cabin, General."

The General looked at Ma. "Mrs. Brady, thank you for your assistance."

Ma took Mrs. Riverton by the arm and started walkin' away. I looked around at the soldiers. There wasn't a dry eye in the crowd. The soldiers didn't move, they all stayed where they were, until we were almost back to the cabin. Death didn't seem as final to me as it had before. The general was right, it was a good feelin'. I was glad that I had gone.

CHAPTER 17

I felt like I was suffocatin'. I couldn't raise my head up.

"It's just me, Bennie boy, your old Grandpa. I come ta fetch ya out'a this here den a snakes. Are ya awake, yet?"

I nodded, yes. He kept his hand pressed hard on my mouth and pushed up against my nose. I could barely breathe.

"Is your Granny and Ma in the bedroom, there?"

I nodded yes, again.

"I'm gonna take my hand off ya now, boy. Ya better not make a peep. That'd make ol' Grandpa mighty upset."

He eased his large hand off my face, then grabbed my arm and jerked me to my feet.

"Grab your boots, boy, we've got some ridin' ta do."

He released my arm and I felt for my boots along the wall by my bedroll. I found my boots and pulled them on. Grandpa was lookin' back and forth between the window and me.

"Hurry up, Bennie boy!"

As soon as I had pulled my boots on, he grabbed me by the arm again and pulled me up next to him; he was speakin' stern, yet quiet.

"Let's go in here and say goodbye to the womenfolk."

He opened the bedroom door.

"Ben, is that you?"

"Yep, and me, too."

Ma and Granny sat up in bed. The moonlight came through the front window and threw our shadows across the back of the bedroom wall. Ma raised her head up, "Daddy?"

Granny sat up quickly, "Chester! How did ya get out'a that jail?"

"Sh...Ya women keep it down. I wouldn't want ta have ta kill anymore of these 'blue bellies' tonight."

"Chester, ya didn't."

"Didn't what, Beth? Save my own hide?! Ya bet I did. Me and a few boys, that ain't forgot where their loyalties are. I ain't got time ta bandy words with ya, I'm takin' Ben with me. I figure I'm after a rat and Ben here will make good cheese. Lizzie, ya be sure and tell that coward of a husband ya picked, that I'll be thinkin' on whether it's worth sacrificin' a little Beck blood ta be sure another Brady don't get old enough to spread the bad name."

Ma reached out her hand to me as she tried to get out of bed, "No, Daddy! He's got nothin' ta do with any of this."

"Get back in that bed, Daughter! I'm doin' what I got ta do ta protect the family name. Ya just tell your coward ta come find me so I can take care of business."

Grandpa jerked me out the bedroom door and closed it behind him. I could hear Ma cryin' and Granny talkin', but I couldn't understand what she was sayin'.

"Let's go, boy, before them cryin' women wake up the whole place."

He opened the front door and quickly looked both ways. Then he stepped out and pulled me out behind him. My heart was in my throat. I was scared! I knew, now, why nobody wanted me to go see Grandpa. We went around behind the cabins and down toward the corral, with Grandpa holdin' on tight to my arm.

"Newt and the other boys got some horses waitin' on us down here. Ya just get on, keep your mouth shut, and ride. Ya stay right on my butt, I'll be leadin' out."

We passed by the jail. I could see two dead soldiers leaned up against the side of the jail. Grandpa noticed me lookin' at them.

"Never knew what hit 'em, Ol' Ike and Jed slit their throats clear ta the neck bone."

He gripped me tighter and started to walk faster. As we rounded the back of the corral, I could see Uncle Newt and four other men mounted and holdin' two other horses.

"Ya got him Pa?"

As we got closer, one of the men led a horse up and handed Grandpa the reins. Another man followed him, leadin' the other horse.

"Son, you let out a sound of any kind and I'll run this Yankee saber right through your lungs."

He leaned over and handed me the reins with his left hand. He held a saber in his right hand. As I took the reins, I noticed the blood on his hands. I turned my head and started gettin' on my horse. "Sight a blood bother ya, boy? You best do exactly what you're told, when you're told or-"

Grandpa rode over between the man and me.

"That's enough, Ike! Let's ride."

Grandpa turned his horse and started at a trot down the brushy slope off the back of the fort. I spurred my horse and got in line right behind Grandpa. I looked back and, to my relief, Uncle Newt was right behind me. The man with the saber was behind him. I couldn't see the rest of the men in the darkness.

"Turn around, Ben Brady. I don't wanna look at yer ugly face. It reminds me too much of yer no good pa."

I turned back around. I was filled with both hate and fear, but mostly fear. We were off the slope and on the flat land now. Grandpa spurred his horse to a run. I did the same. He kept lookin' back, first at me and then into the distance. We stayed at a steady lope for about a half an hour, then Grandpa reined his horse into a small grove of trees. Uncle Newt and the other men rode up around Grandpa and me. The horses were pantin' and sweat was drippin' off their necks.

"How long before it comes daylight, Ike?"

"I reckon about two hours, Chester."

"Where are we?"

Ike leaned toward Jed, "you'd get lost in our barn, that's Ledford Mountain, right there in front of us."

Grandpa looked over at Ike, "Where did ya say ya put Thompson, Ike?"

"Tom's got him out back of Dickerson's mill."

"That's near four miles from here."

Grandpa looked at me.

"Bennie boy, I haven't introduced ya. This here, is Ike and his brother, Jed. Their other brother Tom's, keepin' ol' Jay Thompson company. Newt, get out'a the way!"

Uncle Newt spurred his horse out to my left side.

"Those two, back there, are Ted and Bob. They ain't related ta nobody. Heck, I don't think they ever even had a mother. They don't say much, but they're meaner than a wounded bear. Best stay clear a those two, boy."

Grandpa rode over by Ike. Ike was a red-haired man with a beard. Thin built and wore confederate trousers.

137

"Ike, you lead, now. Since you know where Tom and Jay are, I'll follow you, and the boy will follow me. If we get separated fer some reason, I'll meet ya up Keener Creek at the first fork. These horses have rested enough."

Ike took the lead and I fell in behind Grandpa. We rode the next two and a half hours without sayin' much. Our pace changed from a fast trot, to a lope and back to a fast trot, the whole way. We rode southwest the entire time. About sunup, we turned northwest up Keener Creek. I looked over my shoulder. I recognized Billy's Mountain behind us. Kenneth's house was only a mile or so on the other side of it. Ike reined his horse to the right, out of the creek.

"He's back up in here, a ways."

We rode through the woods and up the side of the hill. I could see two horses tied to a rope, stretched between a couple of trees.

"Right over there."

Ike pointed to a little flat area on the side of the hill just behind the two horses. A man stood up and walked over toward us. He was stocky built with sandy brown hair. He had a long handlebar mustache. He looked older than Ike.

"How's our little birdie?"

"He's fine."

"Did he give ya anymore trouble?"

"No, not after we tied his arms and legs around that tree. With that rag in his mouth, he's been pantin' like an ol' hound dog. He's fattened up since we was kids."

I looked for Jay. Finally, I saw him. He was tied to a tree on the edge of their camp. He had dried blood on the side of his head and his forehead was swollen. He looked over at me. I wanted to get off my horse and run over to him, but I knew I didn't dare. Jay had taken the place of my father for the last four years. He had always treated me like his own son. Jay looked away. I looked up at Grandpa and he was starin' at me. Tom walked over to Grandpa.

"Good ta see ya, ya ol' coot. Looks like our plan worked. Who's the boy?"

"That's Jake Brady's son, Ben, or my grandson; time will tell." Grandpa stepped down off from his horse and tied him to the rope. "Get down, boy, like ya ta meet Tom. He's that other brother I was tellin' ya about."

"Please ta meet ya, boy. Let me have them there reins and I'll tie your horse up for ya."

I released my split reins as he pulled them down to tie them to the rope.

"Did they have you in jail, too, boy?"

I shook my head, no. Grandpa looked back sharply at Tom.

"Are ya kiddin'? They were treatin' him and his Ma like royalty around that fort, while Newt and I were rottin' in jail. Get off your horse, boy!"

I crawled down off my horse and walked over by the small fire in the middle of the camp. Ted, Bob and Jed had tied their horses and walked over by Jay. They were laughin'. Jed picked up a stick and poked him in the ribs with it. "Ya 'member ya used ta hold me down and tickle me till I wet my trousers? How 'bout I tickle you a little, Birdie?"

Grandpa and Newt were standin' in front of the horses with Tom. Tom walked over and looked at Ike's hands. "What happened, Ike?"

"Had ta send a few of them Yanks to the Promised Land, ta get ol' Chester out."

Tom looked back at Grandpa. "That means we got the whole Yankee army out lookin' for us!"

Grandpa put his foot up on a rock and slowly placed his elbow on his knee. He looked at the ground for a moment, and then looked back up at Tom. "That's right, Tom. Just the way we planned it. Hopefully, that coward, Jake Brady, will be leadin' that band of fools and we can pick him off before they see us." Grandpa looked back down at the ground. "I got no use fer cowards, Tom. Only good one's, a dead one."

Tom stared sharply at Grandpa, then turned back to Ike and Jed. "This wasn't the plan at all, Ike. You were gonna go look over the fort and see if there was a chance ta break him out, or if we'd have ta make a trade. We didn't talk about startin' another war."

"Well, big brother, we saw a chance ta break ol' Chester out and we took it. We couldn't just ride off and leave him there with those Yanks. Who knows when they'd have decided ta get a little target practice at Chester's expense."

Tom shook his head and walked over to a log and sat down on it. He put his elbows on his knees and his forehead in his hands. Grandpa raised his eyebrows and looked at Ike. Ike walked over to Tom and squatted down beside him.

"It's too late, Tom. Done killed 'em."

Tom looked up.

"Too late ta not kill 'em, but not too late ta quit killin'! This was about helpin' Chester out of a bind, not about killin' Jake Brady! Count me out!"

Grandpa walked over to Ike and Tom. "Where's your family loyalty, Tom. You can't just walk out on your family."

Tom stood up. He got within a foot of Grandpa's face. "Jake Brady ain't my family, old man, he's yours. I'd say my family's gone far enough. The killin' stops here for us." Tom started to walk toward the horses.

Grandpa cleared his throat. "'Fraid it don't work that way Tom. We've got the boy and ol' Jay over there. They know the whole story."

Tom looked back at Grandpa and then over at me and then Jay.

"Cut'em loose, Ike and let's ride. We can be in Texas in three weeks."

Ike stood back up. He pitched a little piece of bark on the ground. "Jake Brady would be in Texas the next day, Tom."

"Why? We ain't done nothin' ta Jake?"

"He wears blue, Tom. We killed Yankees. I don't care ta live the rest of my life lookin' over my shoulder fer Jake Brady."

"What are ya gonna do after ya murder Jake? Kill birdie and the boy, too? Is that where we're at, Ike, killin' kids? I'm out! You do as you wish. I'm goin' ta Texas."

Tom turned and started to walk away. A shot fired from behind me. I jumped and stumbled over the fire and fell down. When I looked up, Tom was layin' face down. His legs were movin' just a little. Bob walked out into the open with a pistol in his hand. Ike and Jed ran over by Tom. Jed got up. He had tears runnin' down his face.

"What'd ya do that fer?"

"Sorry, Jed. Chester's known me fer years. I don't leave witnesses, do I, Chester?"

"No, that's right, Jed. Bob ain't big on havin' witnesses, and I ain't got no use fer anyone that ain't loyal to their family. Ya might say we're all family now, Jed. We're all in this together. Too bad Tom didn't pick up on that. We coulda' used the extra man."

Bob walked past Jed and over to Ike.

"I shot him, I'll bury him fer ya if you'd like."

Ike stood up. He was much smaller and thinner than Bob.

"He's our brother! We'll bury him!"

"Suit yourself, just thought I'd offer."

I stood up and looked at Bob. Now I knew what it meant to kill in cold blood. I was afraid. I wondered where Pa was, and if he would come soon. Bob walked over and stood across the fire from me. He rubbed his hands together and looked up at the sky.

"Looks like it might rain, Chester. That's good fer us and bad fer them."

Grandpa walked over by Bob.

"Yeah, I'd say so. We need ta have a little sit-down with those boys, as soon as they're done buryin' Tom. We need ta make some plans."

Grandpa looked over at me. His eyes were hollow and empty-looking. He never even looked over at Ike and Jed, or Tom lyin' dead on the ground. Just talked about the weather. For the first time it hit me. Somewhere, Grandpa had crossed the line. He had become a cold-blooded killer now, too.

CHAPTER 18

Jed and Ike were propped back against their saddles, sleepin'. They were tired after ridin' all night, and then buryin' their brother. Uncle Newt was lying asleep on a saddle blanket just below us in the trees. Bob and Ted had left to go up the ridge and scout for Yankees. I was sittin' down leanin' against a large limestone rock. Jay was still tied to the tree. I felt sorry for him, but I knew, and I knew that he knew, there was nothin' I could do. Grandpa walked over and sat down beside me.

"I don't blame ya, Ben, fer me bein' locked up in that jail. I know your Ma's right. Ain't none of this your fault. Ya just got born into it."

I just sat in silence and looked into the campfire.

"What was all that bugle blowin' last night at the fort?"

"It was a funeral."

Grandpa got a grin on his face. He leaned forward and slapped my leg with the back of his hand. "Were they a buryin' that Yank I shot fer trespassin'?"

"Yes." I looked away from the fire, then down at my feet.

"That's why that pot-bellied Yankee general had them soldiers gag me and ol' Newt. He was afraid we might disrupt the service."

Grandpa leaned back on a log, stretched one arm across it and crossed his legs. "That boy I shot, did they say where he hailed from?"

"No, just that he was a Mormon."

Grandpa threw back his head, slapped his own leg and laughed out loud. "Ya mean I got me a Yank and a Mormon all in the same shot! Well, I'll be. That is some good shootin', if I do say so myself." Grandpa shook his head and chuckled. "I guess they'll be blowin' some more bugles fer them Yanks that stuffed that rag in my mouth. That'll learn 'em ta cross a Beck."

I knew I shouldn't ask the question, but I had to know the answer.

"Grandpa, do ya know what happened ta Kenneth?"

"Is that Jay's boy, the one ya run around with?"

"Yeah."

"Ike told me they left him and his Ma tied ta the main beam in the barn. They left 'em for the Yanks, on purpose. Figured that would get the Yanks wantin' ta make a trade with a cryin' woman and child botherin' 'em. I guess they burnt the house just ta let 'em know we meant business."

I looked over at Jay. Grandpa looked up and noticed me lookin' at him.

"Boy, you've got some choices ta make. I need ta know what kinda' blood's a flowin' through them there veins of yours. Is it Beck blood, or Brady blood?"

I didn't know what to say. I was scared of what would happen if I said Brady blood and ashamed to say Beck blood. I sat silent.

"Speak up, boy. It's time ta make a choice. Do ya have any honor or not? Is it Beck, or Brady blood in those veins?"

At that very moment, I remembered what Pa had said about it not always bein' wise to tell all the truth. I looked up at Grandpa. "I got Beck blood in my veins."

He got up and patted me on the back. "Good boy, good! I knew that Beck breedin' was strong. I figured you'd come through fer ol' Grandpa." He walked on over and stirred the campfire around with a stick.

Fact was, I did have Beck blood in my veins, but what I didn't tell him, was, that I wasn't proud of it. I looked over at Jay when Grandpa had his back turned to me. Jay nodded his head and winked at me with his swollen eye. That made me feel good, I knew Jay understood. I heard some limbs breakin' on the ridge above us. I looked up and saw Ted and Bob jumpin' down the hillside into camp.

"Yanks are comin'!"

Bob ran straight over and kicked Ike.

"Get up, boys! Didn't ya hear me? I said, Yanks are comin'!"

Ike grabbed his hat and shook Jed.

"Get up, Jed! Yanks!"

Bob walked over by Ted and Grandpa. He acted excited, not scared. Uncle Newt got up and walked up to us.

"What's the plan, Bob?"

Bob clapped his hands together and grinned. "Well, Newt, I'd say we kill ol' Jake and ride like the wind. Sound good ta you, Chester?"

Ike and Jed joined the circle of men. Bob looked at Ike with a smirk on his face.

"First thing we need ta do, is take care of a witness or two. Ike, ya wanna shoot your little 'birdie' or do ya have the stomach fer it?"

Grandpa looked over at Jay, then at me, then back at the ground. "No shootin'. We can't risk it."

Bob looked at Grandpa.

"Then I'll cut his throat!"

Bob reached for the long knife hangin' off his belt on the left side. Grandpa reached out his hand and put it on Bob's right forearm.

"We don't have time, Bob! He'll die soon enough! First things first. We set out ta kill Jake Brady; let's figure out how ta get that done. How far away are they, Bob?"

Bob slowly took his hand off his knife.

"It'll keep."

He looked over at Jay. Then back at Grandpa.

"About two miles up in the flats. It looks like they're followin' our tracks."

"How many were there?"

"Hard ta tell; eighty, maybe a hundred. There's a bunch."

"Ike, you and Jed start saddlin' the horses. Saddle the boy's horse, too, he'll ride with me. Ted, you and Newt are gonna be the ones ta draw fire. Bob, you can come with the boy and me. I'll give ya first crack at ol' Jake, but if ya miss, the next shot's mine. They're gonna follow our tracks up Keener Creek. Ted, you and Newt stay on this side. Take your horses and tie 'em good at the top of the ridge. Find yourselves a good spot where ya can see the mouth of the canyon. I figure ol' Jake will be ridin' in front. Ya let all the Yanks ride past until ya hear our shot. That'll be Jake, dyin' up in the front. Then ya open fire with everything ya got. After you've stung 'em good, high-tail it up ta your horses and ride east in the trees a ways. When ya start droppin' off the slope on the other side, turn due south and ride straight across the flats about where they're at now. Go up over Taylor's Gap and keep ridin' southeast, Ted. Newt, don't go home, ya head West, over to Round Top, wait there until I come fer ya. Bob and I will be upstream on the west side of Keener Creek. Bob, you'll sit downstream, just a little south of me and the boy. Ya should see Brady, first. Don't shoot unless ya can kill him. Don't forget, I'll be waitin' just up from ya. If I don't hear ya shoot, I'll figure the pleasure's all mine."

Bob pulled his pistol and rubbed the end of the barrel. "Sorry, I'm afraid I'll have ta cheat ya out'a that pleasure, Chester. I've been waitin' a long time ta get this burr out from under my saddle." Bob put his gun back in his holster.

Ike and Jed were still over saddlin' the horses. Up until now, Ted hadn't said a word. He bumped Grandpa on his arm.

"What about those two? We can't trust 'em."

Grandpa looked over at Ike and Jed.

"Yeah, I reckon we may have ta sacrifice them fer the cause."

Bob pulled his pistol out again. He waved it past Grandpa, and then let it hang loosely in his hand. "After I shoot Brady, where are you and the boy goin'?" Bob slid his pistol back in the hoster again.

"We'll go up over Double Knob and hold up over at Kilby Mill. Then when it gets dark, we'll start makin' our way west."

Ike and Jed walked over.

"What's the plan, Chester?"

"You and Jed will ride back down on Keener Creek with Bob, me, and the boy. When we get ta the creek, you and Jed go upstream about a hundred feet. Fan out on both sides of the creek, up in the trees about fifty feet. Ted's gonna be down lower on the east side and Bob and I will be down below ya on the west side. As soon as we open fire on the Yanks, you two ride down ta the creek and fire downstream at the first Yank ya see, then sink spur and ride north up Keener Creek. Take the trail over Joe Gap and keep ridin'."

"Chester, that'll take us right back by the Yankee fort."

"That's right, Ike, and where are all the Yankees at? Down here. After ya go north a ways, turn west and go ta Texas, that's where Tom wanted ta go."

"Yeah, no need ta worry about Brady lookin'over your shoulder. When ya hear this pistol go off, you can assume that Brady's lyin' dead in Keener Creek."

Bob had his pistol out again.

"'Bout time ta cut this 'birdie's' throat, ain't it, Chester?"

"If he's dead now or later, what's the difference, Bob?"

"None, I guess, cept my ol' Pa always said, if ya want a job done right, do it yourself."

"Well, your pa probably didn't have the Yankee cavalry breathin' down his neck. Ted, after ya get through stingin' 'em, ride over here and put a bullet in the 'birdie' for Bob."

"Love to."

"Good thing ya asked Ted ta do that fer me, Chester. I wouldn't a trusted no one else. I thought you was goin' soft on me."

Grandpa looked at Bob, then looked around at the rest of the men. "Let's ride!"

We all went over to the horses and mounted up. Ted rode out first and went past the fire, then past Jay. He pointed his finger at Jay.

"Don't get lonely, 'little birdie', I'll be back."

Uncle Newt followed behind him. We watched, as they rode off into the trees, then we turned our horses downhill back toward Keener Creek. I looked back one last time at Jay. He just winked at me and smiled as much as he could. What did he have to smile about? I'd never seen anything get this man down. He'd smiled and laughed all my life. I turned back around before anyone noticed me lookin' at him. I didn't know what to do. I was followin' Grandpa, and Bob was following me. Ike and Jed were behind him. I thought that my best chance was to wheel my horse to the left and ride through the trees out past Dickerson's Mill and into the flat to meet the soldiers. I looked off to my left to find a clear spot in the trees. As I was lookin', I felt somethin' poke me in the back.

"Chester, your boy's got the jitters. I'd hate ta have ta run this knife up in his lungs, but that's about the only way ta keep him from yelpin' when he dies."

Grandpa pulled his horse up and turned around in the saddle. "He ain't goin' nowhere, Bob, put that knife up."

Grandpa looked at me. "Are ya, boy?"

"No, sir."

"See there, Bob, he's family. He knows where his loyalty goes."

"Family or no, Chester, I may have ta kill him."

Grandpa got a stern, hard look on his face. "Any of my family needs killin', I'll do it!"

"That's what ya said about Jake ten years ago and now I'm havin' ta come do it."

146

"Jake ain't my family. He ain't got an ounce a Beck blood in him. Ya leave the boy ta me, Bob."

"Okay, Chester, okay fer now. We got bigger fish ta fry; or should I say a bigger Brady?"

Bob laughed and put his knife up. Grandpa turned forward again in the saddle and started down the hill. What was Bob talkin' about—ten years ago? Bob had wanted Pa dead for a long time, but why? I knew there was no chance for me to get away, at least not right now. Bob would kill me before Grandpa could do anything about it, if he would do anything about it. We reached Keener Creek.

Grandpa pointed upstream. "Okay, Ike, you and Jed go up there and find yourselves a spot. Bob and I will go up the other side and downstream a bit. Good luck, boys. Maybe, we'll see ya in Texas."

Ike and Jed rode up the right side of the stream that we were standin' our horses in. As soon as Ike and Jed had rode about fifty feet upstream, we started up the bank on the other side.

"The only place I better see those boys again is, in hell, unless your plan don't work, Chester. Then I might have ta help 'em get there."

Bob laughed again. Grandpa never said a word. I could tell he was nervous, I think deep down, he was afraid of Bob, too. We rode up the hill about fifty yards and then turned left and rode south. We came to a small clearing in the trees.

"The boy and I will wait here. I've got a clean shot at the creek and I can go right up through that clearin' in the trees, there, and over the top."

"Ya won't have to worry about that shot. Just be at Kilby Mill."

Bob spurred his horse on past us, and disappeared in the trees ahead of us.

"Get off yer horse, Bennie boy. Let's get 'em tied up." I slid down from my horse, and followed Grandpa back into the trees behind us. He tied his horse and then reached for my reins. "Better tie him, boy. When the shootin' starts, we don't wanna lose our ride out'a here." Grandpa looked at me. "Are ya scared, boy?"

I didn't want to let him know just how scared I was. I didn't want him to think that I would be any trouble to him.

"Yeah, a little."

"Well, don't worry, boy. If things go right, we won't have to fire a shot or look at a Yankee. We'll just hear ol' Bob shoot, then Ted and Newt'll open up across the canyon. After that, those two fools down there will ride out and start shootin' downstream. Meanwhile, you and I will slip out over the top and nobody will even know we were here." Grandpa grabbed his rifle off from his saddle. "Follow me, boy."

We went back out to the clearing. I could see Keener Creek through the trees below. There was a clear path straight up the hill above us. Grandpa walked down the hill about ten feet and sat down behind a tree that had been freshly downed by a beaver.

"This'll work right here. Come sit down by me, boy." He pointed his finger while he kept an eye on Keener creek. "Right there ta the side of me, where I can see ya."

I walked down and sat down where he pointed. I felt helpless to do anything, except what I was told.

"What did Bob mean about ten years ago, Grandpa?"

"Aw, it's nothin' really. Bob's got a mean streak a mile wide. He's been tryin' ta get me ta kill ol' Jake fer ten years. He's afraid Jake knew somethin' that he didn't."

"What?"

"Well, I guess it don't matter much now. Bob killed Jake's father. Jake was down at their barn when it happened. He was just a small boy, younger'n you. Fer that matter, Bob wasn't over sixteen, himself. He figured Jake saw him, but I talked ta Jake enough ta know that he didn't."

"Why did he want ya ta kill him?"

"Well, cause he was over at the Brady place on my account. Jake comes from a long line a cut throats and thieves. His Pa had stole some horses from me; said he paid fer 'em, but he didn't, and when I told young Bob about it, he said he'd go get 'em back. Next thing I know, Bob came ridin' into the place. He had killed Jake's father and left my horses there, ta boot. He left our place on the run. Nobody ever even asked me about the shootin'. Just buried the man, and Jake went ta live with his grandpa. I never thought much about it until Bob showed up one day on my front porch. By then, your darn fool ma had went and eloped with Jake, and I was in a fix. I told Bob, if Jake crossed the line someday and gave me an excuse, I'd be glad ta kill him. Sure 'nough he did. Although, I had hoped that the war would take care of it for me."

"Don't it bother ya ta kill people, Grandpa?"

Grandpa looked up at me with a stern look on his face. "Some folks got a killin' comin', boy. I could shoot a Yankee, coward or a traitor as easy as shootin' a jackrabbit. The only difference is, a jackrabbit's good ta eat and Yankees, cowards and traitors, ain't good fer nothin'."

He turned and looked back down at the creek. "That's enough talk. Settle down behind that log and be quiet. They ought'a be ridin' up this creek, anytime."

I sat quiet. I thought I would do what Granny Beth did when Uncle Newt shot at Pa; I'd hit Grandpa's gun barrel and make him miss, then I would run down through the trees before he could put another cartridge in his single-shot rifle. I didn't know what to do about Bob or how to help Jay. I felt helpless. I didn't know if I could believe any of what Grandpa had told me about Bob, or not. I felt like some of it may be true but it didn't all ring true to me. Grandpa was right about one thing; until this was over, it didn't matter. I listened for the sound of horses or voices or worse yet, the sound of Bob's pistol firin' in the trees ahead of us.

CHAPTER 19

I could hear, in the distance, the sound of horses' hooves breakin' small limbs. It sounded like they were gettin' close. I heard some voices in the distance. I hunkered down further behind the log.

"Sounds like they're a comin'. Bennie boy, don't you make a peep!"

I sat as still as I could. I wanted to hear everything. All of a sudden, the echo of a shot rang out from across the canyon.

"What in the sam hill is he doin'?! He was supposed ta wait on us ta fire before he started up!" Grandpa got up from behind the log and moved to the left, a few feet, and stood behind the trunk of an oak tree. I knew that I had to stay put. We listened and waited. I could hear voices off in the distance, down the canyon. They were yellin', but I couldn't make out what they were sayin'. Grandpa came back over again behind the log.

"They must'a spotted ol' Ted, so he went and took care a Jay Bird and hit the saddle."

My heart sank. I couldn't hold back the tears. Grandpa looked down at me. "Quit your bawlin', boy. He was just in the wrong place at the wrong time. That's life, boy, ya better learn ta live with it; besides, he weren't much count fer anything, anyway."

I wiped my tears, I was scared of Grandpa. I was also angry. I loved Jay, and he did count to me. I had been able to count on him, more than I had Grandpa. I heard horses down below us. It was Ike and Jed. Ike had his rifle lying across his left arm and Jed was holdin' his pistol out to his right side. They were ridin' real slow downstream, toward where we could hear the soldiers comin'.

"What are them dad blame fools doin'?"

Grandpa stood up again. He stayed by the log, leaned over, and squinted his eyes as he watched Ike and Jed. Another shot rang out! Ike fell from his horse. This shot sounded like it came from straight across the creek from us. Grandpa dropped back down behind the log. Jed stared at Ike for a moment, then spun his horse and spurred him hard. He was quickly out of sight, headed up Keener Creek.

"Somethin's gone foul. That shot came from straight across the way, there. If them soldiers got up the creek that far on us, we best be mountin' up and gettin' out'a here."

Another shot rang out, this time from upstream.

"That'd be Jed. He's either shootin' or gettin' himself shot. They must have come in over top of the ridge instead of up Keener Creek. Let's go, boy!"

Grandpa headed for the horses. As I got up to follow him, I noticed a Yankee soldier across the creek about fifty feet above where Ike was lyin' dead in the creek. He was on a grey gelding just sittin' in the trees, lookin' our way. It was Pa! I looked away, quickly, and didn't say anything. I jogged over to the horses. Grandpa had them untied. He handed me the reins to my horse. He was already mounted before I could pull myself on my horse. He kept his rifle out and layed it across the saddle in front of him.

"You lead out, boy. I'll foller behind ya, just go straight up. Go slow up this side, till we top out, then we'll high-tail it over ta Kilby Mill and wait fer Newt. Lessen these Yanks start closin' in on us, then we'll have ta fend fer ourselves. Don't veer left or right, boy, we may have Yanks on both sides of us."

I didn't know about that, but I did know there was a Yankee behind us and I hoped he would see us. I rode straight up the hillside, with Grandpa right behind me. As we topped out, I looked around. I couldn't see anyone. I wanted Grandpa to take the lead so that I could turn and get away through the thick tree line on top of the ridge.

"I'm not sure where ta go, Grandpa."

"Just keep ridin' straight. We'll drop off the other side, here, and go across Howard Creek. Pick it up ta at least a trot, boy. I got a feelin' we got Yanks breathin' down our necks."

I spurred my horse to a trot and started down the hillside. I wondered if Pa had seen us. I wondered where Bob was, and what happened to Jay.

"Hurry up, boy, ya wanna get us shot?!"

My horse had slowed, to go through some dead-fall limbs,

and I had left him at a walk after he had gotten through them. I could see the creek in front of us. I started down the muddy bank and into the creek.

"Hold up, boy! I hear somethin'."

I pulled my horse up and spun around in my saddle. Grandpa had turned his horse sideways and was lookin' back behind us. I could hear a horse runnin' down the hillside behind us. Grandpa raised his rifle and aimed toward the noise. I could see flashes of movement above us in the trees. All at once a horse came bustin' through the brush. It was Bob.

"Ya blame fool. Are ya tryin' ta get yourself shot?"

"Great plan, Chester. So far you've about got us all shot."

Bob stayed at a fast trot, pushed past Grandpa and down by me. He had his pistol in his right hand and the reins in his left. He pointed his pistol at me.

"Ya stay right on my butt, boy!"

As he crossed the creek and started out the other side Bob turned his horse to the right and angled up the bank. He waved his pistol back toward me, again.

"That boy may be our only ride out'a here. Ya make sure he's right behind me, Chester!"

"Follow him, boy!"

I spurred my horse up the creek bank and followed Bob, it was plain that Grandpa was not in charge, anymore. Bob turned back to the left and went straight up the hill. He was ridin' faster through the trees than Grandpa and I had been. He was flipping limbs back as he rode swiftly through the trees. I held the saddle-horn and leaned forward as low as I could, to avoid gettin' hit in the face by the limbs. Bob kept lookin' back, first at me, and then beyond me. Then he would turn back to the front again. As he got to the top of the ridge, he turned to the right and pulled his horse to a quick stop.

"How far is it ta Kilby Mill, Chester?"

"Quarter mile at the most. Straight off this ridge and back to the north, just a little. It sits back in a little draw."

"Is there a place we can hide out till dark?"

"There's a one-room shack just back of the mill. Old man Kilby used ta sleep in it. We could tie the horses out back in the trees."

"You and the boy ride on down. I'll follow the ridge around

and drop in from the backside. Go ahead and tie up out back. I'll stay up in the trees awhile ta see if any Yanks are followin' us. After I'm certain we ain't been followed, I'll come on down. I'll put myself where ya can see me from the back of the shack. If I see a Yank, I'll point in the direction they're comin' from. If ya look out and I'm gone, you probably missed my signal and ya best get ta your horse and ride west."

Bob looked at me

"Boy, ya best stay right beside your ol' grandpappy, here, or I'll hunt ya down and kill ya."

He spurred his horse hard and rode north up the ridge.

"Let's go, boy."

Grandpa pointed down the ridge, northeast through the trees. I was glad Bob had left. I turned and rode down the ridge. This time I kept the same pace that Bob had kept, comin' up the other side. We broke out of the trees as we neared the bottom of the ridge.

"Up there, boy."

Grandpa pointed off to the right. I could see the little shack up on the edge of the hill, in front of us. I got a glimpse of Bob ridin' through the trees on the ridge above. We rode around to the back of the shack. Grandpa rode out ahead of me and got off his horse.

"Jump down, boy. Let's tie up, here."

I jumped down off my horse and followed Grandpa. We tied our horses to a couple of small trees.

"Lets go." Grandpa motioned me toward the shack. As we started to cross the fifty feet of open area between the trees and the shack, I was lookin' back to my left to see if I could spot Bob behind us. Grandpa was walkin' in front of me.

"Well, would ya looky here. The coward got some sand in his craw, after all."

I looked up and Pa was standin' at the corner of the shack, holdin' his reins in his left hand and a pistol in the other. Grandpa reached back and grabbed me by the arm. He pulled me in front of him and slowly took his hand off my arm.

"Ya just stand still, Bennie boy, don't ya move a muscle."

Pa never raised his pistol. He just stood and looked at me, then at Grandpa.

"You can't win, Chester. There's over fifty soldiers comin' up this canyon and a good thirty or more that'll be comin' over that ridge any minute."

"Can't win?! Why, Jake, ya don't even know the game I'm a playin'. I win the minute you're dead. Then the boy and I will worry about them soldiers after that. Ain't that right, Bennie boy?"

I didn't say anything. I didn't know what to do. I was afraid.

"What's the matter, Ben? Go ahead and tell ol' Jake, there. Go ahead and tell him you're a Beck. Tell him you're with me, boy."

I still didn't say anything.

"That right, son? Have ya decided to stand by a man that has murdered in cold blood?"

It wasn't true, but I was afraid if I spoke, Grandpa might shoot me.

"Ya can't call shootin' a Mormon Yankee, murder, Jake, least not around these parts." Grandpa poked me with the side of his rifle. "Go ahead, boy, tell him where your loyalty is."

I looked up at Pa.

"Pa, do ya really want me ta tell all the truth?"

Pa stood silent for a moment. "Yes, Son, I know the truth about what kind of a boy ya are, but I think you're Grandpa Beck needs ta hear it."

I was scared to death. I had hoped that Pa would understand how I felt and I wouldn't have to say anything.

"Your safe son. I won't let anything happen to ya."

I caught the movement of brush off to my left. I turned to look. It was Bob, with his pistol pointed right at Pa. Pa looked over at him, then back at Grandpa and me, then back at Bob.

"How touching. Jake's gonna keep his little boy safe." Bob walked out into the open. His pistol was cocked. He suddenly turned the pistol and aimed it at me. "Drop your gun, Jake, or on the count of three, I'll make a liar out'a ya."

Pa pitched his pistol out in front of him.

"Good, now, boy, get over there so ya can die by your daddy."

Grandpa grabbed my shoulder. "The boy's got no part of this, Bob!"

Bob grinned and looked at me. Then he quickly pointed the pistol at Grandpa. "You don't understand, old man; I don't like witnesses. I thought I told you that. That includes you." His pistol blasted fire and my ears were ringin'. Grandpa fell face down in front of me. I stood still. Bob laughed out loud. He re-cocked his pistol and pointed it back at Pa. "What a pleasure, I get the distinguished honor of killin' three generations of Bradys."

Pa had been lookin' at Grandpa on the ground. He turned and looked quickly at Bob.

"Oh, so the old man was right, you didn't know I shot your dear ol' Pa. Ya see, after I killed him, I looked all over for ya, so I could take care of ya right then and there, but I couldn't find ya. Your pa had some visitors comin' up the lane, so I had ta leave before they found me. But, I promised myself, one day I'd see ya dead, if for no other reason than ta see that we didn't have anymore Bradys around these parts. By the time I caught back up to ya, you'd already spread the bad blood into the Beck family. But, I'll fix that little problem right now. Since I shot your pa first, it's only right that I shoot you next and then the boy. I like things orderly. Sorry, I can't drag this out too much longer, but ya did say we had some soldiers comin'."

Bob raised his pistol up higher and I covered my eyes. "Adios, coward!"

The gun fired. I fell to my knees and started crying. I knew he was goin' to shoot me next. I heard him walkin' over to me.

"How about 'adios' ta you, instead. Ya skunk."

It was Jay Thompson's voice. I looked up. Jay was walkin' up behind Bob, who was layin' face down. Pa was standin' next to me. I looked at Grandpa. Pa grabbed my arm and lifted me up. I was sobbin'. Pa pulled me in with both his big arms and held me tight for several minutes.

"It's better for Grandpa, this way Son. All that he had ta look forward to, was a trial and a rope. Ya know, I think what ya ought ta remember, is that he stood up for ya there at the last."

I nodded my head against Pa's chest. My tears had soaked the front of his uniform. He took his right arm off from me and kept me pulled tightly against his side as we walked over to Jay. Jay had Pa's rifle in his hand and was lookin' down at Bob, lyin' in a pool of blood.

"First man I ever killed."

"Let's hope it's your last, Jay."

"The man was a cold-blooded killer, you'd think it wouldn't bother me, but I kinda feel bad."

"It always bothers good men, Jay. If it didn't bother ya, that would put ya down on his level; just another cold-blooded killer."

"Yeah, I guess you're right."

"Although," Pa paused, "I am glad you finally decided ta

155

shoot."

"Well, until he shot Chester, I thought I'd just slip up behind him and have him drop his pistol. But after he shot him, I figured he might just turn around and shoot a hole through me, before I could do anything about it."

"Did ya get that other one that turned back up Keener Creek?"

"No, afraid not, Jake. I barely could hit this yayhoo standin' still, much less someone runnin' horseback full-speed."

"The one I shot down in the bottom, was Ike Clancy. I assume that the one you missed was either Tom or Jed."

"It was Jed. Ol' Bob here, shot Tom in the back, cause he wanted no part of this deal after Chester had been broke out."

Pa took his eyes off of Jay and looked down at Bob again. "Live by the sword, die by the sword. Those Clancy boys all went bad, but Tom, probably the best of the lot."

"Jake...ah, what about Newt? Did ya see him?"

"No, I never saw Newt. Just some guy, said his name was Ted. He died in my arms as he pointed down toward our old campsite. I figured, when I saw their tracks headin' for Keener Creek, they'd be held up there. So I fell out and came over top of the ridge. I rode right up on this Ted fellow and he spun around ta shoot me, so I had ta kill him. That's when I rode over and found you kissin' that tree."

"Well, I'll tell ya for certain, that tree don't kiss worth a darn." Jay rubbed his swollen face, "I guess ol' Newt must a cut 'n run, then."

Pa pointed at a group of soldiers that were down below us in the canyon.

"I'll let these boys, ridin' up the canyon, here, worry about Newt and Jed Clancy."

Pa rubbed the top of my head, then looked over at Jay.

"I'll have these soldiers take Chester home ta be buried on his place. They can bring this man back ta the fort."

Pa looked at me, back at Jay and then back at me and smiled.

"What do ya say we hit a lope back ta the fort ourselves and see ol' Kenneth, Maggie, and your ma?"

"Yes, sir. I'd like that a lot."

I couldn't think of anything I wanted more, than to see my mother.

CHAPTER 20

I felt something cool on my neck. It startled me.

"Wake up there, Son."

It was Pa's hand. He had ridden up next to me.

"You were swayin' in the saddle, a little. I thought ya might go face down any minute."

"Yes, sir. I guess I am purdy tired."

"Well, it won't be much longer. The fort's up ahead, there."

Pa looked over at Jay. His face was swollen, still, and he looked tired, too.

"What about you? You doin' all right?"

"My butt and my head are sore." He shifted a little in the saddle, "I ain't used ta doin' all this ridin'."

"I wasn't thinkin' about your butt or your head. I know your old hard head'll be fine and I've seen your butt draggin' a third track before; it's your heart I was worried about."

"My heart? What do ya mean, my heart?"

"Oh, you know, havin' ta leave your girlfriend and all."

"Leave my girlfriend?! I'm headed ta my girlfriend. Maggie's waitin' on me back at the fort, ain't she?"

"It ain't Maggie, I'm talkin' about, it's that ol' pine tree." Pa turned back to me. "Why, Ben, ya should've seen him. When I rode up there, it was all I could do ta keep from takin' my hat off and excusin' myself. Jay was a holdin' that pine tree so tenderly, both arms wrapped around her, both eyes closed, with his head restin' on her bark. I was afraid I'd rode up on him at a bad time."

Jay laughed. "Ben, now don't tell Maggie on me, she'd turn plumb green. Why, Ben, she's liable ta get an ax and head straight fer Keener Creek, just ta kill my girlfriend."

I laughed and nodded my head. "Yes, sir." It amazed me that after all we had been through, they could still laugh and joke. I guess they had seen a lot more death than I had.

Pa took his hand off my neck and rested it on his right thigh. "Speakin' of tellin' things, Ben. Why don't ya let me tell your mother what happened today. I think there's a whole lot that don't need ta be said, and a whole lot more that needs ta be forgotten. One of them times that we don't need ta reveal all truth. We'll tell the truth, it just ain't necessary ta tell everything that happened. It would just bring pain. It's called 'keepin' it confidential', Ben. Ya think you can do that?"

"Yes, sir. What about Kenneth?"

"Him too. If Jay wants him ta know, I guess he'll tell him."

I looked over at Jay.

"No, your Pa's right, Ben. No good can come from anybody knowin' what happened this mornin'. I can tell Kenneth, someday, when it's long past hurtin' folks. But right now it'll just cause pain."

"I've never known of a man becomin' a leader that couldn't keep a confidence. They lose credibility fast, Son. A leader would take it ta his grave rather than betray a confidence. Unless of course, more people stand ta be hurt, if the information isn't shared with those who need ta know. Ya understand, Son?"

"Yes, sir."

"I'll tell your mother and grandmother what they need ta know. Is it a deal?"

"Yes, sir."

"I'll hold ya to it."

I could see the fort, now. I was exhausted. I thought yesterday had been the longest day of my life. Today had it beat, in more ways than one. I knew what Pa and Jay had said, was right. What they didn't know was that I had no desire to tell anyone. It was like a bad dream and I just wanted to wake up and have it be over. The other soldiers followed behind us a short distance. As we rode into the fort, the soldiers at the gate saluted Pa. The general walked off the end of the porch, over to us. Pa stepped down off from his gray gelding and I crawled down off my horse.

"Thank God above! You found your boy. Are you all right, Ben?"

"Yes, sir, I'm fine."

The general turned to Pa. Then looked past him at the soldier leadin' the horse carryin' Bob. "Who's that?"

"One of the murderers, sir."

"Anyone else?"

"We didn't lose any of our men, sir. That man over there, killed Mr. Beck for tryin' ta save Ben's life. Jay shot him and I had ta kill two more. Two are still runnin', but Captain Roundy should be bringin' them in soon."

The general put his hand on my shoulder. "I'm sorry, son, that must have been a livin' hell for you."

He was right, it was. I just nodded my head. Jay had gotten off his horse and walked over by us. A soldier stepped up and took all three of our horses and led them toward the corral.

"General Haywood, this is my friend, Jay Thompson."

Jay shook hands with the general.

"How long have you known Jake, Mr. Thompson."

"Jacob Allen Brady; ta be honest, General, I can't remember when I didn't know him. Seems almost like I knew him before we were born." Jay looked over at Pa. "I can think of a lot of times when I was the only one that really did know him."

The general smiled, then looked at Pa. "Yes, I believe you're probably right about that."

The general raised his hand, a little, and motioned toward Jay. "Jake, I've longed for a friend as true as you have." The general started back up the steps to his office. "You men go see your wives. Mr. Thompson, your wife and boy are over with Mrs. Brady and Mrs. Beck. Jake, I'd like you to meet me in my office in about an hour. Jay, you're welcome to come along; you too Ben. I reckon you're grown up enough to hear anything I've got to say."

"Yes, sir."

As we walked to our cabin, I noticed some soldiers down by Lieutenant Riverton's grave. They were diggin' more graves. I felt Pa's arm fall around my shoulder.

"We've seen enough of that, let's go see your mother."

Ma and Maggie came runnin' out of the cabin. Kenneth was right behind them. Ma started cryin' as she threw her arms around me. I hugged her tight.

"Oh, Ben, I'm sorry. I'm so sorry. You're safe now."

Pa stood beside us. Ma looked up at Pa.

"Jake, what about daddy?"

Pa looked down at the ground and shook his head.

"He gave his life, a tryin' ta save Ben's, Lizzie."

I felt Ma's arms loosen around me. She started sobbin'. I was cryin' too. Pa stepped forward and put his arm around Ma. I looked to the side of me. Maggie and Kenneth were huggin' Jay. Maggie was lightly touchin' Jay's swollen face. Tears were streamin' down her cheeks. I looked up and saw Granny. She was slowly walkin' toward us. She had both hands up over her mouth and tears were poorin' down her wrinkled face. Pa looked up and saw her too. He took his arm off of Ma and walked the few steps over to meet her. Pa reached out and put a hand on each of her shoulders.

"Chester?...Newt?"

"Beth, Chester made the ultimate sacrifice ta save Ben's life."

Granny bowed her head and began to sob.

"I don't know about Newt, Granny."

Pa put his arm around Granny Beth. Ma stepped over and Granny turned to her and they held each other. Dad looked back at me. "Ben, get the door for your mother and Granny. Let's all go in the cabin."

Granny let go of Ma and pushed past her to me. She put her hands on each side of my face. "He really was good, Bennie. He really did love you." She took her hands off and hugged me tight.

"I know, Granny, I know." I knew a lot more than I would ever tell her.

We all went in the small cabin. Ma and Pa went in the bedroom with Granny. In a moment, Pa came out.

"Your mother's gonna stay in there with Granny for a minute. Why don't you and Kenneth go check on ol' Dungeon. He's probably mad at ya for leavin' him."

"Yes, sir."

We were all still wipin' the tears from our cheeks. Pa even had to wipe a couple of tears. Kenneth and I walked out the door and it shut behind us. We walked for a moment in silence.

"What happened?"

"If ya don't mind, I'd rather not talk about it right now."

"I understand." We walked closer to the corral. "They burned our house."

"I know."

We walked over to the corral fence and I climbed up on a corner post. I just wanted to sit and think. Kenneth understood. He climbed through the poles on the corral fence and walked over and started pettin' Dungeon. I could hear the sound of the shovels behind me. My heart ached with pain. My eyes had seen both good and evil, and I would never be able to deny that I knew the difference. The sun was goin' down in the west and darkness was settling in over me in more ways than one. I heard footsteps behind me. I turned around. It was the general.

"I dropped by your cabin to tell your father that we'd meet in the mornin', instead of this evenin'." The general rested his arm on the top rail of the corral, beside me. "I figured you fellows had already had a full day. Your Pa asked me to come down here and let you know." He put his foot up on the bottom rail and looked up at me. "He said I'd find you down here trainin' to be a rooster."

I smiled a little.

"I figure that since you're a Brady, you're probably trainin' to be a fightin' rooster. I thought maybe an old war bird like myself, might be able to give you a few pointers. That all right with you?"

I made eye contact with him for the first time. "Yes, sir, that'd be fine."

"Well, Ben, having lived through a few battles, I'm here to tell you that we sure don't get any choice, when it comes to who or what life's gonna throw in the fightin' ring against us. The only choice we have is how we're gonna fight it. First thing is, Ben, not to focus on the size of the other rooster; focus on the time allotted you to fight this rooster. Some fights last a few minutes and they're over. Others last days. Some last a lifetime. All depends on our commitment to the fight. If we just focus on the minor obstacle of the size of the rooster, then we'll never see our goal of defeating him. We won't see our own strengths and the other rooster's weaknesses. Second thing is, do your best to get the fight on your own terms. Fight in a ring that you're familiar with. You'll need friends on your side of the fight. If you have no friends, when the fight's over, sometimes the crowd will be mad enough to kill you. I guess the last piece of advice is, after you learn to fight really well, pick your battles well. They're not all worth fightin'. Go be a barnyard rooster, they live the good life. If the day comes that you need to fight to protect your barnyard, you'll know how."

"Is my Pa a fightin' rooster?"

"One of the best I've ever seen, Ben. If he fights, he fights to win. He's a dangerous man to push into a fight. But deep down, he just wants to be a barnyard rooster. Live a peaceful life and never fight. But heaven help the man that pushes Colonel Jacob Allen Brady into the corner of his own barnyard, thinkin' he can't fight.

While he's backin' into the corner, he's learned everything he needs to know to beat his opponent." The general took his foot down off the rail of the corral fence. "I hope this old rambling general has been of some help to you. I know you've been in a scrap here, that you didn't choose to be in. I just wanted you to know that with Jacob's blood in you, you're bred to win." He clasped his hands together and started to walk away.

"Sir?"

He turned back and looked at me.

"Thank you"

"You're welcome, son. Why don't you come on up in the mornin' with your Pa."

Kenneth walked up by me on the inside of the corral.

"You, too. Come on up, we'll see where we're at in this rooster fight."

The general walked on back toward his office.

"Rooster fight?"

"It's a long story. Let's go on back to the cabin."

As we walked back, Mrs. Riverton came out of her cabin with her little boy, Seth, right behind her. Seth saw us and started runnin' over to us.

"Kenniff, Kenniff."

He jumped and Kenneth picked him up.

"He's a neat kid. He and I have been playin' today, and got ta be buddies."

Mrs. Riverton walked up to me.

"Ben, I am so glad to see you're all right, your mother was worried sick about you."

"Yes, ma'am, I'm fine."

"Come on, Seth; leave Kenneth alone, now. We've got to go see General Haywood."

She grabbed Seth by the hand and they walked up to the general's office. Pa and Jay walked out of the cabin door.

"How's ol' Dungeon?"

"He's fine."

"It don't look much like rain. Why don't you boys sleep out here, tonight?"

Ma stepped out of the open cabin door.

"Jacob Brady, I've already lost ten years worryin' about this boy! You and Jay sleep out here!"

162

Ma motioned for both of us to come inside.

"Thanks, Jake, you done got me throwed out of my borrowed cabin."

Ma looked back at Jay.

"Don't tell me you wanted your son sleepin' out here, too. Aren't men supposed to protect their families?"

"Why, Lizzie, if you hadn't interrupted ol'Jake and me, we'd have done been hid out with our rifles in hand. We were just pickin' our spots, when you came out here. Ain't that right, Jake?"

"Just startin' ta pick mine out, right now. We'll see you two boys in the mornin'."

Ma shook her head as we walked past her. She closed the door behind us.

"Maggie, those two were gonna have these two boys sleep outside tonight!"

"After what we've been through and two men still on the loose? I've a good mind ta not even throw 'em a blanket."

Maggie grabbed a couple of blankets stacked by the bedroom door. She walked over and opened the front door.

"Not that ya two deserve these, but here they are. If I open this door, I better find you both right here close, all night!"

"Et tu, Maggie?"

Maggie threw the blankets. I could hear Jay laugh at himself as the door shut. Ma had a couple of tins with some beans and corn-bread. I was starvin'.

"After you two get done eatin', just lay out right along the wall."

I looked down where Ma was pointin'. It was the same place I had slept last night. My memory of Grandpa comin' to get me last night, raced across my mind. I lost my appetite. I took my blanket and layed down on the floor.

"You not hungry, Son?"

"More tired, Ma."

"Okay, Son, we'll eat a good breakfast."

I closed my eyes. I knew now what the general was talkin' about. Life had certainly thrown a big rooster in the ring with me. I needed to spend some time figurin' out how to fight this rooster.

CHAPTER 21

I slept hard. As I opened my eyes and looked around, I saw Ma and Granny through the bedroom door. They were both sittin' on the foot of the bed. Both of them looked tired still. The sun was shinin' brightly through the front window to the cabin. I had slept late. I looked around for Kenneth, but he was not in the cabin.

"Good mornin', Ben." Ma walked out of the bedroom, "You must have been tuckered out. Go out and wash up and I'll get ya some breakfast."

"Yes, ma'am."

I wiped the sleep from my eyes as I walked out the door of the cabin. I looked up toward the general's office and saw Pa, Jay and Kenneth standin' on the porch, talkin' to the general and Colonel Billings.

Kenneth saw me and came runnin' over to me. "Colonel Billings brought another dead guy in, this morning!"

My heart pounded harder in my chest. I hoped it wasn't Uncle Newt, for Granny's sake.

"He's laid out right over there."

Kenneth pointed down by the jail. "You're Pa said his name was Ted. Ya wanta go see him?"

I breathed a sigh of relief, yet part of me was still saddened. The last time I saw Ted, he was alive and ridin' past Jay. He was a cold-blooded killer and, I'm sure, got what he deserved, but his death still bothers me.

"No, maybe later."

"Is he one of the guys that took ya?"

"Yeah."

"Pa and Jake have been talkin' to the general and Colonel Billings all mornin'. The general said he has a plan ta end this mess and he'll talk to us after the funerals for the soldiers."

I looked up from the washbasin, I could see four piles of freshly-dug dirt down by Lieutenant Riverton's grave. "When're the funerals?"

"He said this mornin', so I figure purdy quick, now."

I dried my face and hands. "Have you already ate?"

"Yeah, I ate at least an hour ago. Ma said it may take a stick of dynamite ta get you out'a bed, so I went on and ate."

"I guess I was purdy tired."

I walked back to the cabin. I had seen enough of death and funerals. I didn't have any desire to go see Ted or go to the funerals for the soldiers.

"Breakfast ain't quite ready yet, Ben. I'll yell at ya in a minute."

"Okay, Ma."

I sat down on the woodpile and leaned back on the cabin wall. Kenneth stood next to me. I looked up at Jay, standin' next to Pa, and then over at Kenneth, standin' by me. I understood why the general had said that he longed for a friend as true as Jay. Kenneth and I had the same kind of friendship; never intrusive, just true, steady, and dependable. Jay came off the porch and started walkin' to the cabin. Pa, the general and Colonel Billings all started in the direction of the newly-dug graves. The soldiers were all lined up in formation with a team and wagon at the one end. In the back of the wagon were four pine boxes.

The cabin door opened. "Ben, come on in. Breakfast is ready." Ma looked across the yard at the soldiers, then looked to her left at Jay, comin'. I got up and Kenneth followed me in.

"Don't shut me out, Lizzie! I can smell that food from here."

"You done ate, Jay Thompson."

"Oh, but ya know how your husband can talk. We chewed the fat up there until I worked up another appetite."

"I declare, Jay, you ought'a weigh three hundred pounds, the way you eat."

"Ya know, Lizzie, you're right. I've always felt a little cheated about that. Eatin' all that good food ta stay healthy and still me walkin' around all gaunt and drawn-up in the flanks."

Ma cocked her head sideways and smiled, "Well, that's stretchin' it a bit."

Jay stepped up in the cabin and closed the door. "Lizzie, you're not sayin' I'm fat, are ya?"

"No Jay. You're welcome ta all we got ta eat. How did ya sleep last night?"

"Like a ba...brave soldier; I put duty first. Why, I was up most of the night, marchin' back and forth in front of this here cabin door protectin' the women and children."

Ma looked up after settin' a pot on the table and raised her eyebrows. Maggie walked over and patted Jay on the back.

"That's my man. Brave and couragous; only has one fault."

Jay looked at Maggie with a curious look on his face, "What's that, Maggie?"

"Ya snore, louder'n a steamship!"

"Well... I said most of the night. Jake had ta take his shift too, ya know."

Jay sat down with Kenneth and me.

"Speakin' of fat boys, that pot-bellied general wants ta talk ta all of us after they've buried them soldiers."

Ma scraped some eggs onto Jay's plate."What about?"

The expression on Jay's face turned to one of sarcasm, "If ya hadn't been so mean ta me, Lizzie, I might just tell ya. But now that you've hurt my feelin's, I'll just make ya wait."

As Ma turned back to set the egg plate down, Jay looked up at Kenneth and me and winked.

"Oh, is that right!'

"Yep."

"Well, maybe I'll just take those eggs right back off that plate."

"Now, I wouldn't advise ya tryin' that on me, Lizzie. That'd be like gettin' between a grizzly and his fresh kill. Ya might get your arm bit off."

Ma and Maggie both chuckled.

"I can wait."

Granny came walkin' out from the bedroom. Jay stood up.

"Mornin', Beth. Here, take my chair." Jay looked over at Ma. "I'm so fat, I was about ta collapse it, anyway."

"Oh, no, that's fine, you go ahead and eat. I just wanted to step outside and get some sunshine and fresh air."

Jay opened the door for Granny and she walked out. He closed the door behind her. "How's she doin'?"

Ma leaned against the bedroom door frame and looked out the window at Granny. "Good as can be expected. Still worried about Newt. She's afraid these Yankee soldiers will shoot first and ask questions later."

"Yeah, I can imagine." Jay got up and sat his plate in the middle of the table. "Maggie, Lizzie, I'd like you two ta hear the general out. My first instinct, when I heard his solution ta this problem, was ta send him back ta Washington with a festered butt, full of my buckshot. But, I held my tongue, thought about why he was suggestin', what he was suggestin', and then looked at all the other alternatives. I'll be blamed if I can think of a more sensible solution."

Ma came off the door frame and pointed at Jay.

"I'll not have a Yankee general, tryin' ta run my life."

"Ya know, Lizzie, that was my first reaction, until I realized he wasn't tryin' ta run lives, just save 'em. Hear him out that's all."

A succession of rifles fired down by the grave site. Jay got up and walked over to the window. He shook his head. "I've sure got my belly full of senseless hatred and needless killin'."

Jay reached and opened the door. Granny came walkin' back in. Jay tipped his hat and looked back at Ma and Maggie.

"Hear him out, ladies, hear him out. I think that's a fair request."

Jay walked out and shut the door behind him. Granny sat down at the table, where Jay had been sittin'.

"It's so sad."

Granny's voice was shakin' and her hands were tremblin'. "It's always sad ta see young men cut down in their prime."

Ma stepped forward and put her hand on Granny's shoulder. "They were Yankee soldiers. They knew what they signed on for, Ma."

Granny slowly stood up and turned to face Ma. She began to tremble even more. Her finger was pointed in Ma's face. "Daughter! Don't let your father's hatred canker your soul, too. I don't care if they were Yankee soldiers or not. What I care about, is some mother, somewhere, put a lot of love and effort, ta make men out of 'em. Look at your own son." Granny pointed toward me. "Would ya care what color his uniform was if he were the one layin' down there in the back of that wagon? I hope I raised a better woman than that!"

Granny walked past Ma and went back in the bedroom. Ma put her left hand over her eyes and walked out the cabin door.

Maggie walked over and started gatherin' up our plates. "You two boys go on out and find your father, Kenneth."

"Yes, ma'am."

Kenneth and I got up and went out the door. Ma was over at the washbasin, washin' her face. Mrs. Riverton was walkin' back from the funeral, holdin' Seth by the hand. Ma watched her as she walked up to her cabin and went in. Kenneth and I looked around for Jay. He was standin' on the steps up by the general's office, so we walked over to him.

He had his knife out, whittlin' on a stick. "You boys get all fattened up?"

"Yes, sir."

"Good."

Jay looked in the direction of the soldiers. Pa and Colonel Billings were walkin' with the general. We could hear something off to our left. We all looked. The gate to the fort came open and Captain Roundy came ridin' through with a group of soldiers following him. The general motioned to Captain Roundy.

"Tend to your horse and then come see me."

The captain saluted him and rode on by. The three men walked up by Jay, Kenneth and me.

Pa smiled at Jay. "Where'd you go hide?"

"Oh, ya know me, Jake, I smelled my way back down to the cabin where these boys was eatin' breakfast."

"We done ate already!"

"I know, but when your wife's a cookin', I'm always available."

Pa laughed, "Ya better watch out, you're gonna get fat enough ta butcher!"

"Yeah, I better watch my nice figure, I guess, or I might lose my new girlfriend up in Keener Creek."

Pa and Jay laughed together.

The general grinned and stepped up onto the porch. "I can only imagine what that's all about. Why don't we all step in my office, or I should say, Colonel Billing's office. Hopefully, I'll be able to give it back to him in the very near future."

The four of them all began walkin' in the office. Pa turned around.

"Ya two boys come on in here, too."

Kenneth and I followed them inside. The general went around and sat down behind the desk.

"Mr. Thompson, have you given anymore thought to my

proposal?"

"Well, yes, I have. It's not your proposal I'm worried about, necessarily. It's the proposal that I made fifteen years ago ta that woman down there."

"I understand, that is your first consideration. Although, I believe that, all things considered, it will be the best thing for her, too. Jake, what about you?"

"I built that home we have, and I cleared the land it's on. But, I ain't attached to the house, just those who live in it."

A knock came at the door and Captain Roundy walked in. The general stood up. Captain Roundy saluted.

"At ease, Captain Roundy. Give us your report."

"Sir, we didn't find either one of them. We went over ta the Beck place and layed Mr. Beck ta rest in the grove of trees out back of the house like the colonel asked us ta do. We rode a mile circle around the place and the only fresh tracks goin' or comin', were ours. I sent Sergeant O'Reilly and a few men ta go see if they could cut sign anywhere, headin' north out'a Keener Creek and I took the rest of the men with me and went to the south. We crossed sign of a horse movin' fast to the southwest, so we assumed that was our man and got on the trail. Sure enough it was."

The captain turned and looked at Pa. "Took us right ta your place, Colonel Brady." The captain stopped talkin' for a minute. It was plain he was at a loss for words. The general walked around and leaned against the front of the desk and the captain looked back at him. "Go on, Captain."

"Well, sir, the place was burned ta the ground. Barn and all."

Jay chuckled, shook his head and looked down at the floor, then back up at Pa, "That'd be Newt. I guess it's a dern good thing that ya don't put much value in the house. The general's offer's lookin' better and better, ain't it, Jake."

"Yeah, except I got the same problem you do. I'm afraid Lizzie was a might more attached ta that house, than I was."

"Oh, no. Our problems ain't the same. Maggie already knows her house is burnt down. No, I wouldn't trade ya places for love nor money."

The general looked at Pa.

"The offer still stands, Jake. I'd like you to make the choice so I don't have to make a tough decision."

The general turned back to the captain. "Did you find his

tracks again?"

"Yes, sir, they went right out back of the place and over the ridge headed straight west. We followed 'em for near ten miles. They never veered north or south much at all. I finally decided ta pull off from them and come back ta the fort for more rations. I met Sergeant O'Reilly on his way back ta the fort, a few miles back. He said that he had cut sign at the head of Keener Creek. Same thing, sir, the tracks turned to the west and stayed headed that direction."

The general looked back at Pa. "Jake, do you reckon they are headed out of the country?"

Pa held his right elbow in his left hand and thoughtfully stroked his mustache, "No sir, I'd have ta say not. Newt's got lots of family in these parts. So does the Clancey boy. I reckon they'll find their way to familiar ground. Newt's not brassy enough ta strike out on his own for long."

The general walked over to the captain. "Thank you, Captain. Go get some rest."

"Would you like us to prepare ta start out again in the mornin' sir."

"Not right now, Captain. We've got some other decisions to make, first. I'll have Colonel Billings get with you this evenin'. Rest your horses and men. You're dismissed."

The captain turned and left the room. The general turned and walked back behind the desk. He had a far-away look in his eyes as he sat down.

"Jake, could you and Mr. Thompson have your wives and two sons up here in my office in about an hour? I'd like to know how long I'm gonna be in Georgia."

"Yes, sir, we'll be here."

"Good, good. Now, if you don't mind I'd like to be left alone so I can think my way around the obstacles and find the goal."

The general looked over at me. "Ben knows what I mean, don't you, Ben?"

"Yes, sir."

The general smiled. He appeared to be very sincere. I could see why Pa respected him. We all got up, left the room and walked out on the porch. Captain Roundy was standin' by the gate to the fort, talkin' with a couple of soldiers. Colonel Billings excused himself and walked over toward Captain Roundy.

Jay cleared his throat as we stepped off the porch. "Jake,

would ya mind excusin' the boys and me, too? We need ta go find us a tree and have a little word of prayer."

"Prayer?"

"Yeah, Jake, we're gonna pray that Lizzie don't kill ya, when ya tell her that her house is burnt down."

Pa got a serious look on his face, put his hand on Jay's shoulder, " Well, thank ya, Jay, I guess it would be askin' too much for ya ta take time ta fast." Pa couldn't hold back the hidden smile, anymore, "Knowin' how you like ta eat."

"No, not at all, Jake, we'll fast the whole time we're walkin' down ta the tree." Jay glanced over at Kenneth and me, "Won't we boys?" We all laughed together.

We followed Jay off the steps and started across the yard. I didn't know where we were really goin', but I was sure it wasn't to pray. I also knew Jay was right; I wouldn't want to be in Pa's' place. Ma cherished our home. I knew she was goin' to be mad.

"Don't forget ta be back up here in an hour, Jay. We've gotta meet with the general."

Jay looked back over his shoulder.

"Yeah, I know, but don't be surprised if I throw a rock at ya the next time I see ya."

Pa stopped and got a puzzled look on his face."Why would ya do that?"

"Ta make sure Lizzie ain't done killed ya and all I'm seein' is your ghost."

Pa chuckled. "Well, don't throw it too hard, your prayers might just work."

Jay had done it again. In the face of trouble, he'd made us all laugh.

CHAPTER 22

Ma, Maggie, Kenneth and I all sat quietly in the general's office. Pa and Jay were outside on the porch talking to the general. Ma had been cryin' again. I assumed that it was because dad had told her that Newt burned our house down. Kenneth and I sat against the wall beneath the window. We could hear Pa, Jay and the general, talkin', but couldn't make out what they were sayin'. Maggie sat by Ma with her hand on Ma's shoulder. We waited almost ten minutes; finally, the door came open. The general had stopped in the doorway; he was lookin' back at Pa.

"Jake, my hands are tied. I understand how everyone must feel, but I've got a job to do and I'm going to do it. Put yourself in my shoes, you'd do the same thing."

The general walked on in the room. He walked past Ma and Maggie.

"Ladies."

They both nodded at the general, as he took his seat behind the desk.

"Jake, you and Jay have a seat by your wives, there, if you don't mind. I had a couple of extra chairs brought in so we could all sit. You boys don't mind the floor, do you?"

We both replied, "No, sir."

Kenneth and I were both nervous. The general had always been pleasant to me, but I knew from watchin' him with the soldiers that he could also be stern. One thing was certain, he was always in control. Pa sat down by Ma, and Jay sat on the other end, by Maggie. The general leaned forward in his chair, placed his elbow on the desk, and clasped his hands together in front of him.

"I'll do the talkin' for a few minutes, if you don't mind, then we can discuss, openly, what I've said or any concerns that any of you may have. First, I must admit, that I have been very humbled by my inability to come up with the perfect solution to the problem at hand. As far as I can tell, there isn't one. The goal seems so clear, 'Stop innocent people from being hurt and even killed—' yet the obstacles seem almost overwhelming. I've been given authority by the President of the United States of America to take whatever action I deem necessary in all such matters as this. I realize that with authority comes the responsibility to make correct decisions. I like that. I like to have the freedom to make a choice, so I gladly accept the responsibility. I've also learned, the hard way, that when I endeavor to force my own will upon any man without his agreement, the outcome is most unproductive, and seldom is the goal achieved."

The general stood up and placed his hands behind his back. He walked over and looked out of the window, a few moments, then he walked back over beside the desk.

"No, the only sure way to lead men, is through trust. I believe that is why men choose to follow God, because they trust Him. Not because he forces them to follow him, but because they trust him. Now, this leads me to one of the obstacles that must be overcome here, today. I believe that Colonel Brady trusts me. Is that a fair statement, Colonel?"

"Yes, sir, it is."

"My problem is, I haven't had the good fortune of working closely with all of you, like I have Jake, to earn your trust. So I can only effectively lead one person in this room, if my premise is correct."

The general sat back down and looked at Pa.

"Which means that trust must be delegated...if there is such a thing as delegating trust. I mean, I must rely on Jake and hope that he has earned the trust of others in this room. Not only does Jake trust me, but I trust him also, so you see it works both ways."

The general stood up again. He walked around to the front of the desk and leaned back on it.

"Now that you understand a little bit about the way I think, I hope that you understand that it is not my wish to force my will upon any of you. What I'm really asking is for you to join me in solving a problem that has brought grief and pain to everyone here."

The general stood back up and clasped his hands together.

"Now, I have made a proposal to Jake as a solution to this

problem. I will detail it to you and answer any questions that you might have. First, I have proposed that Jake re-enlist in the Cavalry for an additional twelve months."

Ma turned and looked at Pa. She was angry.

"Now, Mrs. Brady, I know that you've been without your husband for four years or better. Please hear me out."

Ma looked back at the general.

"Second, I have also proposed that Mr. Thompson enlist for the same twelve month period. He will receive full pay and will, I'm sure, be of great assistance with his horseshoeing skills. Third, I will authorize the purchase of both the Brady and the Thompson farms by the United States Cavalry. Fourth, I will assign Mr. Thompson and Colonel Brady to a company, bound for the Utah Territory. Colonel Brady will be in command. Mrs. Brady, I would propose that you, Mrs. Thompson, Mrs. Riverton and your sons, all join this company. All at the Cavalry's expense, of course. When you have reached the Great Salt Lake in the Utah Territory, Colonel Brady will be responsible for seeing that Mrs. Riverton finds her family, at which time the obligation of both men to the Cavalry will have been met. Your families are free to continue on with the company to California or, independently, go anywhere you please. The twelve months enlistment will be extended only if the Utah Territory has not been reached, which I view as very unlikely, since it's only about an eight-month trip. I will return to Washington and see that the agreed price for your farms is sent to you with the payroll. Colonel Billings will not pursue Newt Beck or Jed Clancey on the grounds of past events. However, if they are caught engaging in lawless behavior in the future, then they will also be charged with the murder of four United States Cavalry soldiers."

The general walked over by the window. He stood in silence for a moment. He turned around and looked at Kenneth and me, then looked over at my folks.

"That, my friends, is the only way I know of, that I could leave here comfortable that there would be no more bloodshed over this matter. I'm open to questions or suggestions."

Ma cleared her throat. "Jay asked Maggie and me ta hear ya out, General, and we have politely listened while ya proposed that we leave the only home we've ever known and traipse across some wilderness to make our home with the Mormons. Pardon me, General, if I don't seem overjoyed at your proposal!"

"I know, Mrs. Brady, that it is going to require a great deal of sacrifice on your part. But may I remind you, that a great deal more has already been sacrificed."

"You don't need to remind me, I'm the one who has lost my father!"

"Yes, ma'am, you have, and for that I'm truly sorry. Jake and I discussed every way possible to keep something like that from happening. But it goes to show, that God did give men their agency to make choices."

Ma got up and walked over by the general. Pa stood up, but stayed by his seat. "Lizzie, the man's tryin' ta help."

Ma spun quickly around and glared at Pa. "And if we refuse his so-called help?"

The general shook his head and walked over to his chair behind the desk and leaned on the back of it. "Then I would be forced to withdraw the hand of mercy and wield the sword of justice. I would have to order Colonel Billings to hunt down your brother and Jed Clancey and see that they were tried and hanged for the murder of these soldiers, I buried this morning. I would then have to withdraw protection for your husband who would no longer be an officer in the Cavalry. I could only offer minor protection that would be given to any citizen. You would be left to rebuild your homes on your own. You'll find the price that I've offered for your farms is ample to cover good-standing homes on them. Unfortunately, I would have to report that the homes were destroyed after I had already made an offer."

Pa walked over by Ma; she turned and leaned against Pa's chest. She was cryin' and her voice was tremblin'.

"Is it ever gonna end, Jake? What about mother?"

The general was uncomfortable seein' Ma cry. He walked over to the door. "Jake, why don't you and Jay take your families back down to your cabin and discuss this some more."

We all stood up, but nobody moved.

"Yes, sir. When do ya need an answer, sir?"

"I'd like to give orders to Colonel Billings in the mornin'. I'm available to hear any questions or viable alternatives, in the mean time. Why don't we make it noon, tomorrow? The sooner, the better though, Jake. If we've got to go find these two, we need to hit the trail while it's hot."

The general opened the door and stepped aside.

"I know, sir."

The general patted Pa's back, lightly, as he and Ma walked out the door. Kenneth and I followed behind. Jay and Maggie came behind us.

"You know, Jay, my offer to you stands independent of my offer to Jake. I recognize the threat to your family."

"Thanks, General, but I reckon we'll stand together."

The general smiled pleasantly, "I truly wouldn't have expected anything else, but I felt it right to offer."

We all walked a few feet off from the porch and stopped. The expression on Ma's face changed from sadness to one of hope. She looked up at Pa, "Let's get Granny and go for a walk outside this fort, Jake. I can't think, anymore, all cooped up." Ma turned around. "Maggie, let's all get out of here for awhile."

"Sounds good ta me, Lizzie. I'll grab a blanket. We'll find a nice little grove of trees and sit down. Is Granny up to it?"

"Yeah, so long as we don't walk too far."

"Ben, why don't you and Kenneth go get Granny and the blanket. Your mother and I will walk over here by the front gate with Jay and Maggie and wait for you."

"Yes, sir."

Kenneth and I started runnin' to the cabin.

"Ya think we're gonna go out West?"

"I don't know."

I didn't know, either. But, I knew we had to do something. Our house was burned and we couldn't stay at the fort, forever. My life had been turned upside down. I had been through more changes since Pa came home, than I'd been through in my entire life. I guess I was kind of gettin' used to it.

CHAPTER 23

We walked for a few minutes down through the woods. It broke out into a small meadow with a creek runnin' through it, where a beaver dam had made a small pond. Ma took a deep breath, looked over the meadow, and then pointed to a flat spot on the ground, just in front of a large log. "This will be fine, here, don't you think, Maggie?"

"Yes, this is a purdy spot."

Kenneth and I spread the two blankets out on the ground. Pa was holdin' Granny by the arm. He walked her over to the blanket and helped her sit down. Ma and Maggie sat down next to her. Pa and Jay stood side by side in front of them, lookin' out across the meadow. Kenneth and I sat down together behind the blankets and leaned up against the log. Normally, we probably would have went off by ourselves and done something, but neither of us wanted to get out of hearin' distance.

"What's on your mind, Lizzie. The boys said ya wanted ta talk to me. Surely, ya didn't walk me off down here ta look at Jake's and Jay's backsides?"

Pa quickly moved to the side, "Oh, I'm sorry, Beth. I'll bet you would rather see the meadow."

Jay stayed where he was standin' and strained his neck around to look at his backside, "Speak for yourself, Jake. I figure I got a purdy, good-lookin' backside."

Maggie burst out, "You get out'a the way, Jay Thompson. I'm the only one that needs ta see your backside."

Jay laughed as he walked off to the side with Pa. Pa just shook his head, "I guess you heard that!"

"I heard it, Jake, but need, and want, are two different things. It's nice ta know Maggie still needs me, she just hates to admit that there's a whole bunch of other women out there that want me."

Jay looked back at Maggie and stretched his suspenders out in front of his belly, raised both his eyebrows, grinned, then looked back out to the meadow. Granny laughed. Maggie and Ma looked down at the blanket and tried to keep from laughin', but they both chuckled a little. It seemed everyone focused on the scenery for a few minutes. Finally, Ma raised her head up, with a more serious look on her face.

"Ma, this fool general, here, has come up with a plan for us to leave Georgia and go out West, ta live with the Mormons. The way he's explained it...well, Jake, you tell her."

Ma and Granny looked up at Pa. He turned around and squatted down in front of them.

"Beth, we've tried ta figure every possible way out of this. When I first heard the general's idea, I thought it sounded crazy, too. But the more I think about it, the more it seems like the right thing ta do. Out West, there's lots of land and opportunity. Here...well, here, I'm afraid there's just trouble."

Pa explained the general's proposal to Granny. She listened quietly and, now and then, would look at the ground or over at Ma. "We'd like ya ta go with us, Granny."

"We? I haven't said I was goin' anywhere, Jacob Brady. I want ta hear what Mother thinks before I make up my mind about anything."

Granny looked at Ma. She sat and stared at her for a minute, "You'll not have that pleasure, Daughter. You're ta stand united with your husband. When the two of ya have reached your final decision, together, then I'll give ya mine." Granny turned back to Pa, "Jake, do you trust this general?"

"Yes, Beth, I do."

"What are the chances that Newt will hang?"

"If we stay, Beth, I believe the general won't leave a stone unturned. He'll hang, or be shot, sure as shootin'."

Granny closed her eyes and looked down at the ground. She was in pain. She raised her head and tenderly looked at Pa, "I have loved you like my own son, Jake. I've never known you ta lie. I prayed for you the whole time you were off a fightin' that war." Granny's voice began to break with emotion, "Nothin's changed. You can't kill a mother's love. I have two sons, you and Newt." Granny looked back at Ma, "I expect, you two will make the right decision." Granny rubbed her eyes with her hands, "Now help this poor, old woman up, Jake, and I'll leave ya here ta make your decision."

Pa reached down and helped Granny up. Ma looked down at the blanket. Granny hadn't said what she wanted to hear. Tears began runnin' down both of Ma's cheeks. Pa motioned to Kenneth and me to get up, "Ben, you two boys walk Granny back to the fort."

"No, Jake, I'd rather walk alone. This is a family decision. The boys should stay here."

"They can come right back, Granny."

"No, Jake, I'm not that old. I can walk myself back to the cabin."

Ma looked up.

"Mother would ya do me a favor?"

"Yes, Lizzie, if I can."

"Would you ask Mrs. Riverton if she would join us down here. I'd like ta ask her some questions."

Granny nodded her head. "That's a good idea, Lizzie." Granny turned and slowly disappeared into the woods.

Ma stood up and walked off the blanket, a few feet. She folded her arms and looked up into the sky. The breeze had dried the tears on her cheeks.

"Maggie, how do you feel about this? Are ya willin' ta stand by your husband, if he decides ta go out West ta live with Jake and the Mormons?"

Maggie smiled, looked down at her feet, then slowly raised her head. She looked up at Jay, then back at Ma, "Yeah, Lizzie, I reckon the general's right about one thing. I don't trust him, cause I don't know him. But I do trust my husband. I've stood by him through all his other hair-brained ideas and, as ya can see, I ain't starved ta death yet. I don't know much about Mormons, but we've lived around Jake, before, and he makes a good neighbor."

Pa and Jay walked up and sat down on the log by Kenneth and me. Ma just kept lookin' out across the meadow, then back up at the sky. Finally, Ma broke the silence, turned around and looked down at Maggie on the blanket.

"I don't know much about Mormons, either, and what I've heard, ain't been good."

Pa looked up at Ma. "Lizzie, this ain't about Mormons. We can live anywhere we take a mind to. This is about us and livin' in peace and bein' happy."

179

Ma looked sharply at Pa, "What if we're jumpin' from the fryin' pan into the fire? We may get out there and them kill us because we ain't one of 'em. I've heard, they ain't even Christians."

"You heard wrong, Mrs. Brady." Mrs. Riverton stepped out from behind a willow tree, just behind Pa and Jay.

Ma looked up with a surprised look on her face, "Oh, Mrs. Riverton, I didn't know you were....I -"

"I didn't mean ta come in unnoticed, but as I approached, I couldn't help hearing what you were saying."

Ma walked over to Mrs. Riverton. Maggie got up and walked beside Ma. Maggie put one hand on Mrs. Riverton's shoulder and lightly held her arm with the other. "Mrs. Riverton, please sit down with us. Lizzie and I would like ta know more about your people. That's why Lizzie asked Beth ta have ya come down here."

Ma looked over at Maggie, then back at Mrs. Riverton, "That's right, Mrs. Riverton. The general has...has offered ta let us go out West with ya. And I've heard...Well, I've heard-"

"I'm sure I know some of the things you've heard, Mrs. Brady. Let me assure you, our men don't grow horns, and don't all have twenty wives."

Mrs. Riverton walked back to the blanket and sat down next to Maggie. She seemed very relaxed and comfortable about talkin' with them.

"We are Christians, Mrs. Brady. In every sense of the word, if being Christian means believing in Jesus Christ and believing that he atoned for all the sins of mankind."

"Mrs. Riverton, I didn't mean to offend you. It's just that I am being asked ta consider movin' to a strange place and bein' with people I have heard nothin' but bad about."

"I'm not offended, Mrs. Brady. May I ask you a few questions?" Ma nodded her head. Mrs. Riverton continued, "Did you know my husband?"

"A little, only while he was at my home."

"Did he ever say or do anything to lead you to believe he was a bad man?"

Ma quickly shook her head, "Oh, no, he was very polite."

"Have I done anything to displease you?"

"Why, no, Mrs. Riverton."

"How many Mormons have you known, personally, Mrs. Brady?"

"Just you and your husband."

Mrs. Riverton smiled. "Ya see, Mrs. Brady. You don't have a bad thing ta say about any Mormon you've ever known. Going off from things ya hear from others is living on gossip and that's not Christian no matter what denomination you affiliate yourself with. We're like any other people. Unfortunately, a bad apple will crop up amongst us, now and then. But, as a whole, I think you'll find upstanding, God-fearing folks."

Ma looked away in thought, as Maggie leaned forward and made eye contact with Mrs. Riverton, "I heard they burnt your homes and ran you out'a Illinois."

Mrs. Riverton took her eyes off from Ma and turned toward Maggie, "That's right, Maggie, they did, and in Missouri, too. Many were killed. Women and children were abused and homes were burned. So our people moved out West to find a place where we could live in peace."

Ma stood up again. "Maggie and I can certainly sympathize with wantin' ta live in peace." Ma walked off the blanket, her arms folded against her, "What about all your men havin' a bunch of wives; isn't that adultery?"

Mrs. Riverton got up and walked out by Ma. Pa stood up, with a disappointed look on his face, "Lizzie, Mrs. Riverton's here because ya invited her, her religion ain't on trial, here."

Mrs. Riverton looked back at Pa and raised up her hand.

"No, Colonel Brady, it's okay. That's a hard doctrine ta understand. It's also one of the most misunderstood things about our religion."

Mrs. Riverton walked out in front of Ma and turned back to face her.

"Mrs. Brady, very few of the men actually have more than one wife. I was the only wife my husband had."

Mrs. Riverton paused for a moment. Tears welled up in her eyes. She looked away, briefly.

"I guess, ta help you understand this doctrine, I need ta ask you a couple of questions."

Ma nodded her head. "Okay."

"Do you believe that God never changes? That he is the same God yesterday, today and forever?"

Ma answered, "Yes, I would agree with that."

"Do you believe that he has spoken, can speak, or ever will

speak through prophets in the future?"

"Yes, I believe he can do whatever he wants ta."

"Do you believe that Abraham was a prophet?"

"Yes."

"Well, Mrs. Brady, Abraham and other prophets, in the same Bible, both you and I believe in, also had more than one wife. So if we believe them to be men of God, we must believe that God allowed it, or surely they would not be prophets. So you see, it only stands to reason that under certain circumstances, for some reason, polygamy is acceptable to God."

"Well, we don't have no prophet, today, tellin' us it is."

"That's what makes the Mormons different, Mrs. Brady. We believe that God does have a prophet on the earth and that he speaks through him. And that he will continue to have a living prophet on the earth to guide his children until the return of his Son, Jesus Christ."

Ma walked over to Pa.

"What do you think about all this Jake?"

"Well, Lizzie, it would take at least a prophet and maybe God, Himself, ta tell me ta take a second wife before I would do it. But I'll tell ya, I saw a lot of so-called Christian men in the war that were unfaithful to their wives at the same time they were cussin' the Mormons for havin' more than one wife. I can't see where what the Mormons are doin' is any worse than that. At least they have the decency to marry their women. I fought a war to help people gain their freedom. I say let 'em believe what they want and I'll believe what I want."

Ma looked at Jay.

"Don't look at me, Lizzie! I feel like a Mormon, already. My wife and child have been abused and my home's been burnt and I still ain't sure why."

Pa laughed.

"Yeah, and he's already got his second wife picked out. She's a big ol' pine tree up in Keener Creek." Pa glanced over at Maggie with his eyebrows raised, "He was sure kissin' that pine tree when I rode up on him, Maggie."

Jay threw the piece of bark, he had in his hand, to the ground, "Now, Jake, ya said ya wouldn't tell on me."

Maggie stood up and pointed her finger at Jay, but looked at Pa, "If he ever gets a second wife, that pine tree will be made into a pine box."

Ma walked back over to Mrs. Riverton.

"Thank you, Mrs. Riverton. I don't know if I believe all your reasonin', but it does help to know why you believe it."

"You're welcome, Mrs. Brady. I'm happy to discuss anything you like."

Ma turned back around and looked at Pa.

"Well, Mr. Jacob Allen Brady, I guess we don't have much of a choice, do we."

Pa shook his head, "We've always got choices, Lizzie. Just that some are better than others."

Ma looked away again. It was plain she was fightin' a battle of emotions. She turned back to Pa, "I promised ya that if ya would do your best to help get my family out'a trouble, I'd stand by ya. My family didn't stay out'a trouble, but I can't say ya didn't try. I reckon I'll stand by your decision, whatever it is."

"Thank you, Lizzie. I was hopin' you'd feel that way. I truly did try."

Pa turned to Jay.

"What do ya say, Jay, are ya up ta one more wild hair?"

Jay looked at Maggie.

"Maggie?"

"I already spoke my piece. I'll stand by ya unless ya decide ya need two wives, then I'll be standin' six feet above ya."

Jay raised both hands, palms up, in front of him, and shrugged his shoulders, "I ain't got nothin' ta stay for, Jake. My business in town has gone down and I won't get a better offer for my place than the one the general has made. Maggie or I, neither one have any kinfolk left that are close ta us. I reckon I'm good ta go Jake, if you are."

Pa nodded his head, "I've thought a good bit on it. I think it's the right choice." Pa walked over by Ma and Mrs. Riverton. He took Ma by the hand, "Mrs. Riverton, would you mind some company on your journey ta the Utah Territory?"

"No sir, not at all. I'd enjoy the company of such fine folks."

Pa faced Ma and reached out and took her other hand.

"Trust me, Lizzie, this is the best move to keep our family together in peace. Let's go see if we can persuade that sweet mother of yours ta come with us."

Ma looked up at Pa. She let go of his hands and put her arms around his chest. He slowly dropped his hands around her. He looked over at Kenneth and me.

"What about you boys? You ready ta go west?"

Kenneth and I both stood up.

"Yes, Pa."

"That's what I like ta hear...Pa.... I'd die a happy man if I could get a few years ta be a better husband and father."

We all walked back to the fort. Mom and Maggie went over to the cabin to talk to Granny. Pa and Jay went to find the general to give him our decision and make arrangements to go west. Kenneth and I walked out to the corral. I climbed up on the corner post of the corral fence. Kenneth walked out and started pettin' Dungeon. My mind drifted back to a few weeks ago, when I was sittin' on the corral fence at our house. My questions had been answered, all of the important ones, anyway. I'm proud to say my name is Benjamin Jacob Brady, the son of Jacob Allen Brady. I have watched, listened, and now know for myself—that's good blood.

The End